ANGEL UNLEASHED

LINDA THOMAS-SUNDSTROM

First Published in Great Britain 2017
By Mills & Boon, an imprint of HarperCollins*Publishers*
1 London Bridge Street, London, SE1 9GF

ISBN: 978-0-263-93003-0

89-0417

Our policy is to use papers that are natural, renewable and recyclable products and made from wood grown in sustainable forests. The logging and manufacturing processes conform to the legal environmental regulations of the country of origin.

Printed and bound in Spain
by CPI, Barcelona

"Now what? You'll disappear again?" Rhys asked.

"Disappearing is what I do best," Avery said.

"I won't let this go, you know," he warned. "You're far too intriguing."

"You'll have to," she said. "I'm already gone."

"And if I were to ask you to stay?"

As fun as this was, it was now clear to Rhys that this immortal wasn't going to volunteer any real information about herself. He was going to have to get those details some other way.

Smile widening, he said, "I do love a challenge."

Rhys took a firm hold on her shoulders and pulled her closer, so that she had to look up to see his face. She did not try to escape from what she had to know would come next.

All that fire...

All that heat...

He was so damn hungry for those things.

Linda Thomas-Sundstrom writes contemporary and paranormal romance novels for Mills & Boon. A teacher by day and a writer by night, Linda lives in the West, juggling teaching, writing, family and caring for a big stretch of land. She swears she has a resident muse who sings so loudly, she often wears earplugs in order to get anything else done. But she has big plans to eventually get to all those ideas. Visit Linda at www.lindathomas-sundstrom.com or on Facebook.

To my family, those here and those gone,
who always believed I had a story to tell.

Chapter 1

The night went wild and never looked back.

An explosion of color lit the dark. Brilliant flashes of blue, orange, green were there and gone in an instant. Bright enough to cause retinal damage, the light show left a lingering imprint in the darkness, much like the aftermath of a fireworks display.

From the rooftop above the alley, Rhys straightened from a crouched position, concerned about this strange phenomenon. Equally intriguing to him was the small, shadowy figure moving through the atmospheric residue.

To most eyes turned in that direction, the figure would have been indistinguishable from the surrounding darkness. Luckily, a Blood Knight's vision was exceptional, and Rhys had a special gift for hunting anomalies like this one. It was his job, his gig. He was good at it. Better than good. He was lethal. A monster's worst nightmare.

Problem was…the figure down in that alley wasn't one of London's usual monsters.

Although it was time for the city's abominations to crawl out of their hidey-holes, the creature with the strange light display wasn't a vampire or a werewolf. The scent accompanying the apparition didn't ring in as blood or damp fur, but something altogether different.

Chances were slim that he had missed a species or two in his centuries of keeping watch on the ever-growing lists of them. However, it now seemed to Rhys as if there could have been a gap in his education.

He supposed mortal Londoners might have chalked up those brief seconds of flashy lights to having had one too many drams at the local pub after work. He knew better. If something new had touched down here tonight, he wanted to know what that creature was up to.

I wonder what you are...

Zeroing in on the alley, Rhys detected another surprise. An odor of power trailed in this stranger's wake. Old power, with a scent reminiscent of an ancient library full of leather-bound books. With the unique fragrance came an atmospheric vibration similar to the hum of lightning striking the earth nearby.

Rhys looked up. No storm clouds.

The sigils covering his neck and shoulder blades rippled in reaction to the stranger's otherworldly vibration. The inky symbols carved into his skin were issuing a warning he couldn't ignore.

Was the newcomer dangerous?

Concern growing, Rhys refocused with another silent question.

Who are you?

He ticked off the rarer end of the species spectrum one by one. Shades and half-casts could be ruled out. A few ancient vampires could manipulate the atmosphere on occasion, but that wasn't the case here.

What else, then? Demon? Some brand-new hybrid concoction designed to confuse the rules and subvert the senses?

Maybe not completely, though, because the vibes this creature gave off were familiar to him on an almost subliminal level, and they kicked his heart rate up a notch or two.

His nagging conscience provided reasonable assurances about having experienced similar physical responses a few times before this, in different time frames and in several places around the globe. Brief blips on his internal radar that came to nothing in the end. Now, though, wasn't the time for pondering the parameters of déjà vu.

One thing was for sure. Tonight had just gotten a hell of a lot more interesting.

Enlisting the full resources of his extensive mental databanks, Rhys searched deeply for images to pinpoint this newcomer. Concentration brought him success. Beneath the noticeable wisp of old power lay another scent that was as different from the grimy London street odors as possible. Perfume, indicative of golden things. Sunrays on the clear water of a fountain. Morning dew on green grass. Fields of flowers.

Sure as hell, no monster he knew of smelled like that.

Shaking his head to clear his mind of images like grass and fountains, Rhys got back to the task at hand. Golden scents were always a distraction because they brought back memories of his days in the light, so very long ago, in another lifetime.

I see you, he wanted to say to test this stranger's awareness levels. *If you're so strong, can you feel me watching?*

Hunting monsters in the mortal world, finding and dealing with predators, had been his calling for as long as he could remember. Hell, with freaks and bloodsuckers increasing in numbers by the truckload, somebody had to take care of the problem so mortals could remain ignorant of what actually lurked in the shadows.

He stared at the alley, and the creature passing through it.

Are you a predator, my fine friend?

A fancy parasite, perhaps?

His inability to determine the answer to those questions was annoying and highly unusual.

"So, what are you, exactly?" Rhys whispered.

The only beings remotely as potent as this one in terms of presence were his brethren, and all six of the other Blood Knights were accounted for. He could touch their minds with his if he wanted to, just as they could touch his. None of them were anywhere near England at the moment.

You, newcomer, are a snag in my nightly rounds.

And it seemed that more surprises were in store.

Small flares, like a medley of tiny shooting stars, appeared to light this stranger's path. Not the steady beam of a flashlight, but some other kind of source. Silvery sparkling particles swept steps ahead of their master as if clearing the way. The night itself seemed to hold its breath as the strange creature with the little fireflies journeyed through the alley.

You're something tricky, then?

Uncomfortable with his ignorance in this matter, Rhys delved farther back into the landscape of his memory, searching for answers. Passing data regarding recent times, postmodern times, Edwardian years, he sailed backward, straining to place the interloper.

The detail he finally discovered was such a shock, he doubled back over it to make sure he'd gotten it right. The stranger in the alley had been flagged as an old soul hailing from a time prior to any of the centuries he had searched through.

Still more surprises were at hand.

This creature's vibe now resonated as feminine. A richly layered female spirit.

By all that was holy, he was looking at a woman. One who was both basking in and shielding her presence from everyone other than a special kind of onlooker with a flair for tracking anomalies in the darkest places.

Impossible, was his initial response. He'd gotten those details wrong. No female immortals existed, as far as he knew. None without fangs and a nasty need to bite, anyway. Yet only true immortals, those with their souls intact and their chests filled with echoing heartbeats, left such an indelible imprint on the world.

Excitement drove Rhys toward the edge of the roof. In spite of everything he had seen and done over the centuries, and though he would have thought it impossible for him to be stunned by anything, that's how he felt right that minute. Stunned.

In all the years since becoming immortal himself, how was it possible that he had never gotten wind of an immortal *She*?

Pulses of excitement pounded at his throat. He felt his blood pressure spike.

What are you doing here? he wanted to shout, to see if her hearing was as exceptional as his and if she possessed the kind of telepathy he and his brethren shared, a connection enhanced by the designs carved into their backs. Blood Knight sigils had been etched with the mingled black blood of all seven of them, fostering true closeness.

Are you friend, or foe?

He could jump down there to confront her with that question. His network of jangling nerves demanded that he did.

Find her. See her. Speak with her, those nerves seemed to whisper to him. Red flags waved in his mind. His sigils were scoring him raw, as if they knew whatever facts he was missing.

Then again, he had no real right to confront her if she wasn't a beast. No universal agreement existed between species that directed them to announce their presence to those already in residence when entering any particular area. Out of necessity, immortals moved around. He had been in London for less than a year, and in many other cities before that. So many cities, he'd lost count.

Is it so with you, my fine bearer of light? Are you a nomad?

As the strange female wove through the alley on this dark fall night, an even stronger feeling of familiarity washed over Rhys. Like a hound dog on a scent, he followed her progress toward the closest street by moving soundlessly above her from roof to roof. At the corner, where the alley met the main boulevard, the woman's accompanying lights winked out.

At least you show some sense.

Fascinated, Rhys watched her slip to the door of a storefront as if that had been her intended destination. When she opened the door, the thunder of loud music poured out.

Rhys saw her hesitate. His body rocked, mimicking the shiver that ran through her as she altered her shape enough to face the mortals inside the shop. Not a shape-shift, just a setting of her real power back to stealth mode.

Mortal was a game immortals often played.

How many times had he done that same thing when confronting the good people of London and elsewhere? Masking his identity, hiding his power, was the only way to walk among them.

The marks on his back throbbed with empathy. This female didn't look forward to going inside. Four walls would make her feel trapped if she was in any way like him. Loud music would be sensory torture for an old soul.

I know, he wanted to tell her. *I know how you feel.*

No one that had come out of Castle Broceliande's gates ever truly became used to extremes. Throughout time, the Blood Knights had been doomed to exist on the fringes of society, sharing the shadows with bad things that preyed on the people of those societies—keeping to themselves to avoid the hustle and bustle of mortals clumping too close together.

And you, my friend, are going to enter a building where mortals hang out. For that, my interest is piqued.

Anxious, Rhys shifted sideways for a better view of the doorway, eyeing the female down there, unable to keep from thinking back.

His Makers had offered no distractions to waylay the purpose of the Knights' quests. There were no female Blood Knights. Finding this feminine soul was exhilarating for the very reason that such a thing was to have been avoided. Females would have been major distractions from the Knights' quests, though they also would have provided a respite from the loneliness of existing endlessly through time alone.

The Knights had been created to serve a higher power. Personal needs had little to do with carrying out God's will.

Who made you, woman?

Where have you come from?

He almost jumped. Nearly did, until patience stayed him. Distance had to be maintained, managed, until he knew more about what this visitor was up to. His brotherhood's existence remained a secret to this day, to all but a chosen few. If this female sparkled her way through London's side streets, what would happen to the secrecy surrounding immortals in general?

What if someone else gets wind of you, milady?

Plenty of creatures on this planet would like nothing more than to take down the immortal Guardians, and afterward enjoy a parasitic free-for-all. More than a few of them had tried.

Thoughts stalled there.

In the light of the doorway, the newcomer's silhouette took shape. Reed-thin and narrow-shouldered, his new prey had the willowy body of an elf. Dressed from head to toe in black, she blended well with street shadows and had covered her head with a hood.

Black for camouflage was always wise. He was dressed similarly.

The desire to see her up close was overwhelming. However, Rhys knew better than to rush things. His hammering heart would have to wait a bit longer for a face-to-face with the enigma down there. The hunger gnawing at him was a none-too-subtle reminder that devils often resided in details, and that things were not always what they seemed.

He smiled sagely.

Giving in to the need to speak aloud, in a normal voice, since he so seldom did, Rhys said, "I will wait here, my immortal friend. I will be waiting for you."

Chapter 2

The bells on the door of Shakespearean Ink, put there to announce the presence of visitors, couldn't compete with the blaring music Avery Arcadia Quinn met when she stepped inside the tattoo parlor. The heavy metal recording made her hesitate just past the threshold.

One glance over her shoulder at the street suggested that she was okay for the time being. Her hope was that no other customers would be looking for a tattoo needle on a cold, foggy night like this one, and that she would be alone. Anonymity was the name of this game. She couldn't afford to attract attention.

Stiff shoulders made her roll them back to ease the buildup of tension. Her black leather jacket creaked as she took stock of her surroundings.

The tat parlor was uncommonly tidy for such a dark, rather seedy, less than desirable location on the London outskirts. A metal counter ran the length of the store on one side. Several cheap chairs crowded the room. Pinned to the milky-blue walls were hundreds of photos of tattoo art, hanging in fairly neat, symmetrical rows.

Bad luck, though. She wasn't the only customer.

In the center of the small space, a padded chair that had been patched one too many times was occupied by another client. Still, it could have been worse. The occupant of that chair was a young girl probably no more than sixteen years old.

Tears of discomfort dripped from the girl's big brown eyes. Her thin hands white-knuckled the seat. No doubt this teen had snuck in here while in the midst of a rebellious streak with her allowance money. A sixteen-year-old's tat of choice? Winnie-the-Pooh.

Avery didn't bother to check the place for tidiness or proper hygiene since those things didn't matter to her. The guy in the faded black T-shirt who was working on the girl's ankle was her target. Rumor had it he was good at cover-ups, with a talent for making things look like something else. He was a fixer credited with being discreet.

"What are you in for?" he asked, addressing Avery without looking up from his work, and waving a small instrument that looked either like a miniature throwback to dark days in medieval dungeons or a super-sized electric toothbrush.

"Tattoo," she said drily.

He did a double take once he'd focused on who had entered. Used to stares, Avery didn't take this personally. She knew she presented a strange picture with her hood pulled up around her face and her mirrored sunglasses reflecting the neon signage...especially since it was after 9:00 p.m.

Snow-white hair, mostly hidden behind the black hood, didn't often stay put. Several pale strands drifted now in the stale-smelling breeze from the open doorway. The sunglasses protecting her sensitive eyes from the lights, as well as the sneak peek of pale skin around them, had to seem freakish in a healthy blond and brunette world, even in the sun-challenged UK.

All in all, though, she fit in better here than she would have in Florida.

"Take a chair by the desk if you want to wait. Feel free to peruse the art on the walls," the guy said. "Maybe you'd like to choose one of those designs."

Peruse. Such a strange word for a century like this one, and odd when spoken with a Cockney accent.

Avery checked out the girl in the chair. The honey-colored bear on the girl's left ankle was a decent rendering of the cartoon and almost finished. She wouldn't have to wait long for a turn with the whirring needles. Still, she was antsy, and anxiously tossed another glance at the street through the front window, half expecting to see someone standing there.

No one was.

Short on square footage, the shop made her feel claustrophobic. Enclosed spaces didn't suit her. Patience had never been her forte, which was odd since she'd had such a long time to try to perfect that skill. Because her energy was untrustworthy and came in wayward steaks and flashes, sitting down to wait her turn was out of the question.

For those reasons and more, it was never sensible to remain in any one place for too long. Nor was it smart to give anyone a good long look at her. Definitely no close-up.

Since she had picked the guy in this shop for his talent and stellar reputation, however, quelling her anxiety was paramount. So was maintaining her human-like persona for a while longer.

With that in mind, Avery headed for the counter.

As he got back to work, the artist barked, "More pictures are in the book on the desk."

When she didn't open the three-ring binder next to her, he looked up a third time. "Ah. The lady already knows what she wants."

Seconds later, he added, "Five more minutes here, tops. There's beer in the cooler."

The girl in the chair spoke up. "You didn't offer me a beer."

Artist guy laughed. "Yeah. Right."

Avery wasn't up for polite banter or alcohol, or for reminding the young girl in that chair, who seemed to be missing parental guidance, about the dangers of being out alone, past her bedtime in a city full of shadows. Nowadays, she wasn't anybody's conscience. Those days were far behind her.

As for the room…

A more thorough scan showed closeable blinds on the front windows and an interior door leading to an adjacent private room, probably used for etching tattoos on a person's backside. She perceived no heartbeats beyond those of the two people in front of her. Those beats were steady and rhythmic.

Just a normal night in the life of a tattoo parlor.

But hell…her shoulder blades were already aching more than usual, as if they knew what she was going to do and also that there would be pain involved. Muscles often retained memories of what had happened to them in the past, especially after experiencing the extremes of agony. And although pain was nothing new to her, Avery always dreaded having more of it voluntarily.

"Take a chair," the artist suggested. "They're more comfortable than they look."

She didn't heed his advice. The lingering odor of hot flesh was cloying. The ink used for the tattoos offered up another distinct scent that tripped more old memories best forgotten.

Nerves bristling, Avery glanced again to the front door, nixing the return of a hazy belief that someone was out there. Anxiousness was likely the cause of her nervousness. An artist in a rundown ink shop was going to see her scars. He was going to touch them—a crime so heinous that no one had ever managed it.

Hadn't she dispensed with the last person who tried?

In order to provide this guy with his next canvas she'd have to take off her shirt. Predicting his reaction to the sight of the multitude of scars covering her body was a no-brainer. Very little space wasn't crowded by the grid of crisscrossed white raised lines. Tat Guy would be fascinated by the old wounds and he'd be nosey, but the stories those grids told were none of his business or anyone else's.

She wished they weren't hers.

"Almost there," he said to her while dabbing at the girl's ankle with a cloth—a benign little bear on a girl's youthful, otherwise unblemished skin.

What would this pubescent girl say if she were to witness Avery's roadmap of scar tissue and the two deep six-inch grooves edging her spine? Humans were squeamish about marred flesh. Other species reacted differently. Werewolves, in particular, got turned on by battle scars and displayed them like jewelry.

So, if exhibiting or touching her old wounds was blasphemy of the highest order and against the rules, why was she chancing this?

She was here because it was her one shot, a last-ditch effort, at soul healing. If this artist could cover the two large wounds on her back with a design that would make her feel like her old self, maybe she'd regain some semblance of balance and a small modicum of peace.

That ever-elusive peace…

The transformation of something ugly into something better, at least superficially, would be an accomplishment terribly long overdue, and one less freakish thing to contend with in the long stretch of unending years to come… if she didn't find what she had come to London to find.

"You still there?" the guy asked, speaking to her.

There was no need to answer him. He was acutely aware of her. She could feel how badly he wanted to take a closer look. The air between them vibrated with that need. He was struggling to keep his attention on the ankle in front of him, and eagerly awaiting the girl's departure.

This was the reason she had to be so bloody careful. The uncanny attraction all humans felt when they saw her was due to the light of the Divine still being there…in her face, her body and her hair. Though the light had dimmed considerably over the years, there was no way to mask what was left of it completely. Throughout time, mortals had been mesmerized by its vibrant energy and lingering afterglow.

"Calm the hell down," she silently sent to the guy to dim his growing interest. He obeyed that directive the way most humans did when she messed with their minds. She'd have to erase this guy's thoughts completely once they were done.

Running a hand along the edge of the sleek metal counter's iron and tin compounds served to sharpen her focus by making her fingertips burn. She blew on them, more for sport than comfort, long practiced in dealing with forbidden metals.

"Two minutes," the artist announced.

Two minutes, and then what? Avery asked herself. Peace actually would descend? Did she actually expect that kind of outcome?

Sound…

Jolted by a sudden lash of nerve burn that instantly heated her face, Avery turned to the door.

"I will wait."

A voice had seeped under the crack.

"I will be waiting for you."

"Son of a..." Striding to the door, Avery rested her hand on the wood. She had been right. Someone was out there. Not just anyone, either. Somebody powerful enough to reach her with a threatening call.

All she had to do was open this door to find out who it was.

Or not.

The flush of volcanic heat and the staccato uptick in her pulse that followed that call paved the way for a streak of fiery intuition. Only one kind of presence in the world had the ability to affect her like this. Seven things, actually...which meant that one of Castle Broceliande's Blood Knights was somewhere nearby. And he had found her.

Fired-up nerve endings were tingling en masse. Avery stifled wicked four-letter oaths. Imagining she could stride through the shadows of this city undetected had been foolish. London had always been overrun by monsters. At least one of those Knights could potentially have been on guard, protecting the city's humans from things that went bump in the night.

While she...

She was a sitting duck in this small enclosed space, if she had indeed been made by one of them.

Damn Blood Knights.

Guardians. Overseers. Monster killers. That's what the dangerous Seven had become. Seven physically perfect specimens of immortal manhood had been created to be as much like her as possible, and their Makers had outdone themselves. Due to their skill with alchemic machinations, the Blood Knights existed unchallenged to this day by any who stood against them—immortals unable to die by any normal means. Immortals unknowingly built on a foundation of pain.

Still, despite the agony the creation of the Knights had caused her, Avery yearned for their company with every fiber of her being, and always had. They alone, out of anyone on Earth, would come the closest to understanding her, and yet could never be allowed to. Misplaced longings for them were never to be addressed. Urges like *want* and *need* had to remain tucked inside her. Only when her mission had been fulfilled would she be strong enough to get what she required from them.

"I know you're there, Knight. Leave here. Leave me. Honor my wishes."

"What did you say?" The tattoo artist asked.

Hell, had she spoken those words aloud?

"Have you changed your mind?" he queried.

"No change," Avery replied.

"Good. All done here." To the girl in the chair, he said, "You remember what I told you about how to take care of this, right?"

The girl nodded and slid to her feet, careful to avoid putting too much pressure on her foot right away. She winced as she rolled down the hem of her jeans. After pulling on her jacket, she headed for the door without looking back.

"Will you look at that. No thank you at all," the artist muttered. "Good thing she paid up front, but what's the world coming to?"

Standing, he turned, careful to avoid meeting Avery's eyes. "Now, what do you have in mind?"

"Wings," she said.

Speaking the word produced a flutter deep inside her chest.

The guy nodded. He would have noted the husky voice she had taken decades to perfect and the slim, leather-encased body only partially hidden by the black leather hoodie. He had to be wondering about the sunglasses.

To his credit, he merely said, "Wings are popular."

His eyes roamed over her—not in a sexual way, but as a painter might look for the best angle with which to fully see a model's potential. Almost strictly business now that her silent directive had calmed him down.

"Lower back?" he asked.

She shook her head. "Upper."

That disclosure interested him. His eyebrows quirked. "Shoulders?"

"A full span."

His gaze shifted to the counter. "I can do up a design for you or show you some pictures so I can see what you have in mind."

"No need. I can sketch what I'm looking for if you have a pencil and paper handy."

Avery wasn't sure which of the two beings in this room would be affected the most when she bared her skin for the needles. Her nerves were like white-hot pulses whispering along over-strung wires.

There was also the question of whether that Blood Knight outside would leave her alone, and if the ward she had set up at the door would protect her.

"Here." She was handed paper and a blue felt-tipped pen. "Have a go at what you mean."

Pen in hand, she began to draw from memory a rendering of the tattoo she wanted. Tonight's session would actually be an act of camouflage, using art and color to disguise the ridges left over from where the real pair of wings had been cruelly cut from her back.

She was going to replace one set of wings with another.

Each stroke of her pen across the paper intensified the chest flutter. Tension balled in her stomach. How long would the Knight give her before figuring those protective wards out?

The artist nodded at the image she had drawn. "I can do this. When would you like to start?"

"Now."

His shaggy-haired head shook. "This will take a long time. Two or three sessions, at least."

Avery pulled out a wad of folded one-hundred dollar bills and laid them on the counter. "Now," she repeated.

He looked at the money and back to her. "No one can handle all this ink at one time, not to mention the discomfort of so much coverage. That design will reach from shoulder to shoulder?"

"All the way across. And I'll manage."

He shook his head again. "I'm sorry…"

His voice trailed off because she had removed the sunglasses and lowered her hood…to give him a first look, a glimpse, a mere inkling of what one of God's angels who had fallen to the Earth centuries ago, and stayed, looked like.

The poor sod's wheeze of surprise was audible, but he quickly got hold of himself with a little mental nudge from her bag of tricks. He hadn't asked any of the questions that had been crowding the tip of his tongue. She also had put a damper on that.

Following him to the back room of the shop, Avery glanced twice more at the front door. Wary, dealing with the craziness of being trapped, she knew that she had only postponed getting caught with her pants down by one of the only beings on Earth who knew what to do about it.

That damn Blood Knight.

Whichever one it turned out to be.

Chapter 3

Rhys's anticipation had spread like wildfire. Neverthe-less, he had to be careful.

At this late hour, people were coming and going, passing the entrance to the alley where he now stood. Predators of the horror movie kind hadn't yet made an appearance, but for them the night was young.

It was 2:00 a.m.

She hadn't come out of the tattoo parlor.

He couldn't imagine what she was doing in there. To be touched by needles would mean exposure. An immortal's blood would be a hefty giveaway of details no immortal could afford to let slip. His blood was black. Possibly hers was, too.

Rhys pushed off the wall he'd been leaning against, pa-tience wearing thin.

"Time's up," he announced.

Three strides brought him close enough to the shop's

front door to feel the buzz of electricity outlining it. The trespassing vixen had set up a defensive ward.

"You did hear me, then," he muttered.

Lips moving with a silent incantation, Rhys shattered the barrier she'd set in place and yanked the door open.

"Nice try," he said aloud. "But I'm no amateur."

Inside the shop, he waved off the burly man coming toward him from a back room with a muttered command. The female he sought wasn't anywhere in sight, and yet her scent, already embedded in his lungs, led him to where she hid.

All those plans about what he would say to her fizzled when he stopped in the doorway of that back room. As if he'd been slammed by a battering ram, his breath hitched.

She was there, sitting on a cot with her back to him, naked from the waist up. Never once had he witnessed anything quite like this. Like her.

The woman on that bench was completely colorless. Pale to the point of being ghostly. White skin. Hair the color of freshly fallen snow. She was painfully thin, but also incredibly graceful in the way her angles converged. Slender shoulders sloped toward a spine where each bone stood out from the lean muscles surrounding it, as if they were pearls on a string.

Ethereal was the word that came to Rhys with that first glance. And *breathtaking.* She was also flawed. Damaged. That, too, was startling. Whitened scars covered her back and arms. Old scars, and plenty of them, proved that she had suffered abuse and had been hurt badly in the past.

She had come for tattoos. Those new tats were vivid, red and raw, adding an overlay of color that contrasted greatly with her skin. She'd chosen wings. Dark blue, light blue and gray feathers with blood-red tips spanned from one of her shoulders to the other, expertly filled in. The result was spectacular.

Rhys stared intently at this incredible apparition.

Strands of her white hair—long, straight, shiny—cascaded over one of her shoulders to partially cover the right side of the tattoo. Both shoulders quaked slightly, not from cold, but as if the violence of the needles used to create the wings had affected her. Her emotional turmoil was discernible from where he stood.

Although she was aware of him, the graceful creature on that cot didn't turn around. Maybe she waited for him to make the first move. Unfortunately, that move didn't include any of the demands he had planned on using for getting to the root of who she was and what she was up to. What bubbled up from him instead was a show of sympathy.

"Bloody hell," he whispered hoarsely. "What have you done?"

Pain sliced through Avery's back as her muscles stabilized; pain reminiscent of another time, only infinitely tamer by comparison and much more civilized.

She didn't have time to try out the feel of her surrogate wings or catch her breath. *He* was here in the doorway, his reflection clear in the mirror across from her. *Him.* Not just any Blood Knight, but the one she had secretly coveted from among the Seven. The Knight she wasn't ever supposed to see in person, face-to-face, was less than five feet away, leaving her breathless.

There was no mistaking this creature for any normal mortal male. No chance in hell. His incredibly handsome, aquiline-featured face had *Blood Knight* chiseled all over it.

There was no use trying to play dumb, either, when they were both far from the classification of *mortal* and knew it.

"What have you done?" he asked again, the deepness of his voice sending shockwaves of familiarity through Avery.

His question seemed intimate, spoken as if he knew her well and cared about what she did, when neither of those things was true. He hadn't known she existed until this moment. She had promised herself things would stay that way until she found the right time to change it.

Slowly, and without answering the impertinent query, Avery reached for her shirt.

"You've been hurt," he said.

It was too late to ask how he had found her, and the answer wouldn't have helped. Like often called to like, and she had gotten too close. But the effect his presence had on her was as unwelcome as he was. Icy shivers crept up the back of her neck. Her insides churned. Blood Knights had been designed to lure the eye and tempt the soul, and angels weren't immune to those things because those seven Knights carried in their souls some beauty of the heavens.

Get out! Avery wanted to shout, studying his image in the mirror. *I don't have time for this.*

As handsome as these Knights had been as mortal men, their famous features had been further enhanced by the grace of the renewed blood in their veins and the importance of their golden Quest. They were, however, ignorant of the fact that some of the immortal blood pulsing through all of them had been hers, unwillingly shared. And that, like a butterfly, she had been captured, ensnared in a net.

This magnificent Knight was muscled, honed, taut, elegant and rugged in equal measures. He stood well over six feet tall, his appearance formidable in every sense of the word. An aura of crackling power surrounded him, announcing that this was a man who had broken from his mortal bonds by stepping into another realm of existence.

He spoke again. "Are you all right?"

His throaty voice sounded like a sweep of crushed velvet, and affected her more than she'd care to let on. They were measuring each other, and she needed time to calculate what might happen next.

She had seen this Blood Knight many times in the past, and always with the same kind of gut-clenching reaction. Frozen in the body of a twenty-something-year-old, he had matured since his inception. His face was more chiseled than she remembered. Bright blue expressive eyes were alight with a worldly, intelligent gleam.

She knew those features well.

In that doorway, too close for comfort, stood the sun-kissed immortal with golden streaks of light in his mane of brown hair whose piercing gaze usually saw through shadows without seeing her.

Perceval had been his mortal name, way back in time. This was one of Arthur's knights, a warrior champion who'd had a coveted seat at Camelot's Round Table and been a major player in the Grail Quest. The intense heat of his observation began to melt her chills.

"What's it to you?" she finally asked, slipping her shirt over her head. "I don't believe you were invited to this party."

Speaking calmly was a chore when this Knight's allure bordered on the mystical. Of all the Seven, he had always been special to her. Her attraction to him had both excited and repelled her from the beginning, and from afar, further complicating the fulfillment of the personal vows she had taken.

Because of that, he was the most dangerous Knight of them all to have found her. She had to be careful, remain calm, when her heart was thrashing. More time was necessary before she turned to face him.

"Who are you?" he asked.

"Who's asking?" Avery returned.

The energy circling the room was expanding, pressing against the walls, humming in her ears. She was trapped, and therefore had to speak to him. No alternative presented itself when he filled the doorway.

She saw in the mirror that he was staring at her back and at the damp towel beside her.

"What's wrong with your blood?" he asked.

"Nothing's wrong with it."

"It has no color at all."

"What's that to you?"

"I've never seen anything like it, or like you."

"No," Avery agreed, sliding her arms into her sleeves. "Other than your comment being incredibly rude, I'm sure you haven't seen anything like me."

Glossing over her feisty comeback, he tried again to engage her. "Where do you come from?"

She was fairly sure he didn't mean the city or region of the world, but something deeper and having to do with her origins…as if she'd blow more of her cover and cough up her secrets because he asked her to.

Turning halfway around, she parried, "Is this an interrogation? Are you London's supernatural sheriff?"

"Only an interested party."

"Where I came from is none of your business."

"Maybe it isn't. What about your scars?"

"Rude again, and definitely not your concern."

Persistence was another well-honed Blood Knight trait.

"Is there anything you can tell me about yourself that might help me to understand what you want here?" he asked in a lowered tone that caused Avery's new tats to ache more than they already did.

"It's late," she said. "Maybe you have a job to do that doesn't include wasting time in a tattoo parlor."

"Not tonight. Everyone got a free pass in your honor."

"Do you suppose the bad guys will thank me?"

Don't let him in. Do not get close, Avery's mind warned. *Remember who you are, and get away.*

None of that was easy at the moment, however. She wasn't just confronting a Blood Knight. She was confronting an old set of wishes long ago tamped down. This glorious creature had always made her want to forget her rage and her vows to keep clear of him and the others like him. The pressure she felt to fight her way out of the room was outrageous.

If she'd had her wings, the real ones, she could have bested this Knight in seconds. Although he was incredibly strong, she would have been the strongest. Wingless, she was unwhole, halved, severed from the rest of her kind with her strength vastly diminished.

"Go away," Avery managed to say.

"Answers first," he said.

Pursuing their prey is what Blood Knights did best, and she was now at the top of that list.

Want to know who I am, Knight?

What if I tell you that your inner light was stolen from me, tortured out of my veins? What then? Would you thank me for your light and for your agile prowess? Someone should.

Stopping the internal chatter was imperative. She felt him tuning in to her. Hers wasn't the only pulse skyrocketing. The rapid beat of his heart added to the tension in the air.

The truth was that in this guy's voice, and in his golden presence, Avery heard the far-off rattle of the chains that had bound her to the Earth in his honor.

"You're immortal, and yet have no sigils," the magnificent bastard noted with a focus hotter than the artist's needles.

Avery hated how he unsettled her.

"I suppose the saving grace is that the new designs look like they belong there," he added. "Somehow, the wings suit you."

Too damn personal...

Avery whirled around. The creature in the doorway had seen the wings, her new talismans, when she hadn't had the chance. He had viewed her bare skin, scars and all. And now that she had lost some of her hard-won control, he had seen her face.

Would she let him get away with that? She had wiped minds for less. She had killed to remain anonymous in a crowded modern world. But none of those things was an option here with someone whose strength so closely matched hers at the moment. She had been sloppy and had not covered her tracks well enough. This meeting was her fault. There was no do-over, only escape.

She did not meet that heated gaze.

"Sigils are in these days. Didn't you know?" she remarked, reaching for her jacket.

"Sigils." He repeated the word. "Was that what you were looking for here, in a place like this?"

"Actually, that would have been useless, don't you think, when you have to be born with those kinds of marks, or be born because of them?"

She was getting warmer, catching the fever that came with speaking about forbidden things. Her shoulders were on fire. Real wings would have taken her away from this confrontation. An inked span was nothing more than make-believe.

Still, the inked wings were an added reminder that if she stopped looking for the missing pieces of herself now, she would never know a moment's peace. If she became distracted after all this time, and after believing she was closing in on the very thing she sought…all the years of searching and hating and destruction that had gotten her to this point wouldn't be worth one single breath.

She wanted to look at him, but didn't dare.

"I wonder if you'll tell me what you are if I ask nicely enough?" he said. "And also who made you."

"I'm afraid you have taken up far too much of my time already." That remark actually sounded breathless. The airless room was stifling.

"Places to go? People to see?" he asked.

Avery ignored the remark. She was in need of fresh air and alone time, and he was in the way.

"I'm leaving." She got to her feet, meeting his gaze at last.

He leaned against the doorjamb as if he had suddenly experienced a moment of weakness. But he rallied quickly. The devastatingly handsome head shook. Blue eyes burned bright.

"They will be waiting for you. London's monsters," he warned.

"They won't find me."

"I did."

"You don't understand…" Avery began, without finishing what she had been about to say. This Knight wasn't to know anything about her quest. The Perceval of old had died, losing his mortal flesh, and had been resurrected by a golden kiss from a holy relic. After feeling Death's black breath, his path had been clear. That had not been the case for her. *And by the way,* she wanted to shout, *monsters no longer concern me.*

"I'm trying to be polite, and you're not making it easy," he said. "What if I came here to welcome you to London, or to warn you about what lurks here?"

"Have you honestly come here for either of those things?" Avery challenged.

"No," he confessed. "I came because I was intrigued by the sudden appearance of a stranger I couldn't place."

The tractor-beam of his blue-eyed scrutiny left Avery feeling as though she were still half naked. She also felt vulnerable when *vulnerable* wasn't in her vocabulary and never had been. She'd been in battles this Blood Knight couldn't even dream of, and had emerged unscathed. Damn straight she could handle this unexpected meeting.

"I owe you nothing, Blood Knight," she said.

As she watched a smile play on the corners of his full, sensuous mouth, Avery realized she had just made a grave mistake. In letting him know that she knew him, and about him, she had trespassed on his purpose for existing. *Blood Knight*, she had said.

That mistake was the mother of them all, and any second now the ramifications of such a slip-up were going to bite her on her leather-clad ass.

Chapter 4

"So you do know me," Rhys said, refusing to let her get past him.

The female, though of an unknown species, was extraordinarily beautiful. She had delicate features and wide-set blue eyes the exact color of a summer sky. Those eyes were the only real color she possessed, other than the tattoo, and stood out dramatically from the flawless paleness of her face. Adding more drama to her features was the way she had rimmed both eyes with black paint, which lent her a modern, edgy look. Not one scar marred that face.

"What if I do know about you?" she asked.

Rhys shook his head. "I wonder if it's possible to get a straight answer out of you."

"Unless you actually are London's sheriff, I doubt it. Even if you were, it's unlikely I would oblige."

Rhys held up his hands in a gesture of submission. "Fine. I get it. You enjoy being mysterious."

He stepped aside. "Would one more question be too much to ask?"

"Yes." Donning her leather jacket, she got to her feet.

Up close, this trespasser wasn't as small as he had originally thought. It was the slightness of her frame that made her seem fragile, though her attitude more than made up for it. He could easily have held her there with brute strength alone. Since he was two heads taller and twice as broad, she wouldn't stand a chance against him. But this strange female was right. She owed him nothing. She had done nothing wrong. Yet.

"How do you know about me? Your answer might be more important than you realize, at least to me," Rhys persisted. "Not many creatures are privy to knowledge of the Seven."

She wasn't going to get close to him, whether or not the doorway was wide open. *Don't you trust me, pale one? Maybe you don't trust yourself. After all, not all immortals are friendly.*

Hell…and again…other than his brethren and a few ancient vampires, he had never encountered another immortal, so what did he really know?

"Blood Knight, you said," he prompted.

She said nothing.

"Perhaps you've met one of my brothers somewhere in this wide world?"

When her eyes met his briefly, the room seemed to fade out of focus. Those eyes were unusually intense and probing. Contained in the blue was the flicker of a far-off light.

A feeling of being connected to her snapped into place as their gazes held. Rhys was sure she felt it, too. Swaying slightly on her feet, the pale mystery was quick to break eye contact.

Rhys caught and held a breath, wanting…no, *needing* to

know more about her. He said the next thing on his mind, shoving aside the answers he most needed in favor of the wave of emotion careening through him.

"Does it hurt?"

She looked up again.

"What you did tonight, here. Does it hurt?" he asked.

"It's nothing." Breathy voice. Lowered tone. Hidden emotion.

"And the other marks you bear?"

"Far worse."

This beautiful female, parchment pale, slight of bone and freshly tattooed, had admitted to being privy to his status as an immortal. She had spoken of his brethren as if she were well-versed in their business, when he remained in the dark about hers.

The situation was unacceptable and there wasn't really much he could do about it. She was intriguing, exciting. Unusual sensations stirred in his chest.

And there was something else…

Something about her that he could not put his finger on, no matter how hard he tried.

The scars that marred her flesh were evidence of battles she had fought. When? Where? They were evidence that she was no wallflower, no innocent maiden or pushover. In contrast to her fragile appearance, she was a warrior of some kind. A fighter.

Her gaze again rose slowly to meet his. This time she didn't back off. She made no move to push past him. Rhys detected in her expression a glimmer of interest that she quickly masked.

Are you as intrigued by me as I am by you?

It was likely going to be a standoff in the doorway until she gave him more information about herself, especially now that she had let on about knowing his purpose in London.

"Why wings?" he asked, breaking the silence.

"Why not?" she returned.

"The tattoos must have been important for you to have come here," Rhys suggested. "I noted your reticence in the doorway of the shop."

"We're talking in circles, Knight. Don't presume to know anything about me. People usually come to a place like this to get their bodies inked. That's what I did."

"Yes, *people* do that," he agreed.

"Are you prejudiced against those of us who don't fit into that category?"

"That would be absurd, wouldn't it, since I don't fit, either."

She continued to stare at him.

"If I step back again, you'll go? Just like that?" Rhys said.

"What's to hold me here?"

"I was hoping my appearance in this doorway might be enough to instigate a real dialogue. You know, immortal to immortal."

"Circles," she reiterated. "When your monsters are calling."

He wasn't going to let up, didn't want to lose her quite yet. Touching her was not an option. Laying a hand on her would be out of the question. But he wanted to do those things and was driven by a strange inner impulse to get closer to her.

"Those monsters will sense your presence the way I did. By now, the news will have spread," Rhys explained.

"Let them come."

"We can fight them together, if you like," he suggested. "Teamwork."

"I fight alone, and only when I have to."

He couldn't keep her there much longer. The stink of death permeated the air, seeping through the seals of the closed windows. Several bloodsuckers were out there, and not too far away.

"Get out of my way," the pale beauty said.

"All right," Rhys conceded without moving.

He couldn't stop staring at this mesmerizing mix of unknowns. She looked like an angel with a purpose. An angel with one foot down in a place not quite as fluffy as the clouds. Her little trailing lights weren't in evidence. The black-rimmed blue eyes were unsettling.

Maybe the tattooed wings make you feel more like an angel. Maybe you imagine you'll use them to fly away.

"Let me help you," Rhys said.

When white lashes lowered over her eyes, he thought again about reaching out to detain her. He wanted those eyes back on him. He wanted to understand her. Nevertheless, he let her brush past him because he was not her keeper, her friend, an actual ally or her lover. With regret, he watched the enigmatic, ethereal immortal female walk out of the room, heading for the shop's front door.

Rhys said, "The monsters will be out there, you know."

She hesitated in the shop's doorway to look back at him with a final word. "They always are."

He had to let her go, let her leave, when his body urged him to bring her back. Once she walked out that door, he might never see her again. Odds for that were in her favor.

Now that he had seen her, spoken with her, having her disappear would leave a dent in his understanding and a hole in his hammering heart. That damn heart was acting like a schoolboy's with a first crush. After just a few minutes, she had become an addiction.

Did he see sadness in her eyes when she gave him a final

glance from the sidewalk? He was sure the light he had witnessed in the blue depths of those eyes now reflected regret. Probably he was wrong. Nevertheless, he was after her in a blur of speed.

On the sidewalk, he stopped. Two mortals passed by. A Night Shade slipped through the shadows and into the alley beside him. That Shade should have been of concern to him, but distraction was a hell of a thing. The female he'd just seen in that shop was gone, leaving no trace other than the lightest wisp of fragrance.

Whispering a litany of curse words, half of them in Latin, Rhys spun to face the next problem. Monsters were indeed rallying. Half a block away, and with the swiftness of an oncoming black tide, vampires were closing in.

Chapter 5

The black tide swept the two mortals who had just passed Rhys into the vampires' vortex of flashing fangs and overruling hunger. One of those unlucky people had enough time to scream before they were on him.

And that was not acceptable to a Guardian.

There in seconds, Rhys joined the fray, pulling a silver-tipped dagger from his right boot and a sharpened wooden stake from his left.

The bloodsuckers were quick, but out of their league when facing a vamp-killing machine from a larger supernatural gene pool. Rhys swung his arms as fluidly as if he had been made for the intricacies of fighting. He had been created with the strength of ten men for just such a purpose.

"Go back to the same black breath that created you," he said calmly, lunging sideways with deft strikes of the blade to take down the first vamp, whose yellow fangs were too near the throat of its young mortal prisoner.

"Rest in peace."

The street exploded with a snowstorm of dark gray ash, which caught the attention of the remaining sharp-canined monsters and made them angry.

"Not what you were expecting?" Rhys quipped, waiting out the seconds until they released the two stunned, but as yet unharmed, mortals.

These vamps' faces were gaunt, almost skeletal. As usual, Rhys regretted that their afterlives had been so cruelly tweaked. Dull black eyes, lacking all hint of their former color, were fixed on him. Grossly sharp teeth snapped with displeasure. All of these bloodsuckers were new to the walking undead status. Hunger ruled them. Feeding was everything. Common sense had departed with their dying breaths.

"It's not your fault. I get that," he said, stepping forward to meet the remaining crush of fang-snapping abominations. "However, you are cursed to be the bane of human existence. You must be aware of that."

His body rocked as the awareness of other company came to him like a moving wall of heat. Without looking for the source, Rhys could venture a good guess as to who had returned. Not many creatures would have been close enough to sense trouble, with the ability to do something about it.

She had come back, as if he needed help with five malnourished fledglings.

"Damn you," she said, appearing beside him from out of nowhere with the ease of having just dropped from the sky.

The sky thing wasn't possible, of course, Rhys knew, since the wings on her back were fake.

He feinted to the right. Simultaneously, she moved left in a choreographed fighting pattern that split the oncoming vamp fledglings into two groups.

"Hell, do I now have to worry about you?" he silently griped.

"I was thinking the same thing. About you," she returned in the same manner.

"You can hear me?"

"No need to shout, Knight."

"You heard things I might have thought earlier?"

"Anyone within a five-mile radius could have heard you."

She went for two of the bloodsuckers as if she had been born to the art of wielding a blade.

Rhys struck the sweet spot in one fledgling's chest with his knife, and that fledgling went down in a flurry of musty-smelling gray ash. Spinning on his heels, he embedded the stake in the second vamp's chest and left it there as the vamp staggered back a few steps before what was left of it became a funnel of ash.

His new fighting partner had taken the brunt of things, with another of the vamps going after what it incorrectly assumed might be the weaker link. Big mistake.

The woman beside him moved like lightning, like a storm in human guise, and with a fighting grace Rhys had never before seen in any but his brothers. Fast, sure, talented, she was all liquid motion. Prepared to jump to her aid, Rhys instead watched at a standstill, his body reacting to each move she made as if he'd made it.

His pulse was again racing. This immortal woman was fast, flexible, canny and dexterous. Tracking her movements roused emotions long compressed deep in his soul. How had he missed this creature's existence? Who the hell was she, and why couldn't he reach the answer to that question when it was buried somewhere inside his mind?

Like a white whirlwind, the female parried, spun and thrust her blade to victory over those ornery bloodsuckers.

And when the street had been cleared of fanged parasites, and the two mortals had run off to safety with a story to tell that no one would believe unless they had seen such a thing for themselves, she turned to Rhys with a stern expression on her incredibly beautiful face.

Speaking with the same throaty voice that had caused his muscles to twitch in the shop behind them, she said, "The mortals won't remember. I've seen to that, and you owe me one."

She wiped her short silver blade on her leather-clad thigh and turned from him.

"You truly imagined I'd need help?" Rhys asked, amused and far too fascinated with the curve of that lean thigh for his own good.

"Well, maybe I just needed to exert some energy," she admitted, turning back. "I was in that damn shop for far too long, and those needles were a bitch."

She was feisty. Sexy. The black leather getup molded tightly to her body, showing off angles and curves Rhys hadn't been able to see when she was sitting down. Her hood had been thrown back. Silky strands of platinum hair crossed her face in the night's moist breeze, partially hiding the features Rhys wished he could see.

"Now what? You'll disappear again?" he asked.

"Disappearing is what I do best," she said.

"Why? Are you hiding from someone?"

"Good thing it wasn't you. Look how that turned out."

Rhys grinned, liking her quick-witted comebacks.

"You might want to can the light show if stealth is your objective. Your appearance in the alley was pretty flashy."

She stared at him with her lips parted for a retort she didn't make—lush lips nearly as pale as the rest of her. He wondered what those lips would taste like, and if she'd use her knife on him if he tried to find out.

When seconds passed and she hadn't spoken or made her retreat, Rhys figured those things would have been points for him in the challenge game, if anyone had been keeping score. Then again, she had known about Blood Knights and had pegged him as one with a single glance, so maybe he'd have to concede some of those points.

Finally, when the silence had grown uncomfortable, the provocative white-haired enigma took a backward step, keeping her eyes on him, possibly afraid to turn her back.

"I won't let this go, you know," Rhys warned. "You're far too intriguing."

"You'll have to," she said. "I'm already here and gone."

"And if I were to ask you to stay?"

The waist-length, silver-white tendrils of her hair had taken on a luminous sheen under the streetlight. Hell, Rhys thought, she looked more like an elf than anything else. Another impulse came to touch her, just to make sure she was real and not a mirage. She hadn't addressed any of his questions, but didn't really have to. What had she said? She owed him nothing.

"Ghosts can't fight. Noncorporeal bodies and all that," he said, thinking hard about which gene pool she might have sprung from and again coming up short. "But you are very good with a blade."

"Hate ghosts." She took another backward step.

"What about Blood Knights? Do you hate them, too?"

"Would you deserve it?"

"You know about us, about who we are. Was that by rumor?"

"Plenty of rumors," she said.

"If you travel in the kind of company that would spread those rumors, why haven't I heard about you?"

"Maybe I'm not rumor-worthy."

"I'm fairly sure no one could forget you after a glimpse.

If your soul had been around for a while, someone would have seen you."

"You're right," she agreed. "They wouldn't have forgotten someone like me, which is why I don't allow them that glimpse."

As fun as this was, it was now clear to Rhys that this immortal wasn't going to volunteer any real information about herself at all, even after sharing in his fight with the vampires. He was going to have to get those details some other way.

Smile widening, he said, "I do love a challenge."

"Good for you. Now, you must let me go."

"Or?"

"It will be a regrettable mistake in judgment."

"Really? When we seem to be on the same side?"

"I value privacy above all other things."

Rhys nodded. "If you stay in London, I will be able to find you."

"I didn't realize Blood Knight was synonymous for bloodhound."

"Scent has strong power," Rhys said. "Smells create memories. I can smell the power in you. Though as yet nameless, what you are rolls in my mind like a misplaced vision, sparking images I can't see clearly. It has to be obvious to you that I need to sort that out."

"Quite obvious," she said. "Which is why you followed me in the first place. You're not sure what I am or who I am. For a Guardian, that kind of void in information would be regrettable."

"You would be curious in my place, I think."

The whittled animal-bone handle of the blade that she clenched in her fist was a further sign of her Otherness. Most supernatural species could not touch any kind of metal.

Rhys wondered if she might use that blade on him if he pursued this line of inquiry.

"I watch here, for now," he said. "I discern friend from foe and try to keep the peace when that task gets harder with each passing year."

She waved her blade at the dusting of fine gray ash covering the pavement. "Yet, aren't you and these creatures you call monsters distant cousins? In which case, one might reason that you and your knightly brothers have an obligation to cull their numbers in order to protect the humans these vampires prey upon."

"More rumors?" Rhys said.

"Aren't rumors often sparked by truth?"

Before he had time to reply, she closed the distance between them. From only inches away, her scent was much stronger. Her next move was unexpected. She touched him.

No, it was her blade that had touched him. Its sharp tip pierced a coin-sized hole in his coat. Rhys looked down at the knife, then at her. He quirked an eyebrow.

She lowered the blade and placed her cool, bare fingertips on his mouth. Rhys swayed and swallowed a rising groan of surprise. He held his breath as she traced the outline of his lips before gently pressing them back. He knew what she searched for and what she saw hidden there. Fangs.

"It would seem some rumors actually are true," he said.

Wickedly placed inside the mouths of each of the seven men who had accepted the vows issued by their Makers at Castle Broceliande, those fangs were, like this female's inked tattoos, not really good for anything. They were merely reminders that blood sipped from a holy relic is what had resurrected the seven men and sent them on a quest.

"This is what the Grail Quest did to you," she said.

"In return for preventing that Grail from falling into the hands of others who might use its power to bestow immortality for another purpose," Rhys said. "Imagine a world where the bad guys couldn't be harmed."

"No rumor, then." She drew her hand back.

Rhys watched this female closely. The effects of her company were incredibly rich for an immortal who had never beheld a female of similar kind. She was enough like him to threaten his moratorium on seeking the companionship of others. Her touch, like her earlier light show, left an imprint, not only on Rhys's mouth, but on his soul, as if she had branded him with the same fire that flickered in her eyes.

Rhys took a firm hold on her shoulders and pulled her closer, so that she had to look up to see his face. She did not use the knife or try to escape from what she had to know would come next.

All that fire...

All that heat...

He was so damn hungry for those things.

Daringly, Rhys rested his mouth on hers lightly, testing his resolve and hers. He waited, expecting a slam of protective power from her in honor of his transgression. But nothing like that came.

Her lips were as cool as her fingertips, and soft. She didn't encourage him. Nor did she pull away when he deepened the pressure, breathing her in, tasting the sweetness of what lay behind the lushness he was invading. She was so very appealing.

She leaned into him and made a sound that was part groan and part whisper. In that sound lay a silent command...not for release, but for more.

He gave her that. And when her lips parted, the uncanny sense of familiarity returned so strongly that Rhys echoed the sound she had made. He knew her, didn't he?

As his mouth captured hers, his hunger raged. Her spirit

seemed to capture his spirit. She bent him to her will, commanding him to forget that familiarity he sought and bury it deep.

But she kissed him back, and the intimacy of the physical connection spiraled Rhys into a world where nothing other than the two of them existed, and the past, present and future became one.

Hell, if she was a demon, someone on the other side knew too much about the longings of a Blood Knight.

A draft of cool air drifted over him when her lips left his. Rhys opened his eyes to find himself alone. In a totally unacceptable move that had to have involved some kind of mind trick, the woman whose lips had so moved him had, like liquid moonlight, just melted away.

He stood beneath the streetlight, looking around, surprised to have been bested by the pale stranger. That was a first.

"All right," he said, retrieving the dagger from his boot. "This game point goes to you, but the game isn't over."

Then he turned to face the vampire watching him from the shadows.

Chapter 6

Avery fled the scene without looking back.

Taking that Knight's mind off her imminent escape had worked a little too well. With his lips on hers and his warm breath in her lungs, she'd almost forgotten what she had planned for these guys, and had escaped only in the nick of time.

Dreams of getting close to him had been with her for so long, remnants of those dreams had nearly been her downfall. By now, she knew him well, although he knew nothing of the woman he had kissed. Still, having the upper hand didn't make her feel better about that kind of closeness, and what a mistake it had been to allow it.

Bad plan. Pitiful timing.

While distracting the Knight had seemed her best way to escape, she now felt a new need to go back to him, have more of him and indulge in the very thing she had always craved.

Hadn't she always craved him?

The line between hate and love, two things seemingly so opposite, was blurring. That had always been the danger of her special bond with Perceval. She was already inside him in an intimate way. Her blood ran in his veins alongside another's, and yet the immediacy of this attraction to him seemed like so much more than blood calling to blood.

But now…

Him…

That kiss.

Avery glanced up at the sky, questioning the heavens. But it had been a long time since she'd had any help from there.

She had heard something, though. The Knight had spoken to her telepathically. She'd heard him clearly because she had left a channel to her mind open. Another slip-up.

"Damn it," she would have returned if she had been able to join in that conversation. *"This is no game."*

They weren't players on some gigantic chessboard. There was so much more at stake here than who might gain or lose a point. This was life. Hers. She'd been a fool to have been so intent on tattooed wings that she hadn't done enough research about which of the Knights she'd potentially encounter if things went wrong in London. Being secretly attracted to this one should have kept her more aware of his travels, even though she'd been loath to remain so close.

It had to be you...

Swinging herself up the side of a building was just one of her many talents. Surprisingly, that also turned out to be a mistake, because the Knight's scent lingered on the rooftop, preventing her from moving on. He must have watched her from here. Below this roof, the alley curved toward the tattoo parlor.

Some new stealth trick of your own, Knight?

Now, she had to regroup. He had threatened to find her,

and would if she remained in this city. Leaving London, however, was not an option. A culmination of the search that had tied up her whole earthly life lay within her grasp. The importance of that could not be forsaken because a Blood Knight was on her trail.

Leave here. Leave him, her instincts warned. *Before...*

Before what? Before she forgot her early hatred for the Seven and their Makers who had caused her so much agony? This Knight was one of them, even if the way things had gone down at that blasted castle wasn't his fault. Still, the beautiful bastard she'd kissed was guilty by association.

Mixed feelings were scary, and she was experiencing plenty of them. Without old hatreds to guide her, what was left? Which direction would she take? She wanted so badly to trust someone, but could not confess her secrets to one of the seven golden Knights.

Leave him.

Must stay away.

"You will never find me," she whispered to her glorious Blood Knight. But those words made her heart ache. They made her feel sick. She added soberly, "Not without an invitation."

Possibly she liked him too much to share the hurt she had suffered. Even more telling than her new turn of conscience was how desperately she longed to have another shot at that kiss—an action that had apparently changed everything after so many years of avoiding him.

Hissing sounds, like static coming over the airwaves, forced Rhys to address the next untimely distraction. There was no mistaking the stink of stale blood permeating the area. Over the years, he'd grown sick of the stench.

"It's rather early for you to be partying, isn't it?" he said to the bloodsucker tucked into a dark corner behind him.

Guttural noises accompanied the vamp's rebuttal, as if the creature wasn't used to speaking through its fangs. "You do not own this city, freak."

Rhys grinned dangerously. "Freak, is it? Me? That's rich."

"I do not fear you."

"You haven't heard the rumors?"

"I have heard them," the vamp snarled.

"Maybe you missed the fight minutes ago?"

"I did not miss it."

"Yet you'll confront me here?"

"Do you imagine I came alone?"

"Yes, actually. I can sense your kind, you know. It's a gift. Or a curse. You're the last vamp crowding my space tonight."

The vampire didn't take the bait of that taunt and showed itself.

"I suppose you're drawn to the scent of this place." Rhys waved at the tattoo parlor.

"As were you," the vampire returned, with far too much insight.

"I'm not attracted to blood, you know. It does not sustain me," Rhys said.

"What does?"

"Current goals. Old vows."

The vampire floated out of the shadows—a middle-aged bloodsucker, turned in his fifties, Rhys presumed. Tall, thin and dressed in a tattered black suit, this child of the night smelled like he'd been in the earth a few years too long. This was no fledgling, after all.

"One cannot thrive on old vows alone," it observed.

Rhys nodded. "I have also cultivated a taste for wine over the past hundred years."

The vampire had no sense of humor.

"You came to her aid," it noted.

Rhys applied new energy to his voice. The vampire had been watching that fight, watching his white-haired companion.

"For reasons you would likely not understand or want to go into," Rhys said.

"Perhaps I would understand. I followed her here, too. I am not immune to what she represents," the vampire returned.

"Would that be dinner?"

"The pale one would be a veritable feast," the vampire agreed. "Whipped cream on a blood-red cake."

Rhys said calmly, "She isn't human, you know."

"All the better."

This bloodsucker had also tuned in to the power the woman radiated. Did the creep believe he could sink his fangs into an immortal and get away with it, when that would have been impossible?

"Trying something like that would be a misuse of your energy," Rhys warned. "Your fangs won't penetrate her skin, you know."

And even if they could, her blood would make this creature choke. White blood, underscoring the colorlessness of her skin.

"Can't hurt to try," the vamp remarked.

"Looking for what? The fountain of youth? You do realize that's a false rumor, and that no such thing exists?"

Agitated, the bloodsucker moved sideways. "Can you tell me this truthfully?"

"No fountain of youth," Rhys promised.

Although the Knights had been resurrected by a blood gift sipped from a golden chalice, they weren't vampires. Though they had fangs, the Knights ate and drank only slightly less than the rest of the world's population. Their blood wasn't a restorative that could heal a reanimated corpse. He and his brethren weren't gods. All seven had been human once.

"I don't think you understand," Rhys continued. "The point I'm making is that this woman is not for you. Not any of your concern."

"Is that not so for you, as well?"

Rhys wasn't entirely sure how to reply to that. Like the vampire, he had left his human existence behind and accepted the invitation to exist forever. But he had done so willingly. He doubted this vampire had chosen his afterlife's direction, or that many would choose to live off the life force of others.

The Seven had been called back to life by a higher power than the black hand of Death. That beginning set them apart. His heart had been restarted for a golden purpose. Only through the miracle of a chalice often referred to as the Holy Grail had his heart and soul been retained.

"I suggest you take your hunger elsewhere," Rhys warned. "Quite honestly, I'm not always this generous with your kind."

The vampire bowed its head. "I find that I'd like to see her again. I will stay out of your way, however, for now, since you've asked so nicely."

With a flurry of kicked-up street grime, followed by the sound of loose roof tiles creaking over Rhys's head, the cheeky fanged bastard disappeared. The way they had of doing things like that was creepy, even to an immortal with equal abilities.

Nevertheless, Rhys's interest in the pale immortal he'd kissed had just increased tenfold. Other creatures had found her twice, for some reason, when their usual MO was to avoid him and his kind. The creep he had spoken with was too interested in her, and that wasn't right. If vampires spread the word that a pale immortal female had taken up residence, other monsters might come calling for reasons Rhys didn't fully understand.

Did they honestly believe the snowy-haired female could help to reinstate their former lives? Change their fate? Too many vamps appearing at once to test that claim might not bode well for anyone on London's streets after dark.

But it suited Rhys.

Taking out a bunch of vampires at once would help those unsuspecting mortal souls stay safe.

It was late. He had taken too much time here. Pulling his coat tighter, setting his intentions on a new course, Rhys followed the whiff of scent and the barely visible ribbon of light that were the angelic immortal female's calling cards, which took him to the alley where she had first appeared.

Glancing up at the building beside him, hearing her warning about not finding her without an invitation, Rhys smiled and muttered, "Who can resist such a sweet-scented warrior?"

He was coming.

Either her powers of persuasion had dimmed considerably, or this Knight's abilities had grown lately. Due to the strength of the feelings for him that she had sealed away, Avery couldn't allow herself to be caught.

The choices were to run or face her dazzling nemesis one more time. Keep her secrets, or tell him the truth and see what he would do.

Roll of the dice. Which is it to be? Go or stay?

It wasn't much of a choice, really. The Knight was right. After finding her, having his hands on her, there wouldn't be anywhere for her to go in this city that he couldn't find if he tried hard enough. One kiss and an old blood bond had seen to that.

But she could not leave London. Leaving would mean losing the opportunity to search for the things so important to her after exhausting her search elsewhere. The things that had been hidden from her, belonged to her, called out with a distant, elusive hum, as if they also craved a reunion. Caution was needed, though. She had been fooled before.

Avery was aware of every step toward her the Blood Knight took.

"You don't own the city, Guardian," she whispered. "You might be its keeper, but you're not mine."

Too late now.

One more time, she told herself. *See him just once.*

She could handle that.

In a ruffle of night air, he was there.

"You keep turning up," she said as he climbed over the ledge.

His appearance on the rooftop might have upset her confidence somewhat, because when viewing the entirety of this guy from a distance, the effect on her system was elaborate.

The third Blood Knight to have ridden forth from Castle Broceliande's massive iron gates no longer donned the golden armor he'd once worn in honor of his Quest. He didn't bear the Knights' red-striped ebony crest of the Grail protectors. But he was always mesmerizing.

The modern duster coat and dark jeans suited him. So did the shorn hair that now only brushed his collar. Where she was white, he was bronze. His luster hadn't faded the way hers had. At times, over the years, she had envied his polished allure.

"Yes. About that," he said, coming closer. "You did leave a trail."

"Impossible," she argued.

"Fortuitous," he corrected. "Because I believe we have

some unfinished business to talk over that rules out distance for the time being."

"Misguided persistence will get you nowhere," Avery warned. "Neither will flattery, so don't bother. The fact is, you have followed me again."

"I did warn you that until I know what and who you are, this city might be at risk and I would be responsible."

"I'm no predator. I would have thought you'd have figured that out by now," she said.

"I don't believe you are a predator. I'm just not sure what you are or why my soul recognizes yours in some way. I'm not sure I can rest until I know why."

Avery took a wide stance with both arms loose at her sides. Inside, she was fluttering again.

"That's quite a line about souls. Do women usually fall for it?"

"Mortal women sometimes do." His tone was light. The situation wasn't.

Avery stopped short of asking him how many humans he'd tried that soul-to-soul business on. She wiped risqué images of him in bed with mortal females from her mind quickly. This bastard was charm incarnate when he wanted to be, and he was turning that charm her way. However, it had been many years since she'd trusted anyone.

"Then I suggest you find someone more amenable to bedroom talk," she said. "The night isn't over. If you hurry, you might find a taker."

After a pause, he said, "Can we cut the crap? I'm not attacking you. I'm merely asking a few pertinent questions."

"I told you I'm not in the habit of telling strangers anything about myself and made it clear I owe you nothing. What don't you get, Blood Knight? Why can't you honor my privacy?"

"I think you have some responsibility to come clean.

There aren't many of us, or beings much like us. I can feel the power you possess. What I can't do is place it. I need to know if you're in any way like me."

"Nothing like you," she replied to get him off her back. That was the truth. She couldn't lie. Not outright. Neither of them could, because of that touch of the heavens they possessed.

Her answer clearly frustrated him. His hands opened and closed, forming and reforming fists as if he might wring the answers from her that he needed. Power meant danger in his world, and as he'd said, she was an unknown. Yet understanding how he felt and doing something to help him, at her own expense, were things on opposite shores of a vast ocean she dared not try to cross.

"Your soul resonates on a similar frequency to mine, which leads me to believe we have some things in common," he said.

Yes. We have that damn castle in common.

We also have the vows that made us into what we are.

You know nothing of my part in that.

"I've seen you before," he went on. "I'm sure I've felt your presence on the edges of my existence in the past."

That news surprised Avery. If he knew of her presence, she hadn't held up her end of the vow she'd taken to never allow the Knights to find her or the truth of their origins until she was ready to spill that news. They might not have accomplished the goals their Makers had set for them if they had known the truth about her and what their Makers had done to assure that the Knights had significant power of their own. As it turned out, the Knights' goals had been good ones, and still were. She couldn't argue with that.

"Your Makers are long gone, I assume," she said, without the probing tone the remark deserved. "Nevertheless, you carry on as though still bound to the oaths you once took."

The eyes studying her flashed with blue fire. "What do you know of the Makers?"

"Rumor. Legend. Fantasy lore," Avery replied. "Legends say the Blood Knights were created by three magicians who were also the earliest form of what we know of today as vampires. If that's true, it would explain a lot about you."

"Rumor is it? What would a bunch of old untruths say about me?"

Avery wiped a finger across her mouth to remind him she had seen the fangs. He watched her carefully with the eyes of a hawk.

"Does the term *fantasy* also explain you?" he asked.

"I'm sure the parameters of fantasy lore cover us both."

"You had a Maker?"

"Oh, yes. An extremely powerful one."

"So why are you in pain?" he asked.

The several feet of distance separating them had not been enough. Somehow he had picked up on the wicked pain that underlined every damn day of her existence and was assailing her now. Seeing this man added to her discomfort, the way seeing him always had. Her heart was beating fast. Speaking was difficult.

"Possibly I can help," he suggested. "I've learned a thing or two about pain and healing."

"You can help by leaving me alone to do what I came here to do."

"Other than the tattoos, you mean?"

"Yes," Avery warily admitted. "Other than that."

She dropped the hand that again had automatically returned to her mouth to trace the lingering impression of their kiss, because this Knight missed little and was analyzing every move she made. She had to be more careful. That was a fact.

She didn't press home the fact that he had fangs. Surely he would have wondered about that.

"We're to pretend nothing happened?" he asked, confirming her fears about that kiss.

"Nothing did," Avery said.

He walked into the light of a moon half covered by dark clouds. Shadows played on his features in an artistic tableau of light and dark. His vivid blue eyes were like searchlights.

Without having ever feared anyone, Avery stepped back. The pressure of being near this immortal was greater than she would have imagined. After circling these Knights for centuries, she had to stumble on this particular one.

Wanting to turn her anger into another kind of emotion wasn't a good sign. Desiring what was forbidden between the two of them was the biggest surprise of all. She could see the outcome of this scenario if they remained in each other's presence. She could taste it.

Avery liked to think she was better than this, stronger than the wayward urges pulsing through her that told her to walk straight toward this seductive male.

"I am no threat to you or anyone else," she said. "I will promise you that."

"You're already a threat to me." His tone was softer now, and much too convincing.

"Forget about me. Move on."

"Yes," he said. "That's what I will have to do."

Relief filled Avery, healing the cracks in her weakening resolve. Remorse was there, too, just as it had been from the start, after she had first set foot on the Earth's hard surface.

Regret topped both of those emotions, coming at her in seismic jolts and due to the possibility of this guy actually fulfilling her wishes by letting her go when maybe he could have helped her, if she'd let him. If she trusted herself to let him. He might have understood what had been done to her, and want to correct old errors.

"More pain," he observed with a keen, appraising gaze. "I can feel it overtaking you."

"It's nothing I can't bear."

He nodded. "Do I play a part in that pain?"

"Do you believe you're so important?"

His head tilted to one side, as if in viewing her from a different angle he might discover something pertinent that would help him to read her. Damn if she'd let him.

"All right," he said. "I'll honor your request and be on my way. It's a shame, though, when we were getting along so well."

Wait, Avery almost cried out, biting her tongue to keep from repeating that ugly earlier show of vulnerability that had resulted in a kiss. For her, vulnerability was rare and dangerous.

When he turned from her, she let him. When he looked back at her over a broad shoulder she had seen many times in secret, from afar, Avery managed to keep her expression smooth. The look she gave him was the same thing as a lie, and also a cover-up. Things had changed. Meeting this Knight face-to-face had softened her stance on the future. Seeing him in person had affected them both.

There was no going back.

Wait, she wanted to say again, because he wasn't the monster she had struggled to believe he was, while knowing better all along. Though he was intelligent and experienced, the man once known as Perceval knew very little about his immortal beginnings. He was continuing to honor Britain's famous old king's credo of using might to fight for what was right. His side was the epitome of doing good. How could she have hated any of that enough to have stayed away?

Damn you...

The desire to be near you threatens to outweigh all the rest.

She didn't utter the curses that stuck in her throat. Not even the worst ones. Weren't the two of them in the same boat, living on and on with no end in sight? Did this man wish his fate had been otherwise, just as she did?

We do have things in common.

Maybe some regrets also haunt you.

Perhaps pain is also your demon?

He had retreated to the edge of the roof and stopped there. "Name's Rhys nowadays. Rhys de Troyes. If you need me, call."

"I won't need you," she said.

He nodded. "One thing I've found in this crazy, over-extended existence is that we never really know how to ask for what we need, even when we do need something. That's the real curse we suffer from."

In a shaft of moonlight, the flash of his golden-highlighted hair was the last Avery saw of the blazing-hot immortal she had wanted so badly to despise, but couldn't. After all the arguing, he had complied with her demands and was going away...like the goddamn gentleman he had probably been before the word *Blood* had been tacked onto his knightly status.

Chapter 7

Moonlight, usually Rhys's ally in his war against the monsters, seemed impossibly dull when *she* wasn't standing in it. The overhead orb's silvery shine didn't matter to him at the moment. Neither did the possible return of the bloodsuckers.

Tonight, for the first time in a long while, he had experienced the kindling of a little thing called *hope.* And the reason at the core of this new emotion had sent him away. She had waved him off as inconsequential, perhaps too wrapped up in a mystery of her own to let a stranger share in that mystery.

He hadn't gotten one straight answer from her, and he had so many questions.

Why the tattoo?

Why wings?

Chances were good that she wouldn't help him out of this quandary, not *if* they met again, but *when* they did. Because he had every intention of seeing her again. In fact, he wasn't going to let her out of his sight completely, in case she used some of that power to disappear.

"Why the kiss, and why would you allow it? Distraction? Moment of weakness? Attraction? Are you as interested in me, as I am in you?"

Given that she could hear at least some of his thoughts and remarks, maybe she'd hear those whispered words. She hadn't gone away. Not yet. Weird as it was, he was able to see the light particles that stuck around this pale vision like the shadows stuck to the street. From where he stood, it was easy to see the faint glow on the roofline.

She was there, all right. She hadn't gone away.

Other things that hid beneath the cover of darkness were moving in and around the square now, as predicted. Most of the creatures in the supernatural world that moved with unnatural speed left a noticeable residue behind in the infrared spectrum. Rhys supposed that he also left that kind of trail. Not the pure, shimmering white of starlight, like hers, though. Seems every damn thing about her was unique, as was his growing need to get to the bottom of her appearance in London.

He had no idea what caused the inner light she wielded and doubted if anyone else did, either. Not anyone living, anyway. As he had told her, some mention of it would have reached him if anyone had gotten wind of that.

The dead were another matter needing consideration. As he had feared, news of the woman he'd kissed under the streetlight must have spread. He sensed the creatures coming. London's vampires might also have seen the light this newcomer projected and been attracted to it.

Being stuck underground most of the time, the dark side probably hungered for light of any kind, including the shine of the Divine. And in some small way, the woman he had met tonight did exhibit a few Divine qualities. Her fake wings might have made her believe she actually *was* Divine.

She hadn't wanted to leave him back on that street. At least he knew that much.

Rhys's awareness picked up a sudden foreshadowing of the future. His sigils were aching. Energy pulsed through the tentacles of inky symbols on the back of his neck, urging him to turn his head.

This was a sturdy reminder that there was a war on, and that more abominations prowled the area nearby. He was needed to help defray the aftereffects of that war and had to resume his post.

But he was torn.

The light on that rooftop was a heady draw and nearly impossible to resist. *She*, whose name he still didn't know, was equally impossible to forget.

"Monsters first," Rhys whispered, hoping he'd actually believe it, because chaos would rain down if humans became aware of what resided in the shadows. For them, ignorance was bliss, as long as somebody in those same shadows took the monsters to task.

He had been that somebody for a very long time.

"So, what do you use your power for?" he asked the empty space next to him, wishing the leather-clad angel wannabe was standing there. Her exemplary fighting skills, seen firsthand tonight, could have helped London's mortal population. The sheer number of scars on her body told him she'd been in many skirmishes. She hadn't shied away from facing vamps tonight.

Studying the roofline above him, Rhys felt more confused than ever. The light up there had dimmed.

"Maybe you're a fallen star in human form? As if that were possible?"

Thoughts sputtered as he perceived another disturbance in the night.

He searched the roofline.

The slightest ripple in the dark suggested to him that her light had not faded on its own, and that his angel had company on that rooftop. Noticeable in the breeze rustling the hem of his coat was a sulfurous odor of rust and freshly overturned earth.

Growls of anger erupted from Rhys's throat. Without considering how many times she had told him to go away, he reached for the ledge above him with both hands and put his boot to the brick.

"Come out," Avery taunted, aware of what was heading her way. "I'm in no mood for playing hide-and-seek."

Her company on the rooftop was a Shade, the ghostly leftover of a nasty human whose afterlife had never been set straight. Unlike true ghosts, Shades could do great harm to the unsuspecting. Like some kinds of Reapers, they sucked the life from their victims for revenge over their own damned fates. They were also cleanup crews for the vampires, picking at leftovers. Otherworldly vultures.

And they had pretty good hearing. As the shadowy form slithered over the lip of the roof tiles, Avery welcomed it with a wry smile.

Gliding on feet that didn't actually touch the ground, the bugger kept to the dark areas cast over the rooftop by the higher floors of the building beside theirs. It was ironic that Shades preferred shade.

"What do you want here?" Avery fingered the blade that could do this creeper some damage if she found the right spot, despite the creature's haziness.

"Speak up."

"Come with me." The response was high-pitched and could have been either a male or female voice.

"I'm busy at the moment. So, no, thanks."

"Important," the Shade suggested, halting where moonlight met the mildewed slate tiles.

"Everything is important these days," Avery said.

"I know what you seek, pale one."

"Doubtful, since it has nothing to do with your kind."

"You speak folly and understand nothing about what's been entrusted to us."

Avery's index finger slid along the razor-sharp edge of her blade. She closely observed the Shade's reaction to the scent of blood. The thing wasn't a vampire, and therefore not fueled by hemoglobin, but the odor it gave off told her it had been in a musty vampire den recently. Things like bloodlust tended to rub off on those who frequented dark places.

Drops of blood beaded on her skin, its whiteness nearly invisible to the naked eye. Smelling it, the shadowy creature leaned forward, nearly taking a step that would have solidified its outline in the moon's light—bright light avoidance was one thing these guys had in common with the bloodsucker population. But it held back.

"We know what you seek," the Shade said, teetering on the brink of pushing its luck with her. "We have news of such a thing. I can show you."

"Really?" another voice called out in Avery's place. "I wonder what that thing might be, Shade."

Avery looked past the creature rapidly backing into the shadows. Her formidable Blood Knight, now calling himself Rhys, had returned and stood with his dagger in his hand, looking every bit like the legends of old had come to life. Formidable. Intimidating to all who might stand against him.

Avery's nerves pinged. Her heart rate soared, as did her pounding pulse. She had known the Knight would find her if she didn't get a move on. So why hadn't she tried to lose him?

Her attention was divided. The Shade's behavior had been more abnormal than the usual Shade bag of tricks. What it had said was interesting. Shades would know better than to attack an immortal, but had it been trying to tell her something that actually pertained to her very private search?

We know what you seek.

Unlike her, and unlike the Blood Knight across from her, most of the world's other monsters lied through their teeth.

"What? No answer?" the Blood Knight said, taking one step toward the shadows the Shade had blended into.

Avery knew he wouldn't pursue the damn thing and that he had come here for another reason. She was that reason. Still, she had to wonder how a Shade could have been aware of the fact that she searched for anything. Believing it had known something would also prove how desperate she was to be reunited with the missing pieces of herself.

All these speculations were moot points, though, since the Shade was gone.

"Saving the day, Knight? You scared that poor sucker," Avery said thoughtfully.

He turned toward her. "Are you into self-mutilation these days, angel? That cut on your hand?"

His use of the word *angel* jump-started the nerve burn that followed. Avery stared back at him, reasoning that he knew nothing.

"Why didn't you dispense with that no-good creature?" he asked, waving at the pool of darkness.

"I didn't have to. You rode in on a white horse."

Her companion grinned. "Would you have dispensed with it?"

"Probably not. It meant me no harm."

"Said no mortal that had ever encountered one of them on a dark street and lived to tell about it."

"We both know that kind of danger doesn't necessarily apply to us," she pointed out.

"The thing issued an invitation for you to follow it home, all cozy-like."

"Yes, it did."

"Are Shades famous for helping others?"

When she didn't answer, he said, "I rest my case."

He was right, of course. Yet, as Avery glanced to the shadows, she wondered why she had felt reasonably sure this Shade knew something that might have helped her quest. The awareness was a gut feeling, with no sound basis whatsoever, but what the hell? Gut feelings were often part of intuition.

Her Knight spoke again. "Was that creature right in the assumption that you've come to London looking for something? You've hinted at needing to be left alone to do what you came here to do. If you tell me what you're looking for, I'll help with your search."

Her inner flutters persisted. At the base of her spine, chills were piling up. Avery had to hide her body's quakes. Because of the amount of effort that took, she was close to telling this Knight what he wanted to hear. She was so very tired of keeping things to herself.

"Who would you rather trust with that information? That hazy black sucker or me?" he said.

When she didn't answer that question, he said, "I see. And I'm sorry you feel threatened."

"Nothing you could do would threaten me."

That statement wasn't entirely true, however, and even

the partial falsehood stung Avery to her core. The handsome bastard's looks alone posed a threat to her many lifetimes of isolation. His hand-picked existence had threatened hers by taking away her freedom. Plus, her heart was misbehaving by beating way too fast, as if all the time she'd spent cursing him didn't amount to squat when facing the real deal.

Discomfort came with his continued scrutiny and from being the central focus of any Blood Knight's attention.

That kiss didn't mean anything.

"I know the closeness back there was meant as a distraction, if that's what you're worrying about," he said.

Words failed her, even in thought, which was never a good sign. Strangely enough, she was weakening, caving to this guy's well-practiced, bronzed allure. While she knew better than to give in, she just couldn't seem to help herself.

This is why I've stayed away from you, Avery wanted to confess.

She kept her mouth shut.

"I will again offer you my assistance," he said in that irritating way he had of sounding chivalrous. "One last offer. Take it or leave it."

Avery considered his offer carefully. She didn't have to like him. They didn't have to be friends. The old vows could stand if she allowed this guy to help her this once. After finding her wings, she would hit the road and curse him all over again.

"If you know what I am, you must also know what I can do, and that I mean what I say," he added.

I know your mission is to do good in this world, endlessly and forever. But can I forget the past long enough to accept your help in such a personal quest?

Major stumbling block. Could she bypass that damn

kiss and how this Knight made her feel, when she hadn't felt anything for countless years?

Maybe he could be trusted. But could she trust herself around him if a simple kiss had sent her running? Former prejudices weren't worth much if they could be obliterated by a pretty face.

I'm not like you.

Not anything like you.

Sadly, that wasn't quite true, either, since the Knight also carried in his immortal soul the light of the Divine. She had been a crucial link in passing that light to him. And damned if it wasn't that same light that made her want to get closer to him now.

"In seeking you out, I wanted to make sure you were all right," he explained. "That's all."

"Liar," she said. Possibly he couldn't lie straight out, but he wasn't telling her everything.

His electric-blue gaze intensified, leaving Avery feeling naked and exposed.

"You're right," he conceded. "I wanted something else as well. Friendship."

"A half truth, at best."

Nodding, he started over. "All right. The truth is I want a lot more than that. So, shall I go, or will you dare to confide at least part of your story?"

Do not give in.

Look away if you have to.

Avery managed to hold to those two inner commands for a few seconds before she spoke again.

"I've lost something that I've been trying to find for decades. My search has been exhaustive and has finally brought me back to London."

He waited for her to go on.

"I had all but given up before being called back to London. I feel close to my goal here and have to give this quest one last shot."

Avery saw how the word *quest* affected the man across from her. For all his glorious Knightness, the guy wasn't so difficult to read. His extended life span had been based on that same concept. *Quest.*

"How much do you know about me?" he asked. "How do you know about Blood Knights?"

"I was privy to that information early on, from a source I can't disclose."

"Can't, or won't disclose?"

"It's the same thing, in the end."

He took a step toward her. "You know my story, and I can't know yours?"

"I doubt you'd want to help me if I told you my story."

"It's that bad?"

"To some."

"Are you a demon?"

Avery shook her head. "That much I will swear to."

"Then you have the advantage, I'm thinking," he said.

"Can you live with that for a while longer and still help?"

He smiled. "I thought you said you knew me."

His smile brought back the deep internal flutter she had experienced earlier. There was no hint of treachery in his expression and no sign of his fangs. Avery wanted to return the smile but wasn't sure she remembered how. Pain had a tendency to darken even the lightest moments. Although this man was part of that pain, there was a chance he could help her rise above the agony of her existence, and at this late hour, set things straight.

If that wasn't to happen, and things didn't go that way, what would fill the empty space inside her that pain occupied? What would happen to the memories carved into her body and her mind? Without those memories, nothing would matter. *He* wouldn't matter.

"You've gone quiet," he noted when the silence stretched.

Don't you see it, Blood Knight? See me?

What kind of creature has white blood in their veins?

How many beings walking this Earth have one boot on the ground and the other in the heavens?

Doesn't my skin tell you something important?

Are you looking deep enough? Hard enough?

Do you not see yourself in me?

Her story? Until the twenty-first century, when whole sections of the human race had gone through phases with names like Goth and cyberpunk, she'd had to stay completely hidden. After that, when pretty much anything worked, fitting in was easier. Her white skin was even envied by a select few. Dressed in black leather, she could skate through crowds if she had to, if those crowds occupied the outskirts of places where normal people gathered.

Parts of her story encapsulated this Knight's story, as well. Neither of them could ever really fit in. The magnificent Blood Knight was hugging the shadows, just as she was. They were freaks because of their unique kind of beauty.

When she looked up, he had raised a hand as if expecting her to take it. As if he was tossing her a lifeline to a better place.

Go to hell, was the response on the tip of her tongue. But that was overruled by another reaction. Because, God, yes, she wanted to take that hand, touch him, believe in him. She wanted those things badly enough to taste the sweet irony of her own stubborn objections. Way back, she had trusted in the power of good, and in those who wielded goodness like a weapon.

The Knight spoke again. "If you allow me to help with

this quest of yours, you'll be doing me a favor, you know. Things can get pretty boring around here. Same old fights. Endless hours. More and more monsters."

Body rebelling, mind reeling with comebacks so indecent they'd send this Knight away forever… Avery took a breath and closed her eyes. Another surprise, one to top all of the others, was hearing herself say, "Yes. Okay. Help me."

Afraid to see his reaction, she kept her eyes shut, figuring a thank-you would have been going too damn far, even if this Blood Knight expected it.

Chapter 8

"Good," Rhys said, though he wasn't sure his new companion wholeheartedly agreed with what she had just committed to. On the plus side, she didn't run away. When her eyes reopened, she turned her head to listen to the sounds he also heard.

"Do we fight what's coming our way first?" she asked. "That's what you're supposed to do, isn't it? Keep the streets safe?"

"It's what I choose to do," Rhys corrected. "You feel the monsters coming?"

"Like a foul wave."

"Maybe facing more of them isn't what you choose to do."

"I've had my moments with the monsters. Far too many."

Was that the cause of her scars? Rhys wondered.

"So we turn back this tide and then we talk about your search," he said.

"Yes. Then we talk."

He walked to the edge of the roof and peered over, joined by this new, unlikely companion whose body language made it clear she wasn't going to get too close to him.

Go ahead, Rhys thought. *Keep your distance a while longer.*

"Ten of them," she noted, her attention fixed on the street. "Vampires. Not so young this time. The odor is fouler, stronger."

"Ten is ten too many to be roaming the streets all at once," Rhys said.

With her silhouette half hidden by her fall of fair hair, his companion gave him a sideways glance. "How many can you take?"

"All ten. How about you?"

"I could leave you one, if you like."

Rhys grinned. "Very generous." He waved at the street below them. "On the count of three?"

"Hell, why wait?" she said, and jumped.

They'd been three stories up. Rhys landed in a crouch on the pavement with one hand on the asphalt. She was beside him. Standing in unison, they looked both ways to make sure they hadn't been seen and then took off at a jog toward the oncoming gang of vamps.

Lucky for Londoners, it was the wee hours of the night, or morning, depending on which way they looked at it. Most people would be tucked safely in their beds. The few roaming around at 3:00 a.m. would have a hard lesson to learn if they weren't careful, and if a Guardian hadn't been watching this particular area.

The woman next to him waved a hand upward, indicating that a couple of the fanged horde had climbed drainpipes to reach the higher floors of the building beside them. Nodding, Rhys headed after those beasts. Climbing as easily as the bloodsuckers had, he reached the roof in seconds, hoping his companion would be able to handle things on the ground until he returned.

Two bloodless faces peered at him speculatively as he approached. Older vampires, but not ancient. Experienced. Hungry. Dull black eyes showed no hint of recognition when fixed on him. Word had not yet spread to this nest about the Guardian in their midst, a being with fangs who came from a larger gene pool.

"Not a good night to be out in this part of town," Rhys said. "Tonight there are two of us to welcome you."

Neither of the bloodsuckers responded with an audible comeback. To Rhys, their thoughts were like waves of chatter. Too hungry to remain idle, both vampires rushed toward him with their fangs exposed. Their taloned hands slashed at the air.

Rhys had the first vamp on the ground before the second reached him, holding it firmly with a boot on the bloodsucker's bony chest. The damn thing snapped and squirmed, struggling to free itself. In this state, the beast could have butchered any human in its path.

Rhys put the vampire out of its misery with a stake to the chest in time to face the second attacker. He was doing the people of London and these creatures a favor. No decent human being would have wanted this kind of fanged afterlife existence.

Vampire number two was wily and halted a few steps from Rhys, taking stock of its formidable opponent. Mouth opening and closing as if snapping at the air, it issued a shrill cry.

"Won't help. The good folks around here need protection, and at the moment I'm their best bet."

The vampire turned its attention from Rhys to the street below them, as if aware of some new threat. Beyond the echo of its cry, Rhys heard what the monster had heard—

the sharp repeat of a weapon going off, followed closely by an echoing howl.

Recognizing the sound, the vampire took off in a smear of speed that would have rendered it invisible to any human that had been looking. Rhys caught the creature by its coat-tails near the roof's rim and spun the bloodsucker around.

"How many more of you are there?" Rhys demanded, his face close to the death mask that was the vampire's face.

Mad with bloodlust and the need to escape, the vamp lunged sideways, biting at Rhys's right arm. With a swift motion born of decades of self-defense, Rhys flung the vampire over the edge of the roof and lunged after it.

He needn't have bothered giving chase, as it turned out. Funnels of gray ash met him on the ground, all that was left of that particular monster.

Standing in a rainfall of ash stood his petite, blue-eyed warrior maiden, silver blade in hand. Rhys saw no other vampires. Their foul scent had dissipated to a faint, odorous stench.

The pale warrior's dark-rimmed blue eyes met his.

"All eight?" Rhys asked, after a beat.

"Nine," she corrected. "I'm assuming you got the other one?"

That was the moment—as Rhys faced the immortal who was looking more like an avenging angel than anything else—that he figured her story had to be one hell of a tale, and that he'd be damned if he'd let her go without hearing all of it.

And maybe he wouldn't let her go, even then.

The way this Knight looked at her had changed, Avery noted with a flare of internal heat. Curiosity had been replaced with something else. His expression was unreadable.

"Really," he said soberly. "Who the hell are you?"

He didn't wait for the answer she wouldn't have given him anyway. Sirens were fast approaching. London's police force was on the way to an incident no doubt called in by the two mortals who had escaped earlier from the vamp attack. Since gunfire was rare for these cops, Avery figured someone else in the area carried concealed.

Her Blood Knight turned, gesturing for her to accompany him. "Time to go."

"We have company," Avery said, striding after him. "The furry kind."

"The moon's not full enough for werewolves to prowl."

"I heard…"

"Yes. One of them, or some of them, don't need a moon to instigate their changes. Lucky for us, those guys are usually the good ones. But then, you probably knew that already."

She didn't confess to knowing a lot more than that about werewolves. In the past, she'd taken a Werelover or two who'd gotten off on her multitude of scars and didn't try to keep her tethered to any kind of impossible relationship. Weres were susceptible to a state called *imprinting* with their mates, which was their version of unbreakable chains. She had known better than to get involved with that. The whole chain thing was grossly unappealing.

Her companion was leading her away from the ash-dusted street and down what she assumed was another road that was often unused at this hour. Confident in his direction, he didn't slow until they had reached an intersection with two alleys branching off. At that juncture, he stopped and turned to listen for sounds indicating they might have been followed.

"Nothing is after us," she said.

Satisfied, he nodded his head.

"I've always wondered where a Blood Knight would

live," Avery said, scanning the alleys. "This dark place isn't what I would have envisioned for one of the golden few."

His gaze came back to her. "Golden few?"

"Isn't that what you are, and what you call yourselves?"

"Only our quest was golden."

She waved a hand. "Is one of these alleys yours?"

"One of them leads to the residence of a friend of mine."

"You have friends?"

She hadn't meant to emphasize that, but it came as a surprise that any of the magnificent Seven would form any kind of relationship beyond their bond with each other.

Her outburst had amused him. He was grinning again, with the kind of smile that would have made a thousand female hearts thunder and that came unreasonably close to doing the same to hers.

It was a fact that he was too good-looking. Not only had this guy scored on that, he had the ability to find humor in a bleak world. After countless years of behind-the-scenes servitude to the unsuspecting masses, without so much as a single thank-you from those he protected, this Blood Knight could smile and enjoy himself.

Rhys was such a simple name to capture all of that.

Avery's gaze lingered slightly too long on his handsome face before she looked away.

He said, "I have a few friends scattered here and there. Don't you?"

Can't lie, and he knows it.

"Nope. Just you," Avery replied, hoping he'd let it go with that.

Bless him, he did.

"Do you have a place to stay?" he asked.

"I'll find one."

"Would you be comfortable bunking with one of my acquaintances?"

"I'd rather not."

"You owe me some explanations, I believe."

"Don't you sleep?"

"I do. Mostly during daylight hours, since darkness tends to bring out the worst in both people and predators."

He was holding back an addition to that statement. Would he have confessed how difficult it was to rest after having experienced brief moments of a more eternal resting state, once upon a time? A sentiment with which she might have concurred if they had truly been friends, and if she knew what that kind of friendship actually meant. In the past, she had substituted sex for friendship. She had used the concept of a climax as an artificial path to a few moments of closeness with a warm body.

Avery wasn't sure she understood this Knight and what he wanted, other than more answers from her. As with the Weres, had the sight of her scars turned him on? Made him want to protect her? Had that kiss kindled a flame that would be hard to extinguish?

That damn internal flutter was back, this time in his honor.

I feel it, too. That kindling of an inner flame. Nothing can happen between us, my fine Knight. Vows and oaths can't be erased as easily as that.

"You make me anxious," she said.

His grin faded. Soberly, he said, "The feeling is mutual, I assure you."

"We can go our separate ways," Avery suggested. "Carry on."

"You asked for my help in locating something."

"I accepted your offer. I didn't request anything," she pointed out.

"Same thing in my way of thinking. And you kissed me to seal the bargain."

The back of Avery's neck prickled. Sparks were tickling her insides. She wanted to argue with his remark, and couldn't. She could not lie. She had kissed him back. The fact that she had liked that kiss made this unlikely liaison doubly dangerous to her ancient vows and promises. Staring at this guy produced warning signals that shouldn't be ignored.

Their chemistry had been immediate, and that was just too bad. How could she fall victim to the Blood Knight's allure when she had helped to create it? Maybe she was attracted to him because of the tenderness in his eyes, she who had been without comfort for as long as she could remember.

Her more-than-passing interest in the tall, sexy creature was her fault, through no fault of her own. No one in their right mind would have been able to resist him.

Tell him the truth and he will go away.

There was another scenario vying for her attention.

Tell him what his Makers did, and the truth might take away his ongoing goals when, as it turns out, the world needs him and his brethren to help keep the peace.

Facing the same old dilemma made Avery want to scream. The look in Rhys's eyes made her want to repeat that kiss.

"Yes. All right," Avery admitted. "I did kiss you."

"If you go, there might not be another moment like that," he warned. "And since you think me rude already, let me just say I'd like a redo, without a bunch of vampires interrupting."

For what felt to Avery like the first time during all her days on Earth, she let in the warmth he exuded. She breathed in his scent and dared to close her eyes in his company, trusting this man when she had never trusted another living soul.

Light to light.

Blood to blood.

She had always wanted him. Only him. She had dreamed over and over of having a moment like this, and how it would go.

Her unspoken secrets stuck in her throat because he didn't deserve the conflicts those truths could inflict, and hurting the innocent went against the very core of her nature.

She looked up to find him standing close to her. No touching, just a physical closeness made to seem more intimate by the bright beam of his blue eyes.

"Stay," he said. "For now. Tell me the things you're withholding and let me be the judge of how I'll respond. Let me help you find what you seek, if that will ease your mind."

Magic words. *Stay. Help. Ease your mind.* Avery believed them. She believed him.

"Your friend with the place to stay might not like the sudden appearance of someone like me." She refused to hold his gaze, confused by the desire to have this immortal, body and soul, right there in this spot, and get it over with.

"My friend is well-used to the likes of us," he promised.

That remark made her glance up at him. Reading the question in her expression, he elaborated slightly. "He's a host of another sort, and unlike you or me."

"Thank God," Avery said. "Because I've had enough of both of us."

The touch came then—a light, cautious, tentative hand beneath her chin that raised her face so that she had to meet his eyes.

Draw back.

Pull away, fool.

Avery tensed, ready to bolt. Running was what she had always done, so why didn't she?

Was it actually time to confront her cravings for him head-on? Could it be true that time healed all wounds and that she now knew this was a good guy?

"You want this?" he asked, his voice gentle for the warrior he was, his mouth inches from hers.

There was no use pretending she didn't understand what he meant. Her first fleeting thought was to wonder if this was a test that would leave him laughing.

What the hell...

"Yes. Damn it. Damn you. Yes."

She waited for a kiss that didn't come, searching the face above hers now that she had given in. He wasn't smiling now. No glimmer of triumph lifted his features. The Blood Knight's eyes bored into hers as if by sight alone he could drink her in. Those eyes reflected a hunger and a passion for something that, like her, he might never have had.

Avery found herself moving without instigating that movement, swept sideways by the man she was with. Every muscle in her body tightened, preparing for God only knew what.

Her back hit the brick wall with a resounding thud that sent sharp stinging sensations through the new tattoos stretching between both shoulders. She had forgotten about the wings.

A hard body was pressed against hers, threatening her air supply. It was a man's body, taut, muscled, tense and unbelievably warm.

His body.

Dreams were merging with reality.

It was all too much.

The sirens in the distance had stopped. There was no one on the street. The only sound left in this corner of the world was Avery's soft, breathless gasp.

Chapter 9

He had her pinned to the wall. All thoughts of decorum and mystery had been tossed aside because of Rhys's need to capture this beauty's essence and hold it in his hands. The need to taste her, feel her, have her, if he was lucky, at least for a while. Whatever special mojo she had going on was like a stake to his heart.

Her lips were closed. The sound he'd heard had passed through those lips as quickly as a sigh. She was as surprised about the suddenness of their needs as he was. In truth, he'd known this would happen the first minute he saw her in that damn shop. He had willed it to happen. The miracle was that she had obliged.

She didn't fight him. Her eyes were wide open, her gaze no longer averted. Those eyes taunted him. Haunted him.

I do know you. But how?

He stroked her face with his fingers, searching for answers to the puzzle of these feelings of familiarity. Cool skin. White. Flawless. Smooth as silk. There were hollows beneath her cheekbones and no furrow lines on her brow. She could have been any age, but looked to be in her late twenties, in terms of mortal years. Rhys supposed he looked a few years older.

The toughness she exuded with every spoken word seemed to dissolve beneath his touch, as if her defiance had simply melted away. But he sensed that defiance ready to make a comeback at any moment.

Although she appeared to like his soft touch, she wasn't to be trifled with or tested, he somehow knew. Nor would she allow herself to be bested by him or anyone else on the planet. No. This one remained in control of herself, as well as how far she'd go in this odd dance of give-and-take between strangers.

His mouth found hers…not lightly this time, but with a pressure that tilted her head back. At first, he got no response. No slap. No shove. And then he felt her lips part. Warm breath seeped into his mouth.

Body alive with sensation, Rhys cradled her face between his hands. He held her firmly while his mouth began to devour hers. His lips explored, tested, tasted, as if by doing so he could positively identify her.

The kiss fast became mind-numbing, far-reaching, more provocative than anything in Rhys's experience. With this merging, Rhys was sure he had discovered traces of the sublime.

She had to feel it. Her body softened against his, while his body hardened. Her hands clutched at his back. Her eyes were closed.

The inside of her mouth was like velvet.

His hands slipped to her throat, then to her shoulders. He liked the texture of her leather jacket and its worn, creaking sounds.

Having his body pressed to hers added immeasurably

to the pleasure of kissing her. They were hip to hip, and as close to chest to chest as possible since he was taller. Her mouth accepted him. Her heat was the ultimate temptation for a creature like him, who, out of necessity, was too often alone.

In the far reaches of his mind, Rhys wondered if he should allow her some time for a breath. The idea fled as her warm, moist tongue slid between his teeth. Startled by his body's immediate reaction, he cursed with a fiery breath that she took in. This lithe immortal was delicious, sensuous, hot.

And yet…

As the kiss took him over, images began to flood his mind, calling for his attention, threatening distraction. The visions were of her.

She was sitting on the cot in the tattoo parlor with her back to him. The rawness of the colorful wings she'd had inked between her shoulder blades stood out as if outlined in bright red blood.

The tattoos sprang to life as he watched. The wings began to pull away from her back, tearing the pale skin surrounding them as they stretched out to crowd the room with a tip-to-tip span of eight feet or more. Beautiful things. Magical. Each snowy-white feather had a bloodred tip.

The wings pulsed in time with the pounding of his heart, as if somehow connected to him. One beat. Two. The woman on that cot turned to look at him over one shoulder, her face partially hidden by feathers. Her flawless features were drawn with strain. Tears glistened in her eyes.

Those huge wings flapped, sending extraneous items in the room sailing. The shop's walls started to topple, as if an earthquake, measuring high on the Richter scale, was passing through. Then she was in the doorway, suddenly, looking out, staring at him. The sensation of their gazes meeting was so realistic Rhys muttered, "What the hell?"

His eyes flew open to find no battering vortex of wind. The building's walls still stood and he was pressing the woman in his arms to the brick.

Rhys took his mouth from hers, pulling back enough to see her face in a slanted shaft of what was left of the moonlight. That face wore the same strained expression he had seen in the vision. Her eyes were trained on him in the same way. Both of their hearts were beating way too fast.

"What—" he began, but had to start over. "What was that?"

Again, she didn't feign ignorance of what he was alluding to when she might have had nothing to do with his dream and couldn't possibly have known what he was talking about.

But she did know.

"That," she said slowly, cautiously and with a slight tremor in her tone, "is why you and I were never meant to meet. Certainly not like this."

Leaning into her, Rhys stared hard, not quite comprehending what she was saying. "Explain."

No tears glistened in her eyes, so had he made that part up?

"We are connected," she said. "Our bond goes way back."

The familiarity, Rhys thought with a rush of relief, was real. The rest of what she was telling him remained hazy.

She went on. "Now you know why I've come here, to London, and what I'm after. You've seen the things I seek, when no one else could have."

"You know what I saw?"

"What you witnessed was a wish transferred through touch—a hope, my hope, for a reunion that's long overdue."

"Explain in plain English," Rhys said. "What I saw was—"

"Wings. My wings."

The moment was surreal, when surreal was also the way Rhys would have described the path through his extended life span. However, her explanation, such as it was, began to make sense. His vision was her version of what she wanted. Big wings. Real ones.

"You believe..." he started to say.

Before he could ask his question, she pushed him back with the strength he'd witnessed when they dealt with the vampires, a strength that defied her size. Although he didn't have to let her do this, he complied with her demand for distance and moved back far enough for her to remove her jacket and drop it to the pavement.

When her hands went to the front of her shirt, he wondered what she might be up to. Forgoing the buttons, she pulled the shirt over her head.

It was, he thought, a strange time for a street-side striptease.

She wore nothing beneath the shirt and stood in front of him partially naked, just as she had the first time he'd seen her, and also in the vision he'd had. And damn it, up close and personal, she was a true vision, one he could have reached out to touch.

Long collarbones balanced her shoulders and a gracefully curved neck. Smooth stretches of bare, pure-white skin surrounded small rounded breasts that were as perfect as the rest of her. The tips of those breasts were pink.

Withholding a groan, Rhys considered shutting his eyes. The moment was incredibly intimate. Painfully so. He didn't really know her at all, and yet they were bonded, she had said. Way back.

Why was she behaving like this?

In full view, she stood for a few more seconds, showing no concern about being undressed in front of a stranger, before turning around to face the wall behind her. Raising both arms, she placed her hands on the brick above her head.

Rhys's gaze went to the tattoos, to the false wings that were unlike the pair he'd seen stretch and flap when his eyes were closed. Beneath his scrutiny, she shivered. Hell, the night was cold. But she was waiting for him to do something, say something. She was waiting for him to fully understand what she was showing him.

Closer. Look closer.

Gaze locked to the tattooed wings, Rhys followed the rows of feathers to where they met the curve of her spine.

What am I supposed to see?

She contracted her back muscles, offering him a stunning replay of the dreamlike vision. These wings were merely inked designs, however. Colorful re-creations of…

Rhys leaned forward, focusing his attention on the spot where those wings almost met the crease of her spine. Did he see something there, almost perfectly camouflaged by an artist's talented work?

Two long scars, darker than the rest of her old wounds and now covered with blue ink, ran parallel to her spinal column. Six inches in length and deeply carved into her, those two terrible wounds made Rhys want to cry out in protest at whatever evil deed had made them.

Were they important? Was the ink merely a cover-up of those old wounds?

Chills washed over him as the unanswerable questions kept repeating. For him, chills often meant truth in the direction he was heading.

Think.

She had lost something, she'd said, and was searching

for it. He had offered to help her find whatever that was. She was showing him her back, showing him the wings that camouflaged her wounds.

As he stared at those incredibly complex tattoos, a kernel of truth blossomed inside him. Was it possible that these wings were representations of the real thing?

"Bloody hell," he said, unable to believe the idea forming in his mind. "The image I saw was real? You actually are an..."

"Angel," she said.

Can't be...

Fighting the urge to lay his hands on her, to feel the scars those old wounds had made and to know what the rest of an angel felt like, Rhys's shoulders twitched with the strain of holding himself back.

Did he believe what she was telling him?

The half-bare woman in front of him didn't move. It seemed to him that she couldn't. He was mesmerized by her. What she had shown him was so personal, he had a knee-jerk reaction that spiraled through his body. So extraordinarily personal, it brought heat.

Giving in to the need to touch this female who was so damn fine and beautiful, Rhys reached out.

"Don't," she warned in a voice that defied argument.

Rhys's hand stopped mid-motion.

"No one touches them," she said. "Especially you."

The way she said that last part made him think they had met before, like this, and that she hadn't liked the result. But he would have remembered that meeting. No one could have forgotten her after the briefest look.

"I want to know about this and about what happened to you," Rhys said, his gaze roaming over her.

The curve of her back was seductive beyond his wildest imaginings. In his mind, Rhys ran his fingers down that graceful indentation, over each vertebra and every freshly inked feather, wanting to believe her and that she actually was an angel. If he was to accept that she was, how had she gotten here? How did an angel lose her wings?

"True," she said, as if reading his mind. "I promise you I am what you think I am."

She was shivering. Quakes rocked her entire body. Rhys pressed himself to her, careful not to touch her shoulders. With his hands on the wall and his mouth near her silky white hair, he said, "It's a good story. Can you prove it?"

Prove it...

Avery had bared her soul to a creature she couldn't mind control into forgetting what he was seeing. His aura and presence had been too vital to fight. That first kiss had been her downfall because she had been dreaming of it forever.

Be careful what you wish for...

"Have faith," she said to him. "Believe."

Can't tell you everything. Not all of it.

He was too close. Too warm. How could she think when she had secretly wanted this for so long? When she had promised herself that a moment like this one would never come to pass?

She had no idea the Blood Knights could radiate so much heat. This one was volcanic. He held her captive with the placement of his arms and hips, and she could feel way too much of the male in him. The quakes rocking her weren't temperature related, but indicative of so much more than being half naked in the cold night air. *He* was causing this reaction. *He* was doing this. The Blood Knight whose closeness she had always craved.

"All right," he said. "I'll take the bait and ask how you know the wings are in London?"

"Rumor."

Her right cheek rubbed against the rough brick. Rhys probably thought she couldn't get away without his permission. Big mistake there, if that's the direction his thoughts took.

"We've already had a discussion about rumors," he pointed out.

"This is black market stuff. Secretive whispers in dark places."

"And therefore highly unstable."

"Not when they call to me here."

After being silent for a moment, the Blood Knight said, "Your wings call to you?"

"Yes." With her face against the brick, Avery couldn't nod her head. She had to speak.

"How? How do they call to you?" he persisted.

"It's hard to explain."

"Try."

Damn you...

"They sing to me."

After another thoughtful pause, he said, "Like in a song?"

"Like vibrations deep in my bones."

"I suppose you'd equate that vibration to a plucked harp string?"

Sarcasm underscored his latest question. Everyone envisioned angels with harps, erroneously. Angels weren't do-nothings who sat around strumming. She had been a warrior. Her instrument of choice had been a sword, but this Blood Knight didn't need to know that.

"How long have you been looking for the wings?" he asked.

"Forever. Seems like forever."

"Then why haven't you already located them?"

"I think..." Avery felt a stab of panic that cut off her

reply. What she had been about to say explained more than she had formerly been able to comprehend. Ideas forming in her mind now were either completely fantastical make-believe strings of thought, or downright miracles, when she had ceased to believe in miracles.

Bond. Connection. Blood and light. Maybe, as impossible as it seemed, she'd been meant to show herself to Rhys here, where the vibration was the strongest. Maybe Rhys was part of that, and he had been the key to her success all along…when she had been either too scared or too stubborn to see it.

She had placed her blood in his veins unwillingly, but was it possible that some good might have been born from that alliance, and that her attraction to him might have been pointing the way? There was a chance the pain of their beginnings had blinded her to what she needed most, and that her oath of vengeance against the Blood Knights and their Makers had kept her from getting what she had needed all along.

Her breath came in rasps now. There wasn't enough breathing space to deal with this revelation.

Blood Knight. Will you help me?

Can you help me?

Rhys.

Those words wouldn't come out.

The calm, throaty voice in her ear soothed a soul so wounded that it had been unable to capture the light it needed for a very long time. His light. And that idea went against the vows she had clung to. So impossible, yet so simple.

"You think what?" he prompted, urging her to finish her remark. "What were you going to say?"

Fear of needing to place her trust in one of the same creatures that had been born as a direct link to her captivity kept the quakes coming. However, the belief in new possibilities had taken root, and the rightness of the path ahead had taken on a silvery sheen.

This had to be the way. *He* would accompany her on the path she was to take.

"I believe," she said, "that I might have found you for this reason. And that reason is to help me see this quest through."

For once, the man holding her there with his almost mystical allure had no question in response, which might have been another freaking miracle in a long line of them.

The centuries-old soul didn't back up or move a muscle. He was breathing as hard as she was, breath being one of those strange anomalies that had been returned to him after Death had stolen it. Avery wondered if he remembered the details of the night he had surrendered his life. Did the pain of those moments live within him also?

There was no way she could have asked him about that, or told him about her own fight for fresh air and freedom from the castle. She didn't tell him that she had caused the destruction of Broceliande after escaping from her iron shackles, dismantling it stone by stone so that no one like her or Rhys could ever be hurt again.

"What do you need me to do?" the gallant Knight asked, as if centuries had not caught him up and then passed him by.

"Find what was taken from me," she said.

"Taken, as in stolen?"

"Yes." That word didn't begin to describe what had taken place in that castle's dungeons. Some things were better left in the dark.

Avery felt his gaze slip to the base of her neck. Each inch that gaze traveled brought more heat. It was odd that she couldn't stop shaking.

"Those two scars," he said. "The deep ones. That's where your wings were?"

"Yes."

"How could you not know who took them?"

"I know." *You can bet your ass on that.*

"Those people are here in London?"

"Those creatures might no longer exist. I can't be sure."

"This happened recently?"

"A very long time ago."

"So, you believe someone else has your wings?" He shook his head. "Hell. You think they are in the hands of dealers from the black market? Is that where the rumors are leading? Those wings exist, and you trust the vibration in your gut to lead us to them?" He hesitated before adding, "You can believe I'm going to help you get them back."

He'd said *us*. Lead *us* to them. An electrified thrill passed through Avery. Her need to get away from this man disappeared, replaced by another emotion that centered on hope. In that moment, all of the years behind her simply faded into one stark realization that she might actually, finally, get what she had prayed so hard for. And, startlingly, that those prayers hadn't only been for the retrieval of her wings.

The new thoughts made her dizzy, needy. Casual sex with Weres was one thing. An attraction this strong to an immortal Knight was another thing altogether.

Her Blood Knight moved, turning her around with a gentle tug. Her back hit the brick. She relished the brief sting of discomfort. The hard body of the man in black pressed against her again before Avery looked up to meet his eyes.

She wanted to drown in those eyes. That had always been the danger.

Whatever ideals about angels she had once possessed dropped away, replaced by a molten tide of oncoming fever sparked by the knowledge that he was going to kiss her again.

Maybe he thought she owed him that as a down payment for his help. And maybe she had willed this moment into existence because dreams were trespassing on reality's turf…and because she wanted what he had to offer so damn badly.

Chapter 10

Rhys saw the flash of light in her eyes that told him she wanted the same thing he did. Her liquid blue gaze never once left his as he gave in to his overwhelming need to kiss an angel. And, in doing so, take away some of her pain.

Admittedly, this probably wasn't the time or place to question the bond between them that she'd mentioned. Who the hell cared, when desire ruled his actions and she looked at him like that?

His mouth on hers was hungry. *Get from me what you need. I can take it.*

Deeply, aggressively, with an almost angry intensity, they went after each other, perhaps looking for a more current physical link to the connections she'd told him about.

Rhys took her mouth in the name of passion and one hell of a long stretch of loneliness dating way back. As an immortal, she couldn't really be hurt by the brick at her back, though he did care about that. Her beautiful skin had been damaged again tonight by ink and needles, and she acted as if nothing had occurred.

Hot, moist, sweet…this little sample of intimacy didn't satisfy him as much as Rhys had hoped. He wanted more of this. More of her. Right now, preferably.

The first indication of trouble came when she turned her head, backing off those brief moments of what had been so incredibly rich.

Breathlessly, she said, "Now you can say you've had it. Had me. A goddamn angel. You can chalk this up, mark it off your to-do list, use those bragging rights."

Rhys studied her closely, aware of her inner agitation. "You think that's what I wanted by kissing you?"

"Isn't it?"

"Not even close."

Blue eyes searched his face. Bruised lips, nearly as blue as her eyes, parted. "My needs both attract and repel this kind of thing. If staying away from you was hard before, it will now be impossible."

"Good. That suits me just fine. But what do you mean about staying away from me before?" Rhys asked.

Confessions were difficult for this angel, it seemed to him. She took her time.

"We wait to search for my wings until they're sure I'm here," she said, avoiding his last question.

Rhys thought it best not to ask her how a pair of detached wings might know anything about who was seeking them. The idea that wings could be alive, on their own, was both eerie and incomprehensible.

Besides, the parts of the story she had already shared created the agitation he saw spiral through the line of the angel's delicate jaw. He wasn't going to let up this time, however. His mission had become to get a straight answer from her about the other issue on the table.

"You said staying away from me was hard before. Have you been watching me? If so, for how long?"

She said, "On and off for a while."

With both hands on her bare shoulders, Rhys held her to the wall, stalling his need to look at the rest of her glowing white nakedness, stifling the inclination to lift her in his arms and take her someplace more private than a dingy street corner. Somewhere they could settle this crazy physical thing between them, once and for all.

"How long is that?" he asked.

Confusion crossed her features. She was shaking again, as if answers were the enemy instead of the cold.

"Tell me," he said.

"Since the beginning. And whenever I could."

Rhys tried hard to understand what she was saying. Surely angels had to tell the truth when confronted, the same as with him and his brethren. Truth was a side-effect of being one of the good guys.

"What beginning are you referring to?" he asked.

"That damn..."

Her anxiety was contagious. Rhys felt cold seep into his stomach. His body was gearing up for a big reveal, hardening, stiffening, the way it always did when he was about to go into battle. All of this in anticipation of an answer to a simple question.

What the hell is so hard for you to say?

"That bloody castle," she said.

Rhys blinked, not sure he had heard correctly. His hands slipped from her shoulders. He stared at her intensely.

"Castle?" he echoed.

The reference could have been about any castle he'd been to over the centuries. He had lived in a few, fought for a few and protected several of them. Just because she had told him she knew about Blood Knights through rumor and secretive legends passed on by a select few, she didn't have to be alluding to the specific castle he dreaded to think about, even in speculation. Broceliande, the white-walled, windowless fortress with its garden of bloodred roses that bloomed only after nightfall. The place where he had offered up his mortal life to honor a higher cause.

Anxiety was nothing compared to sudden fear that Broceliande was, indeed, the castle she was referring to and that an angel might have seen it for herself. No legend he knew of mentioned the place by name. No one knew of its existence, other than the castle's original occupants and the Knights the Makers had created, and then sent out on what had turned out to be so much more than a single golden Quest.

"How…?" Rhys muttered, half to himself, sensing something else was wrong.

When he looked up from his descent into the past, it was to discover the beautiful enigma he'd begun to believe actually might be a real angel had used his thoughts about the past to beat a hasty retreat…for the second time in an hour.

Avery ran, accustomed to using her feet for travel and escape these days. She moved fast, though her heart was heavy. She raced from one alley to another without paying much attention to direction or the fact that Rhys would find her anyway, sooner or later.

What she needed was time to think.

She had given up too much information. She'd had to. Witnessing the change in the Blood Knight's expression when she'd mentioned the castle had made her heart sink.

For sure now, she knew Rhys also held no love for Broceliande. That realization brought her more discomfort. While she had wanted to repay the Knights for what she had gone through in that terrible place, meeting Rhys in the flesh had managed to change that plan. In just a few hours, and in only one night, he had become the single creature in all the world she'd hate to hurt.

Big change of plans.

What to do with these new feelings was the current problem. How to react when her entire thought system had been rearranged. Given that she actually no longer sought revenge on the Knights, her main objective for coming to Earth had been made clearer.

Was he behind her already?

How far was far enough to clear his reach, and to get him out of her thoughts for a while longer?

Climbing to the rooftop of the old warehouse building beside her, Avery paused for a look, sensing visitors on her trail. The wrong ones.

"Damn Shades are everywhere."

The moon was low in the sky and mostly covered by clouds, but the streetlight below her showed shadows passing in and out of its yellow light.

"Have you brought your friends, Shade?" she muttered, angry over losing alone time.

Beyond those slithering shadows, she detected no other presence. No special beat moved the still, stale air. Was it possible that Rhys had let her go?

Avery closed her eyes. "Need time," she said to Rhys, as though he stood beside her. Another thing she needed was to shed the excess energy built up by allowing that kiss—and the desire she felt for having more just like it. All in all, facing the approaching Shades would have to do, for now, to calm her jangling nerves.

"Sorry, boys," Avery whispered as she headed back to the street. "It's not going to be your night."

"I should let you go until you realize I can help," Rhys said to the empty street beside him, thinking hard about how eager the female whose name he didn't know had been to get away from him.

"Or I can follow the parade of ghosts to your doorstep, if you've chosen a doorstep, and help you extricate yourself from their sudden affections."

Maybe she didn't need his help and didn't really want his assistance, but dark things in this city would want to steal her light. Rob her of what made her unique. As for himself, he didn't plan on pressing her to do anything other than cough up a few more truthful answers.

His sigils burned as if the damn symbols were his personal conscience. This was because he had just lied to himself about merely wanting answers from the pale enigma, when he also wanted so much more. If the lie had been voiced, he'd be on his knees, bent over by a terrible, racking pain that one of his brothers had described as similar to the sting of a hundred scorpions.

Rhys rolled his shoulders to ease the discomfort. *Okay. I want more from the angel than a few answers. I admit it.*

The unforgiving marks etched on his back eased only slightly with that declaration, pulsing as if they truly understood those words. Hell, he thought now, maybe her wings were the equivalent of the symbols on his back.

This angel was a puzzle that needed solving. One he looked forward to solving.

His head came up as the scent of Shade slid by him. The creature was using the shadows for cover and had gotten close, when most of the anomalies in this area avoided him, aware of the power he possessed. Some of them went long distances out of their way to skirt the areas he patrolled. Tonight, the damn Shades were coming out of the woodwork, attracted to a kind of being they didn't yet understand.

Hell, he was no better. Leaving the angel alone with her quest was apparently not an option since he was already moving after both of the filmy creatures. He felt he had an obligation to deal with them, one way or another...and they were after her.

An angel had landed in London, and that angel knew too much about him. A damaged angel, hurting, keening for her wings. Rhys hurt for her, on familiar terms with the concept of loss. Setting things to rights for others was his only purpose for getting through his extended existence, the only way Rhys knew of to wade through the ever-expanding lineup of years both behind him and ahead.

He stopped walking.

"Angel," he whispered.

The word caused the rise of a hazy internal warning because an idea was springing to life, along with a possible reason for this angel knowing about Blood Knights.

Could she, having mentioned the word *castle*, be connected to the Knights' original Quest? Could she possibly have anything to do with the holy relic that he and his six brethren had hidden from the world? A relic with strong ties to religion and the vast idea of a Great Beyond? A golden relic that an angel might know about?

Why else would one of Heaven's creatures have known about that blasted castle?

Rhys's heart responded to that idea with a kick. He swiped at the back of his neck, dispersing the fresh wave of chills before glancing to the sky in search of the last remnants of the moon. Dawn would arrive in a couple of hours. Vamps would now be heading back to their nests. Shades had to be careful about traveling too far from their basements and caverns... Which meant that his angel was still relatively close.

But then, he already knew that. He was able to feel her, smell her. Tasting her light had been like capturing the essence of starlight on his tongue.

It was a fact that he had liked that kiss way too much for his own good when he should have been finding a way to help her.

"Too many questions left," Rhys noted, standing on a corner where three narrow streets converged.

"Not enough time," he added with a sense of urgency, though in truth, he and others like him had all the time in the world at their disposal. And so, it appeared, did *she*.

Chapter 11

Dispensing with five Shades had been a breeze. The rest of them had bailed after witnessing what a silver blade in an experienced hand could do. But Avery was so very tired of fighting. Her entire existence had been moving from one battle to the next, driven by the need to get back what she had lost. What she wanted tonight, more than anything else, was peace, breathing room, and to be whole again.

She wasn't an idiot. Running away from Rhys had been the wrong move. Unused to kindness and sincere offers of aid, she had acted like a child. It didn't matter how addicted to him she might become. Once she had her wings, she'd be out of here, off this angry planet and back where she belonged. Rhys would go on as he had before, only without her watchful gaze. He would no longer be her concern.

Waving the blackened blade in the air to dry it, Avery stood on the deserted street waiting to see how long it would take for Rhys to find her. Minutes? Seconds? He'd have the word *castle* stuck in his mind now that she had put it there.

That couldn't be helped. She'd had to give him something. He was so very convincing about wanting to help.

Morning was on its way. The approaching scent of dawn left a warm sensation in her chest. Thankfully, this long night was almost over.

Where was Rhys? Seconds had gone by without him showing his pretty face.

She might take Rhys up on the offer of shelter at his friend's flat, since anyone a Blood Knight trusted had to be worthy of a secret or two. That friend could run interference between her and Rhys. She could rest.

She turned slowly as a wave of familiar heat returned.

"What took you so long?" she asked.

"I had some cleaning up to do."

Her Blood Knight stepped from the shadows as if he, like the Shades, had been part of them.

"Ghosts?" she asked.

"Among other things."

They faced each other without daring to breach the gap of separation. He was as anxious as she was, but wore it better.

"What now?" he said. "Why did you run?"

"I needed to stretch my legs."

"Were you waiting for me?"

"I was thinking about it."

Refusing to dial down the heat of his gaze, he asked, "What is it you expect to happen?"

"A repeat of what happens each time we face each other like this. We got too close, Knight."

She watched his face for the grin she was sure would follow her confession. That grin did not appear. Rhys was acting like a gentleman again, when something far more lethal resided within him.

"Do we stand here, or would you accept my offer for

shelter?" he asked. "I promise no monsters will bother you there."

"Are there so many monsters in London that walk in daylight?"

"Far too many of them to count."

"Humans, you mean. Mortals."

He didn't deny the remark.

Avery nodded. "Very well. I accept."

"Hypothetically?"

"Actually."

He said, "Good. Follow me." He turned from her, took two steps, then turned back. "You might want to pocket the blade first. Your host for the night might take exception."

"And if we meet more unwelcome guests along the way?"

"That's doubtful. I've cleared the path."

"I don't need a protector," Avery said. "I think you know that."

"I do know that," he agreed.

Avery heard him add beneath his breath, "But maybe that's exactly what *I'm* going to need. Protection. From you."

His confession, an acknowledgement of the unnamable thing growing between them, made Avery's nerves blaze. The only hope she had was that they'd soon find her wings, and then her deep-seated attraction to this Blood Knight wouldn't matter.

How often, though, had she thought that same thing? That he would no longer matter to her. It had been so many times, in fact, that by now she should have believed it.

"Is it far?" she asked, not quite ready to move in any direction.

"Yes," he said. "Time to move, angel."

He stopped again to look back at her. "It would be nice to have a name, so I can introduce you properly."

"Names have power."

"Real names do. Somehow I very much doubt anyone knows yours."

"You can call me Avery."

"Avery," he repeated in a deep, gravelly tone. "A form of old English?"

It meant *battle* in old English, but she didn't clarify that point. She merely liked that it started with the same letter as her original name.

"All right, Avery, come along. Night is waning."

Avery wasn't sure she liked him using one of the monikers she had chosen for herself. Vowing to find another name that wouldn't sound so provocative when Rhys said it, she moved up behind him.

Be careful, her mind warned. *You are falling under his spell.*

And what a spell it was. Following him gave her an impressive view of Rhys's commendable backside. In her defense, angels weren't immune to physical perfection any more than humans were.

His pants were tight enough to skim his long legs and lean, muscled thighs. The black coat swung with each stride. Boots that should have made sounds on the pavement didn't—another indication that Rhys wasn't like most of the others in this overcrowded city.

Light-streaked brown hair brushed his collar in a shiny mass of thick strands that Avery envisioned running her fingers through if he were to ever pin her to a wall again. She almost wished he would. After admiring all of this from the beginning, she liked it more now. Rhys was a walking advertisement for the beauty of the supernatural. How many years had she loved him?

Sacrilege.

Treacherous thoughts.

What she wanted to do to this Blood Knight, and with him, produced a warning flutter deep in her belly and an ache between her leather-clad thighs. While times with the Weres had suited her on occasion for a rough-and-tumble, bedding this Knight would be the end of her. He would be a great lover. All that power and calm might entice her to give up and give in.

And in the end, he might not want her. Once he knew the score, the true beginnings of his kind and who his Makers really were, that golden sheen he radiated might dim… and she would have been the cause.

Have to get out before that happens.

Don't look at him. Get this over with.

That's what her conscience said. Her body wanted no part of that. Her body wished for hot sex on a cool night, on a rooftop high above the city where the stars shone brightest. Hell, she almost rubbed her hand between her thighs to ease the ache building there, knowing that nothing temporary would satisfy the spot that needed this Knight most.

Lovers. A damaged angel and an immortal Blood Knight. The heavens would shudder if they weren't already, and if anyone up there was watching this play out.

"Are you coming?" the object of her desire said over his broad shoulder.

Not coming yet, she wanted to tell him. But Rhys, who had also lived forever, wouldn't have missed the double entendre in that remark, and all bets would have been off for pursuing her quest, at least for a while.

Rhys let the heat of Avery's thoughts roll over him. True, he couldn't hear what she was thinking in ways that made sense, but feeling the direction her thoughts had taken was doable. This angel talked a good game. Still, all he had to do was turn and open his arms to get what he wanted. One small move for such a big reward.

And then what?

She would leave without giving him those answers, and he'd go back to his former watch alone and none the wiser.

Who the hell knew what she was really after?

So he kept walking. Down one street, then two, he led her, much like a man with a shadow. She didn't speak to him again, and the silence was filled with wayward energy that had nowhere to go.

Down three more streets and they were back to the place where he had kissed her. Glancing at that brick wall caused a thrill. Remembering the way she had stood there, half naked, baring herself to him in order to prove a point, caused a rustle in the fabric of his being. He couldn't shed the shock of the sight of those tattooed wings and what they hid.

"We're here," Rhys announced, waiting for Avery to catch up.

Big blue eyes outlined in black were on him.

"Up there." He pointed to the top floor of the building beside them. "Penthouse."

"Safe because…?" she asked.

"No creature in London would mess with the immortal that uses it from time to time. In his absence, an Alpha lives there. A werewolf–cop combo is a dangerous mix of both things."

"Another immortal also uses it?" she said.

"A brother."

She nodded, said, "I suppose you mean St. John."

Hearing the mention of another Blood Knight, spoken through Avery's lips, gave Rhys a start. This was a healthy reminder that the angel did know a thing or two about the Seven. That reminder was disconcerting.

Christopher St. John, long a fixture on London's ancient vampire scene, had recently left the city, bestowing the right to his penthouse apartment on the wolf that had helped him bring down some very bad vamps. How the hell did Avery know about that? He planned to ask her as soon as they were off the street.

"You don't have anything against Weres, I hope?" Rhys asked.

"Nothing at all," she replied with a hint of wryness in her tone.

"There's an elevator inside." He waved at the door to the building, a heavy dark green chunk of wood bearing an intricate Celtic design. "After you."

He wasn't entirely sure if Avery would go through that door and sighed with relief when she did. Careful to keep a polite distance, he followed her, glad four specially designed lead-lined walls would contain all that light for a few short hours and confuse the creeps who seemed to be after her. She was strong enough, he gauged, to handle the creature-proof walls.

They shared the small elevator without looking at each other, though the tension of it filled the small space. Neither of them spoke until the ornate gate opened and Rhys gestured for her to exit into the grand room beyond.

The penthouse was a wide expanse of uninterrupted loft space, and just the sort of thing Rhys preferred. Cavernous ceiling. Gray slate floor. Stone covered the lead walls, in places decorated with rare framed art from St. John's extensive collection. Several pieces of fine furniture that weren't too modern for an ancient being's sensibilities were strategically placed.

Avery went right to the bank of glass that covered one

entire wall, as if looking out at the view of the streets and buildings below them would help her breathe easier. Claustrophobia seemed to hound all immortals, though everyone, mortals and immortals alike, needed some kind of safe house and time spent indoors.

"Is he here? The wolf?" Avery asked with her back to him.

"Yes," a deeper voice than Rhys's replied. "The wolf is, in fact, in residence tonight."

Rhys noticed that Avery didn't bother to turn around. Maybe, in this instance, she did actually trust his take on the matter of a host.

"It isn't my preferred form of greeting, that *wolf* thing," continued the large man entering the room. "I trust you're a friend?"

"Avery," Rhys said, "I'd like you to meet Detective Inspector Ellis Crane, the Alpha of London's rough-and-tumble West End pack."

When she turned, Crane said, "Avery..." and stopped there as his appraising gaze met hers. "Welcome. Any friend of Rhys's is a potential friend of mine."

"Potential?" she asked.

"Friendships have to be earned and not freely given, don't you think?" Crane replied.

She nodded in agreement. "Your particular skills would aid nicely in your job as a DI."

"You're alluding to the special senses inherent to my species. And, yes, they're quite a boon. Have you known many Weres...Avery, is it?"

"I have known a few Weres. And yes, Avery is the name I go by these days."

Crane faced Rhys. The Were's practiced cop face was free of all expression and standard fare for a DI, but Rhys easily understood what the detective was silently asking.

"She would have to tell you more, if she wants to," Rhys said. "I know little about her, other than she has solicited my help. We need a night or two here, if you'll agree to that. It seems others in this city are as interested as I am in her sudden appearance in London."

"Vampires?" Crane asked.

"And Shades."

"As a reminder, I am right here," Avery said from her place by the windows. Directly to Crane, she added, "I'm interested in why you came up with vampires right off."

"We've had an uptick in bloodsucker populations lately, which isn't necessarily anything new for this time of year. However, Rhys also mentioned Shades, and that catches my interest."

"Why?"

"We rarely see them nowadays," Crane replied. "I haven't caught sight of one for ages. Maybe a year or longer."

"These few appeared, at least superficially, to be tagging along with the vamps," Rhys explained. "Hot on vamp coattails, anyway."

Crane looked again to Avery. "Does that make sense to you?"

"Not much makes sense these days," she said noncommittally. "And neither of those two species will deter me from my objective for coming here."

"But you know why they might be interested in you?" Crane pressed, in the kind of tone that perfectly suited one of London's lead investigators.

Avery nodded. "Darkness covets light."

"And you are that light," Crane said.

Rhys swore beneath his breath, afraid Avery was going to disappear, if not now, then as the good detective resumed the interrogation.

Crane had pegged her as something special, and that was a no-brainer, especially for a fine-tuned cop used to reading people. But if the detective thought he could probe a grounded angel, especially this one, and get her to dish on the details of her background, Crane had another thing coming. Like the only Blood Knight in the room, he had met his match tonight.

Stepping forward to break up any added buildup of tension, Rhys said to Avery, "Would you like something to eat? Something to drink?"

She shook her head. "Just a place to curl up, if the offer for time here still stands."

"It does," Crane said. "I'm on duty tonight and was on my way out, so feel free to make yourself at home."

"Thank you." She turned back to the view.

"Extraordinary," Crane said as he moved past Rhys, toward the elevator.

"What is?" Rhys asked.

Crane paused long enough to say, "Meeting her in person like this."

Shots of an unfamiliar emotion struck Rhys like a sucker punch to the gut. "Whatever do you mean, Crane?"

"There have been stories about a stranger like her."

"What kind of stories?"

"Still here," Avery said from across the room. "And for the record, Detective, my hearing is as good as yours. Maybe better."

Crane shrugged. The look he gave Rhys when he continued to the elevator left Rhys sensing he had missed something important about his guest.

When Crane had gone, Avery said over her shoulder, "I use them from time to time for recreation."

"Cops?" Rhys said.

"Wolves."

He really didn't like the picture his mind was conjuring up that accompanied her statement.

"What does that mean, Avery?"

"Sex. Among other things, that's what they're good at."

Now he really didn't like the images hurling through his mind. Anger welled up. He didn't appreciate being tied to terms like *jealousy* and *possessiveness.*

"I see," he said.

"I doubt if you do." Avery turned to him. "Weres relate to anger, scars, and being separated from the rest of the world by things beyond their control."

"Things such as being a completely different species?"

"Yes."

"Like you."

Her eyes were very bright in the dim light. "Yes. Like me."

"All right. I get that," Rhys said.

"Do you?"

He threw her own question-for-a-question tactic back to her. "Would you care if I did or didn't understand?"

"More than you know," she said.

Her answer surprised him. Rhys found himself by her side without knowing how he got there. He didn't touch her. He lowered his voice. "Would you care to elaborate on that?"

"Is this another interrogation?" she returned wearily.

"Just the one question, then, because it might help me to understand."

"Understand what, Rhys?"

"Why I can't seem to get enough of you. Why I've been mesmerized from the first sighting of you. And why I feel the need to protect your ass, when you're obviously capable of protecting yourself."

His hand was on her arm, on the black jacket she had

slipped back into after he had relieved her of it in a moment of passion. She met his gaze. The connection, blue eyes to blue eyes, immortal soul to immortal soul, caused his next move. There was no way to stop it, Rhys told himself.

He took her hand in his, pressed her palm to his chest, absorbed the shudders of desire that small touch caused. Flames of greed licked at him, proving he hadn't passed his own test. He wasn't able to separate this willingness to help Avery from his unexplained feelings for her.

Wanting so much more, without daring to act on those desires, Rhys waited, counting the seconds ticking by, until she spoke again.

"I'm sorry." Her voice was hushed, throaty. She didn't break contact by averting her eyes.

Sheets of gleaming white hair curtained the sides of her angular face. Against the black jacket, the long, straight strands looked like a physical metaphor cementing the dark-versus-light theory taking shape in Rhys's mind. That contrast also illustrated the dichotomy between good and evil that wasn't always cut-and-dried or easily explained. White spilling over into black, and vice versa.

"What are you sorry about?" he asked, keeping her hand pressed to his chest, feeling her heat burn all the way through his clothes to leave a fresh print on his flesh.

"You," she said. "I'm sorry for doing this to you."

"Making me want you? Is that what you mean?"

She shook her head, dispersing the waist-length silken strands that Rhys wanted to run his fingers through. His body ached for the next intimate touch, and to feel her breath on his face. This lust for her wasn't usual. He realized that. He just wasn't sure what it was or where it had come from.

"Sorry for…" he gently prompted.

"For your life as you now know it," she whispered, and Rhys's heart, beneath her hand, inside his chest, thudded with a warning about what she was going to say next.

Chapter 12

Avery swallowed hard, stifling the words she had been about to speak. Something else nagged for her attention, tearing it away from Rhys and the scary moment of closeness they were sharing that had been leading to a confession.

Turning her head, she said, "Hell, they're here."

Rhys stiffened and looked past her. "They?"

"Vampires."

The apartment was soundproof, but Avery didn't need to hear the vamp chatter to sense them. She felt those monsters' foreign presence as if she stood on the street watching the parade of bloodsuckers arrive.

Something else. Something more...

"He's there, too. Damn it, we've led them here," she said.

"Who, Avery? Who else is here?"

"Your detective."

"Crane? Christ!"

Rhys was already heading for the elevator. The moment

they'd shared and the confession she had left hanging had to be tabled in favor of a more pressing issue.

Avery was right beside Rhys, relieved about the reprieve and reaching for her blade as the elevator descended. In a loaded silence, they raced from the elevator and out the front door of the building, careful not to say anything else about feelings.

Enemies were massing on the street in the distance. There was no sign of mortals in the area. It was still dark, but had to be early in the morning by now. One hour was much like the next. She rarely kept track of time's passage, having experienced so much of it.

The first howl echoed between the buildings, closer than half a block away. "Werewolves," she said, as Rhys moved past her toward the sound.

"Let's hope they're some of his," Rhys called back, and he took off at a sprint.

She really was sorry…for this, and for allowing herself to be caught in the first place. For nearly confiding in a Blood Knight, even if it was Perceval, or Rhys, as he now called himself.

God, yes. She had messed up, big-time, and now had to deal. She was the cause of this latest round of confrontations. She could not, in good conscience, run away from Rhys now, when he was fighting for her, and because of her. They ran side by side, covering ground in a blur of speed. Vampires were quick. Immortals were quicker. Werewolves were lethal when it came to guarding their territory, as well as fast. No lazy bloodsucker should have dared to come here, where Blood Knights and a Detective Werewolf shared a penthouse.

She ran at Rhys's side to the dark place where some of London's Weres had caught up with their old enemies, knowing that without a full moon overhead, there couldn't be many furred-up wolves in this fray, but the ones who could pull off a trick like shape-shifting at will were truly fine specimens with the purest bloodlines.

Silver blade in hand, Avery lunged into the heart of the battle being fought, a battle that had little to do with species interaction and everything to do with her.

Without her unwilling help in creating the Blood Knights, and that blood gift they had received, there might not have been a species called vampires. From the slip of a Maker's fang, way back in time, after their loss of control over the Knights, one of the Makers had started the vampirism ball rolling by passing the whisper of death and immortality to other humans. One good bite to the jugular and it was bye-bye mortality for the victims. Castle Broceliande had been ground zero for such experiments, and after gaining her freedom from its dungeons, she had demolished that evil place too late.

"Avery!" Rhys was in Guardian mode, and serious about taking the lead.

"Fat chance!" she shouted, hitting the first bloodsucker head-on.

There were too many adversaries for him to maintain his human semblance and get very far, though Rhys tried hard to hold on. Avery, on the other hand, had become light, and beamed the pure white energy of her origins at every monster in the area.

Crane was there in the shadows. Other werewolves were howling, coming closer, keeping to the darker spaces as they rushed toward the spot where Rhys stood. Without a full moon, they had shifted. Like Crane, they had to be full-blooded Lycans. Several huge Weres, half morphed, naked and partially furred up, joined the fight. Two others ran on all fours, which was another sign of ancient Lycan lineage. Savage growls tore from their inhuman throats that would have frightened any living soul.

It was a miracle no one had yet heard the noise and called the police…a minor joke, he supposed, since it was likely some of these guys were the police. Crane's friends on the force.

Led by Crane, they fought the vampires. Bloodsuckers were notoriously nasty fighters, but the unparalleled beauty of werewolves in action made the vamps look like amateurs. The enemies clashing in this alley looked a little bit like Valhalla's gods at war. Not for the first time in his long history, Rhys was glad there were Weres on his side.

As with their prey in the old days, Crane's pack went for vampire throats in a weird turnaround twist. With enough power in their agile bodies to sever vampire heads from their emaciated bodies with one or two bites, at least ten bloodsuckers went down before Rhys could count to five.

He turned his attention to Avery, who was slashing at a particularly nasty fanged freak with her glinting blade. She had severed one of its hands from its bony arm, and the creep didn't seem to notice. Fangs bared, the beast went at her again and again, snapping its teeth, hollow eyes red-rimmed with bloodlust and anger.

But angels were no weaklings, mentally or physically, Rhys had discovered, not merely pretty things with wings. Avery held this sucker off without a single groan of protest, choreographing her moves with precision and an almost effortless ease.

She could handle this. That was obvious. But Rhys felt sick watching her. He hated seeing how that monster's yellow fangs got close enough at times to graze the collar of Avery's jacket and how tightly her pale fingers gripped the blade.

Although she might be angry about it, he was beside

Avery in a flash. He caught the snapping beast by its coat and spun it around to face its new dancing partner.

"Mine," Avery called out, already moving up between Rhys and the bloodsucker in his grip. Confused by the diversion, the vamp looked at her too late. Avery's silver blade pierced its chest cavity in a direct hit to the spot where this vampire's heart once had been a beating, living organ.

Surprise overtook the monster's gaunt features before it exploded into a storm of ash. All motion in the area seemed to slow to a standstill as the gray flakes rained down.

The Weres had the situation well under control. The foggy, water-saturated London air stank of dusted vampire remains. There would be no remnants of this fight left to be found. No missing persons reports would be filed, because vampires were no longer people.

Rhys stood back-to-back with Avery, absorbing her tension, feeling electricity spark off her. Neither of them moved.

The area cleared quickly. Crane's Weres were disappearing as fluidly as they had arrived. That left only Ellis Crane, who growled a greeting to Rhys, tossed his head and took off after his pack.

One lone Shade, either brave enough or stupid enough to glide from the shadows with malice on its mind after the main event had concluded, was the street's only ghostly reminder of what had gone on.

"This one's mine," Rhys said.

Stake in hand, he welcomed the gauzy apparition with a wave.

"You do know that stake won't harm this guy," Avery warned as the Shade rushed in.

"Trying to tell me how to do my job?" Rhys quipped as the Shade advanced.

"Just a friendly reminder," Avery said.

In what seemed like a slow waltz with a shadow partner, Rhys let the Shade get close enough for him to smell its fetid breath. Sidestepping Avery, who was watching him intently, he whirled, ducked and straightened again with the blade he pulled from his boot.

Fighting a Shade was like fighting a dark mass of jelly. The thing had no face that he could see. Its arms stuck out from its body like liquid spilling from a pool of ink. But between those arms lay its vulnerable spot, and Rhys angled his blade there as the thing's cool, moist presence came at him.

The attack was weak, at best. In seconds, the malignant shadow figure dissipated as if it had been composed of nothing more than a bit of compressed fog. No hint of it remained. There wasn't a spot on Rhys's knife.

"Well, that was just too easy," Rhys muttered. "I wonder why the damn Shade had bothered to show up."

"Maybe it was trying to tell me something," Avery said thoughtfully. "Easy, was it?" she added, with a sardonic nod to his Knightly prowess.

She was smiling wryly when Rhys looked at her. Riled up, tense and with his sigils crawling on the back of his neck, Rhys reached her before she had time to wipe the smile from her pale, perfect face. With his hands on her jacket, and a small surge of the power he rarely used and never openly displayed, Rhys picked her up and tossed the angel through a partially boarded window beside them.

Sounds of breaking wood were muffled by the heaviness of the fog. Rhys jumped through the opening after Avery, who lay on her back on the floor, uninjured and still smiling.

Had she liked this show of strength? Whatever the reason for her welcoming expression, he found her too damn inviting. The surge of lust searing his insides was also a genuine surprise.

Rhys was beside her on the floor before her next blink, thinking that in the old days of chivalry he would have spread his cape for her to stretch out on, and that tonight their bed would have to be rubble.

He could have found her mouth without any light to guide him. He would have done this no matter what. Hungrily sealing his lips to hers, he perched on his elbows above her, ready to take however much of her she was willing to give, while also half expecting her to shove him away.

She didn't offer up a protest. None at all.

On the dirty wood-splintered floor of an abandoned shop, and with the last howls echoing faintly in the distance, Rhys tore the leather jacket from Avery's lean body without his lips leaving hers.

He stroked her shoulders through the soft, worn fabric of her shirt as the kiss deepened, before tearing the shirt apart with his hands. The sound of ripping cloth was sinful, provocative and sexy as hell. He was hard in all the right places to follow through with this particular meeting.

Avery's mouth was moist, hot and malleable. She was not only willing to let him get this far, she was encouraging him.

His hands followed the roadmap of scars covering her torso to her breasts, which, like her face, were smooth beneath his palms. When he brushed their raised buds with his fingertips, she made a soft sound. A sigh of acceptance. His angel wanted this as much as he did. Who would have guessed that angels considered a good fight as foreplay?

This was to be no plan made by careful lovers, however. There was going to be no slow lovemaking session tonight, and no tender exploration of the glorious being beneath him. It was entirely possible there would never be another moment like this one. Conceivably, this was their one shot at taking the edge off an attraction that had them hungering for each other every time they met.

Hell, Avery felt like a woman to him. She kissed like a woman, with passion, little darts of her tongue and fiery determination. Jealous, Rhys fought off a disturbing pang of uneasiness that had his sigils squirming. She had kissed before. What else had she done?

Oh, yes. She'd mentioned playing with the wolves.

His need to possess her overruled those questions. With his mouth on hers and her sweet angelic breath in his lungs, Rhys's fingers moved to the zipper on her tight leather pants.

Surely she would stop him now?

Each inch that zipper traveled was a new revelation about time, and a fresh thrill. Rhys's pulse pounded as though someone hammered away at him. His sigils, antsy only seconds ago, had gone still.

Avery snaked her arms around his waist, under his coat. Her touch sent shockwaves of longing through him that made Rhys wish he was already undressed and inside her.

Too many clothes in the way...

Her hands were strong, her grip on him firm. She was seeking a way inside his shirt, and he wanted to help her. But the zipper had reached the end of its metal track. His fingers burned as he slid through the opening he had created in the leather, heading for what awaited him there and almost afraid to find the damp heat he so desperately sought.

Her skin was feverish. Her next sigh nearly sent him over the precipice of withholding his desire for what now lay within his reach. Rich. Succulent. Sexy. Did anyone think of angels that way?

The smoothness of her face and breasts extended to what

lay beneath his fingers. Her belly was concave, stretched tightly between two blade-sharp hip bones. Touching the mound of skin and bone beneath that was like running a hand over a newborn's back. And angels, he discovered, did not believe in underwear.

Hell with this!

He drew back with reluctance, missing her mouth as soon as he'd left it. Cool air rushed in to fill the space between them, but did nothing to cool his ardor. Braced on one elbow, he began to press her pants downward, imagining the delights he'd find, crazy with longing for this angel.

Avery sat up. She gripped his wrist. Pale blue eyes met his in the dappled darkness.

"You'll stop me now?" Rhys said.

Clearly, she had other ideas. She got to her feet, but not to get away from him or halt what was going to happen. With her hand clamped to his wrist, she urged him to stand. She helped him to remove her pants, kicked off her boots and shook her head to scatter locks of white hair that were starting to tangle.

Fully naked, she stood in front of him, open to his curious examination. Rhys couldn't help but stare. Certainly Avery felt like a woman made of flesh and bone, but seeing her like this, bare from her face to her feet, he wasn't so sure about his own earlier perceptions.

White skin gleamed with the same light he had seen radiate from her before. That extraordinary sheen bathed her, encapsulated her. Undressed, it was easy to see the real thing. The real Avery.

She was mind-blowingly beautiful.

Avery looked exactly like everyone's version of one of Heaven's denizens. It was all there. So much so, Rhys half expected her to use those new tattoos and fly away.

Angel. Yes. No argument from him. She was a walking miracle and beyond belief. At the same time, though, Rhys found this image tragic. Hers was a unique exquisiteness that hurt the soul of whoever witnessed it.

It hurt him.

He refused to close his eyes.

The scars she bore added to his discomfort. Someone had wounded her, branded this heavenly creature who had, for some reason, turned earthly. Only her eyes, dark-lined and curious, vied for his attention over every other incredible detail.

What happened to you? Rhys wanted to ask her.

Why are you here?

Unable to look at her any longer, lost in the blue of her eyes, he drew her into the circle of his arms. Wanting to give comfort, and at the same time wanting so much more than that after all the years of being alone, he reasoned that this angelic being was in his arms for a similar reason. She also sought comfort, wherever it could be found in a cold world where the population remained ignorant of what went on beyond their everyday lives.

He would give her that comfort. He would accept the invitation in her eyes and in her exquisite nakedness.

Without asking her permission or being mindful of what would happen to them afterward, he lifted Avery, wrapped her bare legs around him and, with his hands on her small, rounded backside, pressed her into the wall across from them.

"Okay," he said. "You and me. Here. Now."

Holding her there wouldn't do, though. Merely feeling the extreme heat between her legs through his jeans wouldn't do. Turning slowly, keeping her tight to him, he took her back down to the floor, careful to lay her on her jacket. Her grip on him did not ease. Her mouth was waiting when he again found it.

With only enough room to unleash himself, and still fully dressed, he found what he wanted—the heat and the welcoming dampness that aided his first entry into that inferno.

Sure he would lose his mind, Rhys paused, exhaled a groan and waited out the few seconds it took for his pulse to catch up with his breathing. That hesitation didn't suit the creature in his arms. A wickedly sensual, unangelic grinding of her hips against his deepened his position inside her. As his cock slid deeper into the blistering heat, the black blood in Rhys's arteries began to boil.

He wondered briefly how something from Heaven could be so hot. Her body molded to his, took him in, massaged his length to greater and greater depths.

No more time for thought of any kind…

Avery's hips had a silent language all their own. Her encouraging moves were undeniably right and perfectly timed to drive him mad. Her willingness left him no alternative but to get on with it, see this through.

So be it.

All right.

Backing off slowly, Rhys then eased inside her again, barely able to absorb the shock of what he was doing and what he was finding at this angel's molten core. This was something altogether new, exciting, and it came with an unexpected current of feeling that made him finally close his eyes.

She was pure electricity wrapped in flesh, underscored by bone. Touching her made his skin buzz, caused his body to ache in places he hadn't known existed.

As he plunged into her again and again, Avery's fingernails trailed down the back of his shirt. When his next surge of pressure reached the core of this angel, her nails cut deep grooves in his skin. A hurt for a hurt. Pleasure and pain were mingling.

She dug in with both hands, holding on tight, making sure he didn't stop what he was doing. Hell, he wouldn't have tried.

My wild angel...

His sigils felt as if they had burst into the kind of flames usually reserved for a warning that he was heading in a wrong direction. But Rhys didn't pay attention to what that might mean. He was exactly where he wanted to be. Inside Avery. Sliding in and out of the soft petals of her sex as if they'd been longtime lovers, and as if they had something further to prove.

It was all he could do to hold on when she was so very succulent, so sweet and otherworldly. Sensation ruled. Touch was everything now. Avery's heat. Her soft skin. Her lush mouth. Building up a rhythm, Rhys's body gave in to those things. His body took over, driving in and out of Avery, striving for levels of ecstasy he'd never known were possible and certainly never thought existed.

Sighs escaped her with each fresh physical assault, rising from deep in her throat. Whips of her internal flames licked at him. Lashes of fire turned him on, drove him on.

Tethered to those outrageous sensations, Rhys felt more alive than he ever had. He had an unquenchable desire for more of whatever this was. More of her. His mouth ravaged her mouth, leaving bruises of possession that marked her as his. His hands on her hips held her steady, so that each thrust met its intended mark.

And she gave back, aiding each thrust, drinking him in with her talented mouth while her light engulfed him. He breathed in that light, reveled in the sparks inside him that it created. Nerves hummed. Muscles twitched with the effort to satisfy her, and in doing so, himself.

No longer content with raking his skin, Avery pounded at him with her closed fists. She nipped at his lips with her tiny white teeth and whispered words he didn't understand.

As the pleasure grew to monstrous proportions, Rhys felt a rumbling vibration start to roll inside her. Tearing his mouth from hers, he arched his back. One final thrust, one last good stroke, and he held her there, to that rising internal drumbeat. He held her until that earthquake reached its peak, and rode out the climax that threatened his hold on sanity.

The pleasure went on and on, ceaselessly. Waves of electrified pulses came, crashing over and over until Rhys finally opened his eyes.

Avery's eyelashes fluttered as she writhed beneath him, moving, stretching, until her own internal quakes finally calmed. Breathing shallowly, uttering a moan, she opened her eyes to look at him.

Beneath the golden glint in her sky-blue eyes, Rhys felt himself begin to sink. He was inside her, and her light was inside him. He had been moved, robbed of breath, transfixed to the point of being nearly mindless, and he wasn't sure how that kind of complete takeover could happen.

All that light brought a surge of memory with it. Memories of Broceliande, where he had traded one life for another.

White stone walls reached toward the moon, surrounded by a dark garden at their base. Windowless towers of quarried limestone rose, tall, formidable, creamy in color and pleasing to the eye. He knew this image, was intimately familiar with Broceliande's beautiful outer shell.

In the distance came sounds: water in the golden fountain, clouds moving in the wind. But beyond those things he heard…screaming.

"No!"

The command came from outside of himself to scatter the dream.

"Not now." Another insistent demand.

It was Avery's voice. Her tone. His angel was speaking to him. He had become entangled in her light and was having a hard time extricating himself.

New chills merged with the extremes of the heat he had sampled. He wanted to understand why his thoughts would go back there, to the castle, now, of all times.

A warm hand on his face brought him around. Avery was looking at him. Their bodies were entwined, their legs in a tangle. Both hearts were racing.

"That's not for you," she warned with that throaty, serious tone. "I thought it would be, at one time in the past. I see now that I was wrong."

Her expression was both sober and pained. Did she regret what they had done so soon?

"I've hurt you." Rhys eyed her bruised mouth.

It wasn't like him to be fuzzy or out of focus. No one knew better than he did that nothing he could do would truly hurt this angel. Her wounds would heal as quickly as his did. The bruises would disappear in minutes, and she'd feel nothing in the morning.

He had shoved her through a boarded-up window, and that action had served to ignite the sparks that had sealed them together. That moment had made them a unified whole.

She spoke again. "I didn't show that picture of the castle to you. You have no right to it."

In the back of Rhys's mind, the scream he had heard in

the dream echoed. Tendrils of his inky sigils writhed in response to the reverberating sound.

Warning...

Waving red flags.

"Are you suggesting that flashback wasn't conceived from my memory?" he asked, thinking her comment absurd. Only the Knights knew about that blasted castle and what had gone on there. The information this angel said she possessed about him and his brethren had to be based in rumor, as she had said.

But then, how had she known about St. John, his brother? She had brought up his name in regard to the penthouse.

"The light comes with consequences," she said, holding his attention with her big blue eyes. "I didn't mean for you to experience that, but I...I had to have you, have this. We had to get it over with."

She wasn't making sense. Light still surrounded her and, by default, him, as if there was a hole in the ceiling and moonlight shone through.

"Nothing is over," he countered. "This was merely a great beginning. Hell, I already want a replay."

His body was in agreement with that.

"Can't happen," she said. "I have to go. I've told you already, we've gotten too close. This was a mistake."

"Too close for what? Why would this matter? To whom would it matter?"

"It matters to me."

"I liked what we did. You liked it."

"I..." she began.

"Where do you have to go?" Rhys interrupted, already guessing the answer. She had come to London for one thing and had gotten distracted. They both had. Time had passed, when Avery's mission might be time sensitive. Taking hours out of that schedule for some long-overdue pleasure probably hadn't been on her to-do list.

Her hands were on his chest, on his shirt. He was dressed, and she was naked, on her back in the dirt. He had just shared the most intimate of acts with an angel and couldn't get enough of her. Would he be damned for that? Would she suffer the consequences?

One thing was for sure. Angels were bloody well addictive.

"All right, Avery." Rhys backed to his knees, got to his feet, put himself to rights before offering her his hand. "I'll play along with what you want. Now that we've gotten this out of the way, as you said, where do we start the search for what you need? What will make you happy?"

Before she replied with another question that wouldn't have given him any satisfaction in terms of understanding her, a pesky, persistent thought came to him.

If that memory wasn't his, and the castle where he and his brothers had given up their mortality lay inside it, whose memory was it?

How the hell could it have been hers?

Chapter 13

Avery liked being bare. Nudity was her natural state.

She liked the feel of the draft on her limbs and the imprint of the buttons on her jacket cutting into her back and buttocks. Craving sensation after going without for so long made her relish the leftover burn of the friction of having had Rhys inside her.

It was no dream this time, though she had imagined mating with him many times in the past. She had known it would be like this if they met. She might even have imagined the look she saw now on his handsome face—a look that told her he was not going anywhere anytime soon, and that his pledge to help her search had become part of his agenda. His tender expression, when translated, meant they'd merely gotten started in this new relationship, and he anticipated more moments like these.

The problem was how much she wanted that same thing.

I'll be damned before letting you see that, Blood Knight.

Giving in to her emotions now would get her nowhere

and lead to a backward slide in her plans. This man, after all the centuries that had passed, had made her question those plans.

"Too powerful," she said, without explaining the remark.

He tilted his head in question.

Avery missed how his warm breath had filled her lungs. With their mingled power surging through them, the creature now calling himself Rhys had somehow been able to share her memories. He had dialed up old images still stuck in her mind.

She might have wanted that kind of mental mingling before tonight, allowing him to see what demands that castle had imposed on her. But she had told Rhys the truth about changing her mind. In person, she found him worthy of better treatment. He deserved more than to share in the pain of her past.

"This is my fight," she said to him.

"What fight are we talking about?"

Admitting her centuries-old love and admiration for this Blood Knight would be the end of her. With her wings, the real ones, she would be free to go home. Rhys would be left behind. She'd have one thing she wanted at the expense of something else that she had always secretly coveted.

Those things were at odds with each other.

"I'm going to find out what that Shade on the roof was talking about," she said.

"That's crazy, and you know it."

"I have to go alone. They don't like you. Your reputation precedes you here."

"This is because you actually believed that abomination and that the Shade has knowledge you need?"

"That's the downside of rumor, isn't it? In order to find how much truth a rumor contains, the seeker has to explore all avenues toward that end."

Her lover hadn't moved, though his body had tensed. "Are you regretting what we did here?" he asked. "So much so that you'd ignore common sense just to spite me?"

"Yes." The pain of uttering that lie struck hard and fiercely, nearly doubling her over. Avery hadn't entirely convinced herself that tumbling on the floor with this Blood Knight had been a bad idea. The honest truth was that she liked everything about what they had done. Liked it way too much.

The magnificent beast beside her nodded his head, perhaps recognizing the symptoms of the lie she had told. Each lie dimmed the light she carried and made her sicker inside.

"It's easier to answer a question with a question than it is to suffer the effects of an untruth," he noted. "Do you think I don't know what you've been doing by evading my probing and by keeping me in the dark about the specifics of your quest?"

"It's best if you don't know everything. You will have to trust me on that."

"No one said you had to tell me everything. If I'm going to help you find the things you seek, though, shouldn't I know all that entails?"

"No. Not yet," Avery replied. "Maybe you can start helping me by handing me my clothes."

She didn't especially care for the grin he was showing her. But she did know what to do about it.

"I will hurt you in the end," she warned.

"If that's what it takes," he said.

The old promises she'd made had been transformed. Avery couldn't bring herself to hurt the man across from her, who had become her incredibly talented lover. However, there was no way to stay with him without hurting him. The only way to remain true to her quest was for her to leave

Rhys behind. Now. Sooner rather than later. Avoiding more pain for both of them.

If that meant forgoing Rhys's help when it might have been beneficial, she would have to be okay with that. Anything would have to do to stop the madness that struck her every time she looked at him.

"Will you pick up my clothes?" she repeated, wanting to lie back down on the floor and open her arms. Wanting to forget about secrets. Wanting him to take her again, fast and hard, and leave her panting. Wishing he would chase away the demons in her past and free her of so many old burdens.

None of that could happen here.

"I go alone to the Shades," she reiterated. "I find those ghosts by myself."

The grin she had loved for the brief seconds she'd seen it, had already faded from Rhys's face, replaced by a seriousness that was equally devastating to her. Rhys was handling this lovemaking session better than she was. He was all in on helping her, and what she wanted most was to have him back between her legs.

Avery thought about slapping him for ensnaring her with his beauty and for the deviation in her agenda this Blood Knight, in all his glory, had caused. She raised her fists to pound on his chest, but he caught them before she could.

"All right," he said, at last. "If that's what you want, I'll give you your freedom."

They stood for some time longer, looking at each other, measuring each other in terms of what would happen next. When he released her hands and leaned over to retrieve her clothes, as she had asked, Avery whispered an honest "Sorry," and slammed him with a beam of light that made him stagger.

As he dealt with that unexpected blow, Avery swooped

up her pants, jacket and boots, and jumped through the open window.

Rhys would only be frozen for a few seconds more while his body absorbed and then adjusted to the light she'd used as a weapon against him. What she'd done wouldn't slow him down for long, since his soul also housed light.

After a few seconds of feeling stunned, you will be all right.

It was strange how important his welfare was to her all of a sudden, and how much she dreaded leaving him. While Blood Knights had beating hearts that bled and broke like everyone else's, those hearts were both the Seven's salvation and their curse, as Rhys was going to find out when she disappeared.

"Sorry," she repeated.

With the wind in her hair and the cool night on her bare back, Avery ran from Rhys and from what they had done, willing the inked wings on her back to aid her retreat. No amount of distance was going to stop her own heart from breaking, no matter which way this went, now that she had finally remembered she had one.

Rhys straightened quickly with a fresh intake of breath. In his mind, he heard the echo of Avery's *Sorry* as he used the window for his own escape.

"You didn't play nice," he said, as much to her as to himself.

Once he hit the sidewalk, he began to run. Sprinting cooled his overheated face while offering a temporary respite from thinking about what he and Avery had done. One long stride after another took him blocks from the room where their bodies had joined in several all-consuming moments of physical bliss.

Hell with forgetting about it; he wanted more moments

like that, right now. His loins pulsed with longing. His muscles were far too tense.

He had to find her.

Listening to the beat of the night, he traced the disturbance creating a disruption in the atmosphere. If Avery was so damn smart, why didn't she know about the trail she had left? Anyone with enhanced abilities could have detected the direction she had taken. All around them, monsters dwelled. Too damn many of them.

"Helping you is my duty," he said, needing to speak those words out loud, wondering if she'd hear them. "But can I wait to do that, as you've requested?"

He didn't want to postpone the next meeting. Avery was going to face a creature that had formed an alliance with vampires, and that kind of partnership was unprecedented and sick. The two species had been on the same street more than one time tonight, and that didn't bode well for anyone.

Better yet, an alliance between a Shade and an angel would be the highlight of the century. And that just wasn't feasible.

How could you think they have information you need, Avery?

No one in their right mind would trust the ghosts.

"We had a deal," he growled. "A deal is a deal. You should know that by now."

Darkness had never been his friend, only a necessary ally. The fact that he missed days in the sunshine was a secret he kept to himself. In Avery's light, those memories had been rekindled. Sun. Flowers. Green grass. Water. Landscapes stretching in all directions, completely visible to everyone. Staring into Avery's eyes, he had relived those days, and he had, for perhaps the first time in his lengthy tenure on Earth as a Blood Knight, experienced a few moments of what felt like freedom.

Turning back was not an option.

As he had lain embedded in Avery's lush body, with her heat surrounding him and her nails on his back, he had almost accepted the notion that his long existence had led him to that very moment, and that going forward might actually be worthwhile if she was to be part of his future.

In spite of her protests, leaving Avery to the bad guys went against everything he stood for. She had not disclosed the secrets at the core of her quest, and because of that, he was still in the dark. Her pain, transferred to him through her touch—the blood she had drawn with her nails and her raised fists—had been a terrible thing, a burden she must have carried with her since whatever had happened to her had set her on this present course.

You never belonged here on Earth, my angel. I know that.

I cannot ask you to stay if freedom is what you seek.

Her quest?

That quest was centered on her wings, and how she had lost them. Rhys felt certain now that she had not willingly given them up, because what could possibly have been worth the trade-off?

"Whatever gross event has left you grounded has to be the bane of your current existence."

He doubted Avery could hear him speaking, but that was irrelevant, because Rhys couldn't keep his thoughts inside.

"That event is also the reason, the impetus, that sent you to me. The secrets you're keeping are tied to why you inked the new pair of wings on your pale, scarred flesh. Do you miss the real ones? Do you ache for your birthright and pine for what you've lost, the way anyone else would pine for a missing limb?"

Considering that scenario, Rhys thought his heart would break.

He relived the last moments on the floor of that abandoned room and the incredible climax they had shared. His body ached from the power behind the act and the desire to have Avery beneath him again.

"You can't have it both ways, my angel. Either you like me, or you don't."

His thoughts turned to another dilemma. Would a successful quest mean she'd fly away? Ascend to wherever she came from, leaving him here to fight on, alone?

He wasn't sure he could forget her. He wasn't sure he wanted to. *Not now. Not after...*

"Avery. I need to understand what happened to you. Only then can I take away some of your pain. Only in sharing can we solve this puzzle of our unexpected attraction. Why won't you trust me?"

An answer came to him on the wind, or in his mind, as if she had heard him.

"Trust is not for this world we find ourselves in. It has played no part in my existence here."

Avery had answered, proving they remained connected. That was enough for the time being. It wasn't everything on his wish list, but it would have to do.

Veering to the east, Rhys picked up his pace. Avery was somewhere up ahead. Not too far away. The bond that had snapped into place between them allowed him to almost see her. Her scent, carried by the night air, drove him on.

Tuning in to those things, Rhys allowed some of the power he kept suppressed to rise to the surface. As that power sparked, his nerves fired up with a white-hot surge. Beckoned forward, some of his outer layers began to peel back, shedding the semblance he had, out of necessity, taken as his own. He might need an extra kick of power when he found her.

The sensation of freeing his real countenance, letting

out what had so long been hidden, was exhilarating. Muscles rippled. The crack of his spine made his sigils whine.

Bit by bit, Rhys unchained what lay at his core, unveiling the special creature that had cheated Death so long ago. One of the chosen few who had sipped from a golden chalice with his final mortal breath—a chalice that had captured the blood of a holy man on a cross.

The mortal Rhys had been born again anew. Not an angel like Avery, but half man and half something else that had no name, other than one, to explain the phenomenon.

Blood Knight.

He was a holy warrior fighting on the side of right and defending those in need. And what could be more right than helping an angel in distress?

"Don't you see?" Rhys asked aloud. "You and the place you come from are the very things I have fought for all this time. I am on your side, Avery."

Breathing came easier now that his lungs had expanded. Old scars that had been carefully concealed began to reappear, crossing his torso as if made by the merciless lashes of an invisible whip. Sight cleared, bringing into focus the way the air ahead of him glittered with tiny obsidian particles that were Avery's personal stamp on the night.

"Have you left a trail for me to follow, despite your arguments to the contrary?" He sent the thought to her.

"Without trust," he said through the fangs that had dropped in honor of this chase, "we have nothing."

Swear to God, he thought he heard Avery's soft, muffled cry of protest in response to that statement.

Chapter 14

On top of a trash receptacle seven alleys over from where she'd left Rhys, Avery crouched on her haunches. Even at this distance, she heard Rhys's comments, plain as day. The dangerous thing she'd feared had happened. Sexual antics had sealed them closer together, threatening the rest of her ability to disappear. Behind the beating of her own heart, she heard his. The light in his veins beckoned to her with a pull that set her teeth on edge.

Morning was coming on the heels of one of the longest nights she had endured. Streaks of crimson backed the clouds over her head and were welcome, along with the quiet that had settled over this part of London.

The beasts were gone. The Shade she sought would be hiding, but she'd used that as an excuse to get away from Rhys. Just far enough to breathe.

Rhys would find her any minute. He had offered her shelter, and she had run away. Rhys had offered his help with her quest, and she had run from him due to her tumultuous feelings for the gorgeous Blood Knight.

God, yes. She had feelings for him. Her kindred soul.

Stomach in knots, she waited for him to find her. The new tattoos only stung slightly from the abuse she had taken after receiving them when she moved her shoulders. Hurts on the inside clung as if they had talons.

No longer good, like you, she wanted to tell Rhys. *I have made others pay for what happened in my past. I had planned to make you and your blood brothers pay.*

And now. Well, now she was screwed. A centuries-old vendetta had been sacked simply by meeting Rhys face-to-face. Old vows of payback, always edging a precipice where this man was concerned, had been shattered after going groin to groin with him. An appropriate second tattoo would be to have the word *sucker* inked on her forehead so that everyone she encountered could see it.

Not a very angelic thought. But Avery's angelness had long ago begun to pale, along with the color of her skin.

Her head snapped up.

Rhys was closer, his imminent appearance as certain as the dawn. And here she sat, feeling much too needy, too earthly.

She needed shelter and a safe place to rest. She prayed for rain or a decent shower to wash away the tentacles of Rhys's rich, masculine scent. That scent damned her, coated her from her face to her ankles. The magnificent hardness of what hung between his thighs haunted her still.

One night in his presence had changed everything. Rhys and his outlandish allure. On that floor, she had wished, not for her lost wings, but for time to stop. One of God's angelic emissaries had succumbed to the pleasures granted to the mortal species populating the Earth. Sex and long, deep, lingering kisses had been the province of humans lucky enough to experience such things. Until tonight.

She had been too long among the mortals, and her time was nearly up. This was her last chance, her final chance to become whole again. Rhys couldn't do that for her, in the end.

No place to go. No way to escape, Rhys.

I've done the unthinkable, and it's too late to correct the mistake.

What other option do I have but to wait for you, without leaving London altogether? If I were to leave without my wings, like the color of my skin, I will eventually fade out of existence. There will be nothing left of me. I used to welcome that thought... And then there was you.

Moist air stirred with the Blood Knight's approach. Avery's hands curled into fists. Speaking was tough.

"Bravo. You found me," she said.

"The sun soon rises," he observed, taking a wide stance and playing the chivalry card by failing to mention the body-numbing stumbling block she had hit him with just minutes before.

"Angels don't fry like vampires do," she reminded him.

"Still, you must be tired."

Avery nodded. *Tired* was an understatement.

"You didn't run far," he noted.

She let that comment go unaddressed.

"And you led me right to you—purposefully, I think," he added.

Yes, she supposed she had done that again. Covering her tracks completely was out of the question after they had coupled in such a fierce, gutsy way.

His next question also avoided mention of what had happened between them. "Do angels eat?"

It took seconds for Avery to follow the mundane direction of this conversation.

"On occasion," she said, eyeing Rhys warily, waiting for a punchline.

"Would this be one of those times if I knew where to take you for food?" he asked.

The big bad Knight was being uncommonly tender in dealing with her when her list of wants didn't include sustenance at the moment, but something far more wicked and much too telling about her state of mind to say out loud.

You. More of you is all the sustenance I require.

"Back to the cop-wolf's lair?" she asked, shaking her head to dislodge the sheer madness of skirting the real issues at stake here. She knew he wanted to ask her about what an angel was doing on Earth, and how she had gotten here. Unspoken thoughts trailed every lull in their stilted conversation.

It was, though, too early to share secrets.

Rhys nodded. "Crane keeps the place well stocked. Wolves are perpetually hungry. Fast metabolisms, and all that. St. John's apartment is the safest place in this city for us to rest. Besides, you don't actually intend to walk around London looking like that, do you?"

"Like what?" Avery challenged before realizing she had forgotten to put on her clothes. Rhys's gaze had let her off the hook about that by never once straying from her face.

"I'll wait," he said, "if you'd like to accompany me and start over."

Damn straight she'd like to start over, and either shore up her skill at avoiding this Knight or restart the clock twenty minutes ago in that abandoned building.

Her current wish was for a big bed in Rhys's blood brother's penthouse, where they could replay on a continual loop their incredible sexual exploration.

Her core thrummed with that last thought. Taut muscles twitched. This Blood Knight had taken her to new heights of passion. He had shown her what sex could and should be like between two consenting beings who feasted on sensation. Back there, in Rhys's arms, she had nearly lost touch with missions and vows.

"Well," he said. "You can come along or not. This time, I won't press the point. What happens next is entirely up to you. If you truly don't want my help, I will withdraw the offer I made and back off. I will leave you alone."

"You'll leave me alone because you now trust me?" Avery queried.

"Because if you want that, it's the right thing to do."

That said, he turned and walked away, leaving her to stare at the sheer grace and beauty of the way he accomplished such a simple move. All that molded muscle was working in concert. There was fluidity in his long limbs and in the way his golden-brown hair brushed his collar.

Rhys's golden allure had never been stronger than it was right then. Avery's breath caught. She closed her eyes. Something was definitely wrong with her for so badly wanting more light, passion, comfort. *For wanting love.*

"Okay," she said. "Let's try again."

He paused, without turning around or acknowledging her remark, before walking on.

Hopping from her perch, Avery slid her arms into her jacket, pulled on her pants and boots, ditched her torn shirt in the Dumpster and started after him. This was a new beginning. A fresh start to an old tale. Hatred of Rhys's kind had grayed, replaced by lust, respect and a secret love that had, at long last, twisted her heart into submission.

She loved him, and she wasn't entirely sure what to do with that.

Rhys didn't wait for her to catch up, and Avery didn't

try to, fearing that if she got close to him now, the dirty sidewalk would be the place of their next sexual tryst. Willpower had dimmed, along with her list of promises, and the future was up for grabs.

Quite possibly, and in the span of a few short hours, her soul, along with her direction, had been transformed.

Quite possibly, she wasn't going to go forward alone.

"I liked it," she heard Rhys mutter. "Each and every damn second."

Hearing that confession, Avery's heart, so rarely buoyant, danced.

Rhys didn't have to look at Avery to know she was sleeping. He instinctively knew this. The tension between them had eased. At last, he could breathe.

She had rested for two days straight, as if dead to the world she'd found herself in. With her eyes closed, she seemed almost peaceful. Even then, however, her fists were curled. Was that due to old pains? Hurts so deep, only Avery could feel them?

What would finding her wings do? Could they be reattached to her back? He had begun to ache for her and rolled his shoulders.

Lying beside her wouldn't have been right or welcome, he supposed. By closing her eyes, she was showing she trusted him. He didn't plan on breaking that trust anytime soon, however much he wanted to be with her.

So he studied her from his place by the windows, afraid that if he closed his eyes, he'd wake to find her gone. Rest was overrated anyway, and he'd had more than his share over the centuries.

Now and then, when he drifted off to sleep, his thoughts spiraled back to the past and to the castle where he'd taken his last breath as a mortal man. Incredibly, after so many years had passed, that image often still troubled him. This new pale-faced addition to his routine also troubled him in a similar way, as though the two things were attempting to make a connection in the recesses of his mind.

He could almost see Avery in his past, dim, hazy and in the distance. The sense of familiarity came back in waves.

Connection with an angel was absurd, surely? Other than one of his Makers and a sorceress with far-reaching predictions, there had been no women at Castle Broceliande. Certainly there had been no heavenly female. In his long tenure on Earth, he had never encountered a being like Avery.

She'd said she thought she had been meant to find him, and that together they could accomplish what she'd set out to do. Maybe she was right about that. He wanted to be a part of it.

However, proper reasoning, Rhys found, wasn't working when so many thoughts and memories plagued him. His attention on the sleeping angel intensified. He wondered if there might be another reason for her appearance, one that involved rescuing his soul from its long, endless span.

He didn't like being in the dark, or confused. It wasn't like him to be so restless when there were so many years ahead of him to wade through.

"Maybe you can hear me," he said to the slender form curled up on the furniture.

When she didn't stir, he kept talking. "None of this explains my attraction to you. Cravings are not part of my pattern, and yet I can hardly look away. I find you so very difficult to resist."

In sleep, the warrior side of this angel was no longer evident. She looked vulnerable and had curled in on herself, as if the pain she carried had become too much to bear. That pain was here in the room and tangible. Like a twang of overextended nerves, his own body shared the fire running through Avery's lithe body. And it was bad. It was terrible, and it was her secret.

Drawn to her automatically and for no real reason other than their unprecedented mutual physical attraction, he glided a hand over her, inches above her body, careful not to touch her, searching Avery's aura for an explanation.

She did stir then. Her big eyes opened. "Need peace," she whispered. "Give me that."

Rhys nodded.

Backing away slowly, he returned to the bank of windows that were tinted so the rising sun only lightened the room a little. Although he could easily tolerate daylight, just as Avery said she could, sunlight had become merely a luxury. A remembrance and a dream.

But she…this angel…was a reminder of how far things had fallen from the norm. She shouldn't have been here in the land of mortals. Hell, neither should he.

"Perhaps that's at the root of our bond?" he wondered aloud. "Two misplaced immortal souls trespassing in the world of men."

That was as close as he could get without delving deeper into Avery's situation. In order to learn more about what was driving her, he had to earn more of her trust.

Hungering for her, longing for their limbs to tangle and their bodies to join, Rhys quieted his anxious desire for Avery with a smile and a brush of his fingers through his hair. The smile dissolved when she made a sound in her sleep. Just a faint cry that matched a sound Rhys was sure he had heard before.

Equally strong and pitifully plaintive, her muffled cry took him again to Avery's side. Her eyes were shut tight. Her fingers clutched at the pillow she rested her head on. Shoulders, so recently tattooed and covered with her worn black leather jacket, quaked slightly. For her, also, dreams offered no respite from reality.

She looked small on that couch, and helpless, when she was neither of those things. Rhys kept himself from enfolding her in his arms. Avery didn't want that and he was a fool for wanting it so badly.

Long white lashes fluttered. Milky-white strands of straight, silky hair draped over the dark cushions as if the contents of a glass had spilled. The reed-thin body Rhys was observing shuddered once. All of that served to widen the cracks in his formerly unreachable, unbreakable heart.

How long did he stand there, observing her?

In this apartment, there was no real way to tell how far the sun had risen over the world outside. That world lay beyond the tinted, tempered glass, and beyond Rhys's notice. Fatigue hadn't overcome him. As usual, he felt strong, and stronger yet in his determination to help the creature on that couch.

Morning came and went. Afternoon shadows were there and gone. When the darkness of another new night returned, Avery finally opened her eyes.

Those blue eyes met his, blinked once, opened wider. She said, "I suppose this is what you do. Stand guard." Breathy, sleepy voice. No hint of the cry he'd heard her utter.

"I choose my…" he began.

"Prey?" she finished for him without sitting up.

"As far as prey goes, would you say you qualify?" he asked.

"Not in the least."

"Then who in their right mind would assume you needed a Guardian, unless you asked for it?"

"And now that I have asked?"

"I'm all yours."

What he'd said had disturbed Avery in some way. A crease appeared on her brow. Tiny networks of fine lines spread from the outer corners of her eyes. Sleep hadn't completely replenished Avery's energy. She hadn't rested enough, and wouldn't want him to comment about it.

Her gaze shifted to the windows.

"Where do we start on this search of yours? Without enlisting the guidance of a Shade," Rhys asked.

"Black market." Avery sat up. Lean leather-clad legs dangled over the edge of the couch casually, as if she had no bones at all.

"You know where that is?" he asked.

"That Shade might."

"Finding one particular Shade in a city this size is unlikely."

"And unnecessary, since that Shade will find me."

"You know this how?"

"I'll set a trap so it will know where to go."

"On the rooftop?"

Avery nodded.

"And the trap?" he asked.

"Blood."

The back of Rhys's neck prickled. His sigils stung in protest at what she was suggesting.

"Whose blood, Avery?"

"An angel's. Think what price that would bring on the black market, and what a Shade might do with such a reward."

Rhys didn't have to think about that. The idea was appalling.

"Whoever has your wings might also want your blood?" he asked.

"A few drops of my blood would animate my wings and cause quite a show."

"That would be a damn circus act. And the Shade would be tortured for information as to where it got the blood."

"Yes."

Rhys stared at Avery, understanding the plan with a rush of insight.

"So," he said, exhaling slowly, "we don't even have to search for the bastard who has the wings, because he will come to us."

Rhys wondered if he was dreaming when Avery got to her feet and stretched by spreading her arms wide. Sparks of light played on each bare part of her exposed anatomy—hands, neck, face. That light caressed her, as much a part of her as her skin. She'd been born of light, and in that moment, when she was perhaps rejuvenated by rest, her heavenly origins showed.

"What happens when we get the wings back?" he asked without actually wanting to hear the answer.

Her gaze swept over him, causing his sigils to ripple with anxiety. "I go home," she said. "If I'm still welcome there."

Chapter 15

It was the third time the Blood Knight had turned his back to her, and Avery knew why. Observing how his muscles stiffened beneath his dark shirt and the way he rolled his broad shoulders made her wish she hadn't added the part about going home. Rhys didn't like that, and at some point, with more sessions on her back, on a floor and in his arms, she might have treacherously started to agree with him.

From the other side of the room, his voice caused an echo. "Why are you here, Avery?"

Before she could answer that, if she'd been willing to do so, he added, "What brought you here in the first place and left you vulnerable to what happened with the wings? I've seen what you can do, and how you fight. I realize it would have taken an army to take those wings from you if you didn't agree to let them go."

Still not finished, he continued after a beat. "So who are you, really, and why are you here?"

Possible ways to feed Rhys small bites of information

filtered through her mind before Avery decided to spill part of the truth. This could have been due to the way he was looking at her and that disconcerting trait he showed of seeming to care.

"I came here to get the Grail," she said.

His response was abrupt. "What did you say?"

Exposing even that much of the secrets she carried caused her breath to hitch, and yet she went on daringly, trusting Rhys, tired of bearing her burdens alone.

"I was sent to Earth to take the item you call the Holy Grail to the only true place of safety for such a powerful relic."

Silence followed that startling statement. Truth had been spoken at long last, and truth had power. Rhys was struggling with that, and how to comprehend the full extent of her meaning.

His voice rang with emotion and skepticism in equal measures when he demanded "Who sent you?"

Again, he didn't wait for her reply. He had worked out the answer to his own question quickly. "Your Maker sent you?" he asked, with a touch of reverence for who that Maker might turn out to be if she was an angel.

Avery nodded, observing Rhys's reactions closely. He had lived with a belief system based only on half-truths.

"Why would you have come to take the Grail when we had it and the situation of hiding it under control?" he asked. "Guardianship of the Grail is what the seven of us were created for. Keeping it safe and out of all mortal and demonic hands is our continuous objective. Surely an all-seeing creator would know that."

They were getting too close to the real problems here, and Avery dreaded having to hide so many more of the answers Rhys sought. She was growing sorrier by the moment for her vendetta against the Knights. Anger and rage had been her driving force for so long, it was hard to let that go.

Yet Rhys and his blood brothers had never been the crux of the problem surrounding the Grail Quest, only the end result. They had been guilty by association with their Makers, but had, indeed, held up their end of the bargain to protect the Grail.

"The chalice didn't belong on Earth then and doesn't now," she said. "You and the others who tested its powers must realize this, and no matter how well hidden you believe it is, the Grail will someday be found. Its powers will be discovered and abused."

Rhys's voice lowered further with a dangerous edge. "You know far too much about our creation to have been fed that information by rumors only."

"I know everything," Avery confessed, convincing herself to leave it at that.

Rhys didn't need to know that after escaping from her chains in the Castle Broceliande dungeons, she had taken out her anger on the Knights' so-called Makers. It had taken her less than an hour to destroy their beloved castle and their dreams of controlling the seven Knights. As satisfying as that destruction had been, it hadn't gotten her any closer to her original objective for coming to Earth, however, since the Blood Knights charged with the Grail's safekeeping had taken the holy relic away, and she had lost her ability to do much about that.

Her wings had disappeared, and these Knights had been sent into the wide world, tasked with hiding and protecting the Grail. They had cherished the chalice that had captured the blood of the heavens from a man on a cross. That same chalice's powers of resurrection were what had been used to reanimate the Knights after Death had claimed them.

Without her wings, she wouldn't have dared to try and

take the holy relic back. Minus the ability to ascend, her efforts might have jeopardized the safety of the Grail's temporary guardianship.

Rhys might not have been to the place the Grail was buried, but he'd know where it was hidden. The sigils carved into his back that connected him with his brothers were, in essence, a supernatural GPS system carrying within their intricate scrolls all the information she'd need when the time came.

"Which came first, Avery?" he asked. "You followed the Grail, and that led to knowledge of us, to knowledge of my brethren and me, or you're hoping to follow us to the Grail?"

"Both."

The earnestness of her answer drew Rhys to her side. His expression was sober, questioning. He was wary. His nearness freed her tongue more than she would have liked.

"I had found the Grail early on," she said, despising herself for admitting that. Rhys would pounce on the unspoken part of her story. His features rearranged as his thoughts churned.

"And I was lured by the beauty of the castle belonging to those who had the Grail in their possession, just as you were," she admitted.

It was too late to withhold more of the truth. Rhys's eyes probed hers. His tension could have set the room on fire.

"Didn't you ever wonder how your Makers got hold of such an important artifact, Rhys?"

The question stumped him. Possibly the Knights had been taught not to question their role in the Grail Quest. Maybe the castle's occupants had erased those kinds of questions from the minds of the Knights as they manipulated a way to give the seven men new life.

And maybe his current name, spoken by her, played a part in affecting him, the same way it affected her. Some things, even now, remained camouflaged by the weightiness of the secrets at their core.

Rhys's eyes were on her, steady, level. "You gave the Grail to them? The Makers?"

She shook her head. A line had been crossed. The only way she could have avoided what was coming next would have been to disappear, as she had always planned on doing before meeting *him.*

"And the wings," he said solemnly. "Your wings. What happened to them? Did removing them occur before or after you had the Grail in your possession?"

She saw that Rhys didn't like the ideas forming in his mind. There was more than one possibility here, and his instincts were to consider them all.

All right. You want this. You've asked for this.

"The wings were severed from my back so I couldn't keep the Grail or interfere with Castle Broceliande's plans for it."

Sickness followed that disclosure. In her. In Rhys. But there was only one more question to ask, and he asked it.

"Who took your wings?"

An expression of horror crossed his handsome features as one of those ideas rolling around in his mind fostered an evil image.

"No," he said with a forceful head shake. "Not possible. They wouldn't."

But, of course, the image he was seeing was the way things had gone down, so Avery waited for the next phase in his understanding to fade some of the color from his bronze, chiseled perfection…the way it had faded hers.

"They wouldn't."

The protest stuck in Rhys's throat. Roiling waves of enlightenment struck him hard, when what he was thinking was unbelievable.

He stood beside Avery without moving, close enough to hear the rasp of her breath. Because he wanted to shake more fantastical explanations from her with his bare hands, his voice was harsher than it should have been.

"How would they do that, Avery? How would the castle's occupants take either thing from you—a holy relic of such importance or your wings?"

The question went unanswered, but it was too late for keeping secrets. If Avery wasn't keen on filling in all of the blanks, he couldn't make her. Nevertheless, it was frustrating to comb his way through all the possible scenarios piling up that might have explained those nasty gouges on her back.

"Not the time for full disclosure," she warned, her voice merely a whisper and always a temptation he wanted to explore.

He wondered if she did whatever she was doing to him on purpose, in order to lead him away from the hard answers. Her eyes, when they met his, had lost some of their shine.

"Did you come to London to find me, Avery?" he asked, needing a few more things resolved.

"Only the wings," she replied. "That's the truth."

"And you will take the Grail back to wherever you came from, when and if you were to find it again?"

"I made a promise to an entity for which promises count."

"But the wings come first."

"Yes."

"And you believe I'm going to help you find them."

She blinked slowly, as if waiting for bad news. As if she assumed her explanations, as brief as they had been, would change his game plan and he'd rescind his offer to help.

Obviously, she hadn't mentioned all of the grittiest parts

of the story, because he felt the anxiousness wafting off her. So far, there was no real reason for her to believe he wouldn't have helped her.

Secrets…

What aren't you telling me, angel?

What's so important that I can't be in on the deal?

Am I more to you than a helper coming to your aid?

"The moon has risen," she announced, carrying things way off course.

Rhys glanced to the window, taking his gaze from Avery so that he could think more clearly. "So it has."

"You haven't changed your mind?" she asked.

"I also am an entity for whom promises count, Avery."

Her relief was palpable. Slowly, the shine returned to her eyes. "We should go now."

"Yes. We should," he agreed.

Neither of them moved. But thundering heartbeats, swirling tensions and anxiety caused a vacuum that threatened to bring them together, and wouldn't be ignored for long.

"Avery…"

She was in front of him and looking up by the time he'd finished saying her name. For an angel, her heat was extreme both inside and out. He knew this firsthand.

"It's important to you," he said, already reaching for a firm grip on her slim hips.

She placed a finger on his mouth. Through that fingertip, he felt the rapid beating of her racing pulse.

"Important," she said. "You will never know how much."

He pulled her to him. Hips to hips, and with her chest against his, Rhys withheld a sigh of acceptance. They would locate her wings and she would go. She'd search for the Grail and take it beyond anyone's reach. There was a reason she was so adamant about that.

"You can do that?" he asked. "Take it away for good?"

"Yes," she replied, standing straighter so she could say that with her lips just centimeters from his.

"I can't stop you if your reasons turn out to be the wrong ones?" Rhys said.

"No one can."

"And if I don't want you to take it, or take yourself away?" he asked.

She shook her head. Her face softened, as if his question had affected her in a way she hadn't been expecting.

Seeing that, Rhys's desire took over, flooding his cells, firing up his nerves with a blistering adrenaline rush. No one could have stopped him from taking the thing he wanted at that moment. Her. And all that incredible angelic fire she was composed of.

He wanted to keep that softness he saw cross her features and the almost pleading look in her eyes that she quickly covered up by closing them. Her lips were waiting. If she didn't want him to kiss her, she'd move away. But he was sure she did want this. Passion underlined their every look and hid in the recesses of each move they didn't make.

He was going to break down that damn barrier.

He took her mouth savagely, deeply and as if there might never be another chance. Who knew that Heaven's warrior angels had so many talents, seduction being one of them?

And, Lord help him…he found her willing.

Chapter 16

Thoughts of quests faded.

Promises. Vows. Wicked four-letter curses.

He was all that mattered. The man filling her vision. The man running his hands up her spine and into her hair. This was the magnificent creature she needed inside her so badly, on any surface that was handy. This was the magnificent creature with the power to make her forget her struggles for a time.

Rhys's mouth ravaged hers unforgivably, and she fought back with equal intensity, tearing at the back of his shirt, seeking a way to reach that tense molded flesh where he likely had scars of his own to display. She wanted to see those scars because wound to wound is how she'd meet him. Hip to hip, groin to groin, front, back and every position between. Their first round had been mind-altering. This second chance would be even better.

She was already wet. Her heart was racing.

In an instant replay of the night before, his hands had

managed her zipper and slid beneath to find out just how much she wished for this to happen.

Releasing her anger added to the pleasure of his fingertips on her sex. Because they were crushed together, his hand was trapped and unable to explore further, so she pushed him away, half expecting Rhys to question the move the way he questioned everything else.

He didn't.

Instead, he twirled her to the couch, onto cushions far too small for coping with the degree of their lust for each other. Eyeing her for mere seconds, breathing as hard as she was, he tugged her to him again, so they were on their feet, standing.

There was a bedroom forty feet away, but they wouldn't have made it. It was a race to see how fast they could remove their clothes while remaining close enough to each other that they could not easily accomplish that. Every time Avery tried to pull Rhys's shirt over his head, his mouth returned with more force and a fresh set of demands. His kisses had grown as dangerous as the Knight himself, and still she wanted more.

When her palms found the patch of skin on his back she had been seeking, Rhys sighed with an indication of the sheer pleasure her small victory gave him. She got the impression he wasn't often touched, and seldom let anyone in, in spite of his earlier remarks about mortals and bedrooms.

She planned to kick the asses of all the women he'd ever been with, and hated all those to come. Anyone lucky enough to have been on the receiving end of one tenth of his ardor was going to have to pay. Rhys was hers. *For now, anyway*, she kept reminding herself.

She wanted to climb inside him, swallow him whole, and nothing was going to stand in the way of that objective.

When her back hit the cool glass of the windows, Avery

prayed those windows were strong enough to hold the force of the impact. Even that thought slipped away as they fell to their knees, going at each other like two possessed beings.

At last, the front of his shirt, laden with buttons, had been ripped to shreds. All that flammable skin of his—still golden, for all his nights spent on guard here in London and elsewhere—was there for the taking.

Ending the kiss reluctantly as she urged him onto his back on the cool floor, she straddled his waist. Her hands roamed over each delicious inch of his chest, and the striations defining his spectacular abs. In the dim light, shadows hugged him, adored him, loved him, just as she was going to do.

Pants to pants, Avery ground her weight into him with a friction that was only a precursor to what lay ahead. The room was hot. She was hot. And she was unreasonably needy.

She nipped at his skin like an animal in heat, taking small bites from his neck to his waist. The man beneath her liked it all. His warm fingers found her breasts and brushed the raised tips before moving to her back for better traction. Tugging her closer, so that their heated gazes connected, he said, "All or nothing, angel."

His brute strength flipped her onto her back. He was on his knees now. In a flash, her boots were gone, along with her pants. So were his. He waited for her to look at him, for her eyes to take him in. Then he sank down next to her with his weight on his elbows and moved once more, so she felt the exhilaration of having his hardness push against the soft folds of the place that would soon welcome him.

The night blurred. The room blurred. Avery heard a sound and realized she'd made it as he entered her with a single stroke that filled her with his hard length. Instead of withdrawing, he stayed there, waiting, watching her with those piercing blue eyes.

"Angels don't beg," she whispered.

"No one said they have to," he returned.

But she couldn't hold still for much longer. Her core was humming. Far off, that familiar drumming had begun, with no more effort on his part than this first physical hello.

"No," Avery complained, her voice husky, weak. "Not yet. Not like this. Need more. Want more."

His grin was a wicked thing, and full of promise. "Do not assume I don't know how to please an angel," Rhys said. "Because that would insult me."

As he began to move, dragging himself back only an inch, Avery halted him with her nails in his skin. She dug in deep, drawing blood she knew was as black as the darkness outside the bank of windows.

With another slight movement of his hips he played with her core, taunting, teasing, daring that drumbeat he had to feel rolling inside her to find him.

"This," he said, pulling back at last, "is for keeping things from me."

He drove into her depths while maintaining eye contact. But Avery had had enough, and she had learned a thing or two from the werewolves she'd used for sport.

"Who's strong now?" she sent to Rhys, rolling out from under him and again straddling the spot where his belly met with the origin of his talented cock. *"Who is in charge?"*

Using one hand, she inserted him into her body. After briefly closing her eyes, she began to move up and down over him, reveling in the look on his face.

Take and retreat. Give and accept. Avery rode this beautiful creature whose soul was dipped in warm, familiar light. Softer. Harder. A pause before coming back for more…

She teased the thunder inside her, bringing it closer before easing the shudders back into the distance, all the while coaxing Rhys toward the climax he had been determined to keep from her.

When that climax finally arrived, she let herself meet it. With the flames of Earth and the heavens meeting as one, a surge of emotion overtook her. Throwing back her head, uttering a cry well-timed with Rhys's final desperate groan, Avery let herself go.

And she fell… Not into Rhys's arms, but into the past, as his hands reached the two deep scars between her shoulder blades that old traumas had marked her with.

A strange sensation crept over Rhys when he heard Avery's impassioned cry. Instant recall told him he had felt the effects of that sound before, not only once, in that abandoned building down the street, but a few more times. That sound was getting clearer in his memory and was something he had stored there.

It wasn't just passion he'd heard in Avery's voice, but a more potent example of feelings that harkened back to the pain she harbored. She had unleashed that sound, let it out, set it free, and it disturbed him in ways Rhys couldn't have explained.

A dazed expression had taken over her beautiful, colorless face. Her eyes had glazed. Her swollen mouth was slack. To him, it looked as though freeing all that emotion she had tucked inside had spiraled Avery into another space, one he couldn't join her in.

"Avery," Rhys whispered to her with his hands on her rib cage, afraid to release his grip. Afraid she'd disappear in some miraculous way and he'd never see her again or know another moment like the one they had just shared.

"Avery." He spoke louder, careful to keep his voice calm when his insides were tightening.

She didn't pay any attention and seemed to be elsewhere.

"Angel," he called to her, willing her to hear him and respond. But she was gone, if not in body, then in spirit.

Cautiously, Rhys sat up and gathered her into his arms. Getting to his knees, then to his feet, he lifted her up. She didn't protest. Her eyes were half shut.

Unsure of what to do, he took her to the bedroom, and to the bathroom beyond it. Turning on the shower, adjusting the temperature to hot, he stepped inside with his pale bundle cradled in his arms. Letting the water run over her arms, then her shoulders and back, Rhys waited, willing her to come back from wherever she had gone, calling her name over and over with the cadence of a chant.

It took several minutes for her attention to return and her eyes to focus. Steam rose around them, trapped by the shower's heavy glass doors. Inside the gray, humid space, Avery's hand moved. Her fingers curled into her palm in a gesture he'd seen before. Her thin shoulders twitched, as if feeling was returning after a lengthy numbness.

"What happened, Avery? Where did you go?" he asked, racking his brain to recall the exact moment she had left him…tracking back to the incredible climax they had ridden out in tandem and the breathlessness of a passion that had overcome them both. She had been with him on that. She had been there.

"What am I missing, Avery?"

He'd had his hands on her, on her back, planning to explore every glorious inch. He had held her in place as they tapped into the ecstasy of a complete physical merging.

Hands on her back…

Hell, he had touched her scars. The two big ones. Had that sent her over the edge of an invisible precipice?

He set Avery down, making sure she could stand on her own two feet. Water ran down her hair, her cheeks, as she raised her face to accept it. With her back to him, Rhys caught sight of movement he might otherwise have missed, sure he had to be wrong about what he was seeing. When her skin quaked, his gaze traveled to Avery's new tattoos.

Stepping back only far enough to study those tats, Rhys froze. His sigils began to burn the way they always did when confronting something spectacularly out of the norm, something that lay beyond the easiest classifications of the supernatural.

The damn wings, inked on her shoulder blades by an artist in a nondescript shop, were moving, when that was impossible. These weren't real wings. Avery had lost those. They had been stolen from her, she'd said.

Swear to God, there was nothing wrong with his eyesight. The inked vivid blue and gray feathers on her back undulated as if they were coming to life. Each feather's bright red tip stood out like it had been dipped in fresh blood.

Rhys took another step back, puzzled, not understanding the reasons for or ramifications of what he was seeing. Avery turned her head. Through a curtain of soaked white hair, she said in a hoarse voice, "They're here. Close. And they're calling."

Relief washed over Rhys for about five seconds before he again remembered touching those tats and the grooves they had been meant to cover. Had he helped her along by adding his strength and senses to hers? There had been an earlier mention of Avery's new belief about having been meant to find him.

Whatever the reason for the catatonic state Avery had slipped into, he had no choice but to recognize that the next phase of the game was on, and that like Avery, and whether or not he truly was willing to put her through more, he would see this quest of hers through to its conclusion without touching her again.

"Where did you go?" he repeated.

"To the place where they are," she said.

Brushing soaked strands of hair back from her forehead, and careful not to touch any other part of her, he asked, "Do you know where that is?"

"Yes."

"Can we find it?"

"Yes."

"We're to start now?"

Her eyes were wide and on him.

"All right," Rhys said. "Show me."

Chapter 17

The night carried the scent of a nearly full moon, an earthy smell with silvery overtones recognizable to all creatures comprised of Otherness.

In one more day the craziness that moon wrought would begin. Poor Detective Crane, who had allowed an immortal and an angel some time alone in the penthouse, might then be out of commission himself, due to the DI's own tweaked, very wolfish DNA. Tonight, however, the shadows contained fewer monsters to trip things up.

Following Avery up one street and down another, careful to remain as inconspicuous as possible, Rhys stayed silent. Avery's hood covered her damp hair and most of her face. Used to drawing stares, Rhys made sure not to make contact with any of the people passing them.

Tonight, mortal was a part they both had to play. Still, he felt eyes turn his way and thought about detouring to the rooftops where he and Avery would be safe from unwanted scrutiny.

They presented an interesting picture—two immortal beings walking down a public street as if they belonged to the world they had found themselves in, instead of merely being pasted onto that world. They were creatures whose origins set them apart from the rest.

"Is it far?" he queried after they'd gone five blocks.

"I don't know." She didn't slow her pace or look at him. "I follow the song until it gets stronger."

Right. The *song* was her form of angelic GPS.

"And now?" he asked.

"Faint." She glanced to her right, at the narrow street branching off this one that was littered with pubs only the locals of this area would know about.

"In the apartment the signal was stronger?" he pressed.

"Infinitely stronger."

"So we might be heading the wrong way."

Avery shook her head. He couldn't see her expression with her face covered up, but figured that determination and excitement would have set her features.

City smells were always overwhelming to his senses, and London was one continuous odor. What he could detect easily enough was the stink of vampires slithering around in the dark spaces of the road Avery was heading toward.

"Vampires," he cautioned.

"Only four of them," she said without moving her attention from the road ahead.

"Piece of cake," Rhys muttered, wary of this latest distraction.

Avery paused long enough to look at him from beneath the black leather hood. Her eyes shone like jewels in its shadow.

"Current vernacular doesn't suit you, Rhys."

"One must adapt. I'm particularly fond of nineteenth-century curse words."

Tuning his mind to vamp static, he said, "And here we go again."

"No time," was the response Avery tossed his way with an abrupt change of direction that moved them toward a second side street.

"Tell that to the unsuspecting people of this city," he remarked, hesitating, plagued by the red flags his sigils were waving at him.

He wheeled around in slow motion to face the threat. Avery rested a hand on his arm, her touch burning into his skin, even through his clothes.

"Hurry," she advised, gesturing up the street.

"There are too damn many of these mindless bastards," he said. "Tonight they're pressing their luck by appearing so soon after sundown."

He strode forward with one shoulder brushing the brick of the closest building, moving through the same shadows vampires used to spring their deadly surprise attacks. But the vamp chatter suddenly ceased, as if someone had changed a radio channel. Perhaps they knew he was coming for them and had scattered. Clearly, they wanted no fight.

Slipping around a jutting corner that smelled like stale beer, Rhys entered a dark, mostly deserted side street. Assuming a wide stance with his hands fisted at his sides, he called out to the bloodsuckers. "I thought you knew better than to trespass in this area. Come out and deal with the consequences of trying to get away with that."

None of the vampires came forward. Of course, Rhys hadn't expected them to. He waited out a beat of time, listening, inhaling the stale, humid air, before realizing the odor of putrefaction that heralded the presence of the bloodsucker population had gone.

That fact was disconcerting.

He turned around uttering one of those favored curses

to find the pale vixen with the undulating tats wasn't there, either.

"Damn it all to hell and back..."

As he took off at a sprint, Rhys was starting to believe his angel had duped him again. Avery might have brought him this way on purpose, to a place where vampires often hid, in order to deflect his attention from the path she was actually taking. The angel would realize he had to take care of the mortals. She understood he couldn't allow human lives to be in jeopardy when there was a chance they'd become dinner for the fanged hordes.

Damn her white hide...

If, like him, she couldn't lie, this misdirection came awfully close to being the same damn thing. And she had suckered him into falling for it. He was beginning to think Blood Knight manipulation was high up on an angel's list of talents. It was also very unlike heavenly behavior. He planned to tell her so.

Uttering a stream of curses didn't make a dent in the anger growing inside him as he sent his senses outward, in search of his angel.

She hadn't meant to leave Rhys like that, and wouldn't have if handling vamps hadn't been one of the things he did best...other than his more obvious proficiencies. Like kissing. Like mind-blowing sex.

Leaving him produced feelings of loss and of being constantly out of breath when she needed enough air to fuel her run. Getting to the end point of this quest had always been her goal, and that end was at long last within her reach.

It seemed to her that the inexplicable flapping sensation of the inked wings on her back was helping to point the way. It was a disturbing reminder that the most important part of her objective for coming to London was near. In spite of that, her heart ached for Rhys.

God, yes. She ached.

The speed of her sprint ate up the ground, creating more distance between herself and the glorious Knight whose lovemaking had only whetted her appetite for more of the same. With her back stinging like a son of a bitch and a left-over thrum for Rhys nestling deep inside her body, Avery took a route less peopled than the main streets.

She refused to slow her pace until the tattoos finally stopped nagging and the song she'd been following was suddenly silenced. Was this due to being in close proximity to the real wings? Had she gotten close to one of the black markets she sought?

Coming to a stop on the sidewalk, Avery became quiet to carefully soak up the scene. Nothing registered as abnormal or as a safe place for the bootlegging black market bastards to ply their trade, unless they weren't on the street but above or beneath it.

"Yes," she whispered. "I'm close."

The ground beneath her boots shook slightly as two cars drove by. Avery stared down, deciding whether or not the street could be like a layer of skin covering a large, hollow space carved under it, and if that might explain the rumble.

Had she been unable to locate her wings before this because they rested in an underground location protected by chalk, stone walls, dirt and several layers of pavement?

A smattering of people were coming and going now, probably on their way home from work. Stepping in front of a young man in a gray trench coat, she stopped him mid-stride, careful to keep her face hidden.

"There's something under this street, right? I'm curious as to what that is. Do you know?" she asked, pointing at the ground.

Once the man got over his surprise at being halted in such a way by a hooded, leather-clad female, he caught on to what she was asking. "Kilometers of tunnels run under this area. Twenty miles of them."

"Sealed off or accessible?"

Was that a weird question to pose? The guy's eyebrow quirked.

"It's a creepy place that attracts tourists at certain times of the year. There are others similar to this one in other parts of the city. Catacombs and the like. I haven't been down there, but you can buy a pass to see some of them." Seconds later, he added, "During the day."

Avery didn't ease up on the questions. Excitement had become a cruel companion. "How old are the tunnels?"

"I'm no history professor," he said obligingly. "But they are supposed to be ancient. Predating the Druids, some say. Other sources suggest the tunnels were carved much later, for mining chalk and flint."

That was all Avery needed to explain the flutter of her tattoos and the sudden urge to jump down a manhole. What better place could there be to conduct some black market business than a system of underground tunnels, at night, when no tourist would venture down there to interrupt?

What safer place could some savage bastard have for keeping a pair of angel wings?

"Thanks," she said to the guy, remembering to be polite, but turning away quickly so he wouldn't continue the conversation hoping to get a closer look at her or assume her behavior was flirtatious. Fact was, she didn't know how to flirt or waste time on mundane mortal male-female issues. She was a warrior. Fighting was her specialty.

Listening to the sounds of retreating footsteps, Avery again studied the street, feeling sick and exhilarated at the same time. Angels detested closed spaces and she was going to have to go deep into the earth to get what she wanted…a move that would take her steps closer to the burning pit-fires of hell.

Rhys hadn't followed, wasn't here beside her. She was sorry she'd had to ditch him. Yet, because the Blood Knights never went back on their promises or lost their intended prey, Avery figured she had fewer than five minutes, if she was lucky, to find a way into those caverns, as nasty as they sounded. She couldn't afford the distractions Rhys provided if she hoped to maintain her focus.

Rhys…

If I don't come out, please find what's left and send me home.

That thought wasn't voiced aloud. Some things were, by their very nature, too personal, even for lovers whose past created a bond between them that was holding fast.

"It's best to cut our ties now, before…"

Her statement dangled, unfinished. She reverted to thoughts, wondering how tuned in Rhys actually was, and if he would understand her current dilemma.

"Without my wings, I am not very much stronger than you are. I must be whole again so I can succeed in accomplishing the task assigned to me, however long that takes. You, of all beings, know the power of a promise."

She caught and held a breath that no longer contained Rhys's musky, masculine scent, and her heart sank. Had he let her go, believing that's what she wanted?

"I can't involve you further or take a chance on hurting you, when lingering longer in this world than necessary is not to be my fate."

She needed more air and couldn't seem to find it.

"My goal is to take from you and your brethren the very item you have protected all this time. The item you were created to protect and that aided in your transformation."

She hadn't pressed the link directly into his mind. It was time to get on with this next part of her mission.

"Now or never," she muttered.

There was no wind on the street to cool her feverish face as she searched for an internet café. Finding a way into those underground tunnels was the new puzzle to solve. She was opposed to computers, as well as most modern technology, but nonetheless had to have computer access to find the entrance to the tunnels. There were twenty miles of them, the guy on the street had said.

Barring internet access, she'd have to start digging.

Squeezing her eyes shut helped to internalize the struggle she had hoped to avoid. A Blood Knight lay at the core of the struggle she was experiencing, and he had once again taken something from her.

Her heart.

In an eerie reboot of the déjà-vu moment when he had first seen Avery in the alley, Rhys silently observed her on the street below his perch.

I still have a few tricks of my own, he mused. *And I can read your intentions loud and clear, angel.*

Most of the people who had lived in London for some time knew about the tunnels. As soon as Avery had looked at the ground, he realized what kind of information she had gleaned from the guy in the trench coat.

He had eavesdropped on their conversation, jealous of the man's closeness to her. His jaw was tight now with the strain of holding himself back from jumping down there.

The messages he was sending to her were working. Mind bending was a gift he had long ago perfected. In utilizing this gift, Avery didn't see him or sense him. He could observe her without being noticed, angry she would try to outdistance what they felt for each other.

"You have come for the Grail, and that is the province of my brothers."

While he understood the Grail would be the safest among her kind, removed from the Earth and its many temptations, Avery had been put through hell in order to find it, and that hell was ongoing. Something was in her way, successfully blocking her mission. Which side was it?

"Who took your wings?" he whispered, thinking hard. "Who would do such a thing?"

Reason suggested a few scenarios, and none of them were good.

Had someone known Avery was after the Grail, and taken her wings to make sure she didn't succeed?

How could anyone purposefully harm such a beautiful creature who was also part of the heavenly host? A violent act like that would have to be executed by an evil entity powerful enough to trap an immortal warrior maiden who was here on a golden mission.

True, there was plenty of evil in the world. But only a handful of possibilities capable of something like that came to his mind. Whoever had done this to her had taken her wings and the Grail, so the Grail had to be the central focus. And after that, his Makers had found the holy relic and charged their Knights to protect it.

Hadn't they?

Jerked bolt upright by the surprise of the sudden flow of insight and a needling sensation that swept across his sigils, Rhys stood.

Avery had made him wonder how his Makers had gotten hold of the Grail. Either in words or in thought, she had posed that question. Or had he imagined it?

Questions arose, one after the other, in rapid succession.

How the hell had those who dwelled at Castle Broceliande kept that relic if an angel was hot on its trail?

Why wouldn't they have handed over the Grail to Heaven's emissary instead of creating seven Knights to hide it?

She had told him she had found the Grail early on…the same relic his Makers had kept submerged in the fountain at the center of Broceliande's magnificent midnight gardens.

Rhys stared down at her.

She had said the wings were cut from her back. How had that kind of atrocity fit in with her Grail Quest?

The fact staring him in the face was that she could have taken the item she sought from that fountain while it rested at Broceliande so long ago, if in fact she had found it there…unless she had been detained and de-winged, held hostage, kept from her quest by the kind of creatures who knew both how to do that and what they had in their midst.

Shock came swiftly to him with that realization, striking hard, tilting his stance. Avery had mentioned his Makers because she had met them. She hadn't taken the Grail away from them because his Makers hadn't wanted Avery to have it.

Christ, she had laid the foundation for his understanding of the problem, and he hadn't made the connection. How could he? Castle Broceliande had been the growing grounds for all of this—him, her and the Knights' original Grail Quest.

His goddamn Makers had done this.

They had to be the monsters responsible for grounding Avery.

With bile in his throat and a chill brought on by pieces of the puzzle snapping into place, Rhys began his descent to the street below.

Chapter 18

Not used to being caught unaware, Avery stumbled back when Rhys landed beside her. Ready to protest his latest stealth trick, she hesitated when he held up a hand.

"Why didn't you just tell me?" he demanded.

Chills passed over her.

"You were there?" he asked before she could rally. "We aren't rumors to you. You knew about the Blood Knights because you also had been to the castle?"

She nodded, catching on to the reason for the stern look on Rhys's face. He had figured out some pieces of this strange story and was processing that information.

"I was there," she said.

Just as strong as Rhys, Avery didn't have to face him like this. She didn't have to allow him to put his hands on her or push her backward, away from any stray onlookers that might have been lurking. But she did allow it. What she couldn't have escaped from was the hurt in Rhys's eyes. The showdown between them had arrived with very bad timing.

"Did you give the Grail to the Makers or did they take it from you, Avery?"

The crux of this whole ordeal was coming to light here on the street above the tunnels she had to get to. Rhys was waiting for the speech she dreaded making.

"The Grail was my mission. Once it was in my possession, I would not have offered it to anyone," she said.

"So they took it from you." It wasn't a question. "I wonder how they managed to do that when you were so strong, and if you were on the side of right."

The hand that agitatedly pushed his hair back also dragged down the side of his face. His eyes closed for a beat of time in which Avery's heart continued to pound.

"And all this time…" His remark took effort. "All this time, I thought our Makers were the good guys."

Avery failed to find the energy to address that statement. This is what she had waited centuries for, and also what she lately had feared after meeting Rhys in the flesh. He would now go deep inside the story to ferret out details of that time, pondering whether his existence as an immortal had been based on treachery and deceit.

"Did they also take your wings?" His tone was dangerously hushed, barely controlled.

She could not lie. Didn't dare. Not now. She felt sick enough.

"Look how you turned out," she said, instead of replying to the question he had asked. "All of you. Seven good things came from what happened so long ago. That's something, but isn't enough to deter me from fulfilling my obligations."

His gaze was intense.

"Maybe your brothers will be glad to be rid of the Grail," Avery continued. "No one in the world, even if looking for it, will never be able to lay their hands on such an important relic. Its powers won't be used again. The Blood Knights will be free of its curse."

Its curse to bestow immortality.

"The Makers were to take their own lives after sending us into the world as Guardians of that holy relic," Rhys said. "The seven of us were to be their replacements. The new Guardians of the Grail. Tell me if that turned out to be true, and if we were fighting on the correct side."

Avery hesitated a few seconds too long. In that time gap, Rhys read the reply she would have made, had she been willing to say it.

His tension transferred to her. Avery choked more words out of a constricted throat.

"You've never been back there, Rhys? It didn't occur to you to check on the Makers' pledges, visit that place or follow up?"

Shaking his head didn't lessen the palpable tension in the air. "Never. None of us returned."

"Because you didn't care for your new role, or because you knew in your soul that things weren't actually what they seemed?"

"Because…" He started over. "One life ended there, and another, more unnatural, one began. I embraced my Quest wholeheartedly, seeing the need to do so. I still embrace it. But I didn't want to see those tall, white, windowless towers of stone, or the strange night-blooming roses that I can smell to this day. I had no desire to go back there."

"You trusted them," Avery said.

"I suppose we all did. What other option did we have, with what was at stake?"

Avery wondered if he'd want to find that castle after this conversation. If Rhys were to learn the truth about the world's first vampires, the three unearthly, beautiful creatures of Castle Broceliande that called themselves Makers because they had made seven more creatures like themselves, the golden Grail Quest might seem like a much darker pledge.

Rhys's Makers had been powerful, deadly beings whose fault had been their ignorance of what might happen if their captive angel got loose and brought that castle down around them. But she had not killed the Makers. They had disappeared, along with her wings.

"Something else kept me from returning," Rhys said, eyes glazing as he thought back. "Hints of memory I can't quite recall surround that time. Sounds I've been unable to process."

As he eased her to the wall behind her with his hands on her shoulders, Avery's breath whooshed with a sound of immense sadness over the timing of this confrontation and the way Rhys was connecting the past to the news she had shared. His ideas, the promises he had made and his memories of that time were clashing. His breathing was harsh.

Avery let him go over things while her internal clock ticked away passing seconds as if there weren't many seconds left. Her back stung. The fake wings were motionless now.

She stifled a groan.

When Rhys's focus returned, he brought his face close to hers. He was searching her features, hoping to spark that elusive memory. He was looking for the truth.

"Like you, I cannot lie," she whispered to him. "You understand that."

He looked away, then back. Artfully chiseled features whitened as his eyes again found hers. "Is it you I hear in my dreams, Avery? Do you haunt me?"

She sensed he had more to say.

"Is it your cry that trespasses on my memory from time

to time? Was yours the sound that has evaded explanations for what I might or might not have heard in that castle garden?"

Avery blinked slowly. *No escape. No way out.* For the second time in her long life span, she found herself trapped by one of Castle Broceliande's immortals. The difference here was that, like his six blood brothers, Rhys, though as dangerous as any powerful being could be, had a heart of gold.

His Makers had unknowingly done themselves a disservice by capturing her. The difference between Rhys and his Makers was that Rhys and the other six Blood Knights also had her blood in their veins.

One small infusion of light had made all the difference between the actions and intentions of Rhys's Makers and the Knights they had sent into the world. His Makers had not counted on that. What they had planned for was full control of the Grail's magic through a six-pack of immortal fighting machines. Rhys, aka Perceval, Lancelot, Galahad and the other Blood Knights.

The thought of what she had to do next was what haunted her. Encourage Rhys to let all of this go? Could she have let it go, in his place?

No.

"Did they do this, Avery?" Warm hands tugged her closer to him, then slid up her back heading for the scarred spot that ached not only for what had been removed, but also for the immortal breathing life into what remained.

Soft lips moved against hers when Rhys spoke again. "This dreadful, unthinkable thing was their doing?"

Do not tell him everything, her mind pleaded.

Save something for last.

That was sound advice, if she were to manage to take it. In Rhys de Troyes she had met her match, and she had from the start imagined a moment like this one. She had longed for contact with him with every fiber of her being.

When his mouth landed on hers, moving over her lips with the slightest puff of air…

When his palms worked their way up her spine slowly, agonizingly, from bone to bone, heading toward the two deep grooves he was in some way connected to…

As he held her tightly to his taut chest, the world began to spin on the sidelines…and his question rang in her ears…

"Is it you I hear in my dreams? Do you haunt me, Avery?"

She breathed words into him, regretting it too late.

"Yes. It was me."

Rhys found Avery's lips rigid at first. She was as shocked as he was by his response to the knowledge he had just uncovered.

Shocking, yes. Disturbing.

What she had told him so far went against everything he had held up as truth. And now…now, he had to fight that knowledge. He had to wrestle with the demons inside him that had been created and manipulated by what? Creatures that might have had something entirely different in mind by hiding the Grail from the rest of the world? Creatures whose ulterior motives now, even so far in the future, had to be questioned?

Avery's pain rested on the foundation of that truth. He saw that now. The loss of her wings was tied to the time of his creation. And all he wanted to do was kiss away Avery's past. Taste the truth. Grasp the rest of the story she seemed to be on intimate terms with.

Her cry, in that blasted garden, was the sound he had imagined he'd heard. God, would he next ask her what had caused it or how his Makers had accomplished their treacherous act?

Would he ask how she could be standing here today, after centuries had passed, with her mouth and her body tight against one of the souls who might have most benefited from her capture and possible incarceration?

Hell, Avery! Maybe you were right when you said I might not want to know much of this.

You told me I might not want to help you once I knew the truth of your past.

But you were wrong.

Christ, angel. You were wrong.

Her lips parted, as if she had heard his thoughts. It was entirely possible she had. In the kiss lay the proof of the bond they had formed. The fact that they hungered for each other despite events that had taken place in a time relegated to distant memory momentarily took precedence over everything else.

Hunger and desire ruled here. Nothing else mattered to Rhys except this one, seemingly unending kiss that had to end eventually.

What Avery had told him would suffice for now, and only served to encourage him to help her. He hadn't heard it all. Darkness rode in the unspoken details. Nevertheless, he had heard enough to share Avery's deep ache for her losses and to accept some of the guilt for what had happened to her.

Locked together in a shadowed corner of this London street, Avery's mouth accepted his as if this were a battle to be fought. In this particular battle, no one would emerge the winner. By kissing her like this, Rhys's blood oaths strengthened. He was a Grail Guardian, and an angel had come to relieve the Knights of duty. She wanted to take that relic home.

There was no way to refuse her, and no need to do so.

The world spun in circles around them, coming apart at the seams. His mouth was sealed to hers. His soul shook. Black scrolling sigils whined.

The only sound that could possibly have broken into his thoughts now, did. From somewhere in that dark, swirling mass of moving reality he stood in, with his lips on Avery's, came a nasty chucking comment meant for him.

"Thank you, Guardian," a Shade's wispy voice intoned, "for making this so easy."

Chapter 19

Avery reacted in a crackle of speed, spinning around with her knife in her hand. Rhys did the same. Shoulder to shoulder in fighting stances, she and Rhys had the location of the ghostly vulture pinpointed before the echo of its raspy voice had faded.

They lunged forward in unison, moving as one body. But the Shade disappeared before they could confront it, replaced by several more shadows that quickly surrounded the puddle of light she and Rhys found themselves in.

"You're not thinking straight," Rhys said to those shadows, as they both waited for what might happen next.

"It's you who have slipped your tethers," another voice returned.

Avery recognized the dusty odor and the slight hiss of a vampire speaking through sharp fangs. The bastards had to be careful with those fangs since they didn't like the taste of their own regurgitated blood, preferring warm, red, fresh fare—which she and Rhys did not possess.

"Be off," Rhys directed, as motionless as if he was carved from marble as he added, "before we decide that tonight's agenda can be postponed in favor of a close-up kind of monster hunt."

"In fact," the voice cut in, "that agenda of yours is exactly why we're here."

The remark had Avery's full attention. Rhys's head came up as if he recognized this voice.

"You realize that it doesn't matter how many of you there are," she said. "And that you're no match for either of us?"

"Now who isn't thinking straight?" the vampire challenged. "We haven't attacked, and have come to offer a truce."

"Vampires have nothing to bring to the table," Rhys said.

"What if we do?"

"Not going to happen," Rhys concluded.

"Perhaps not all of us are the monsters you hunt down and stake. I believe you know this."

"I have met a few old souls among you," Rhys admitted. "But I don't sense anything like that here."

"Then perhaps your senses need tuning."

Avery broke in. "What is it you want?"

"A deal," the vamp spokesman said.

"What kind of deal?" Rhys snarled.

"Perhaps we can offer assistance with the things your companion seeks," the vampire suggested.

Avery knew the vamp was alluding to her.

"In trade for what?" she asked.

"For a *taste*."

"A..." Rhys began.

"Taste," the vampire repeated. "Of her blood."

Rhys moved. His shoulder brushed hers as he positioned himself in front of her as if she were a damsel in distress and in need of a champion. The knight of old had reappeared, ready to fight for her, or in her place.

Hell with that.

Avery stepped up beside him, flashing the knife she wielded. "How do you know what I seek?"

"We have been watching for you," explained the vampire, who had far too many of its wits intact to be anything other than an old bloodsucker. "We are guardians in our own right, you could say."

"Anytime now you will start to make sense," Rhys suggested wryly. But Avery felt his attention sharpen. Rhys also recognized that there was something different about this vampire.

Deep inside her, a premonition formed that sent chills cascading down her back. Since arriving in London, more than one monster had mentioned her quest.

"Where are they?" she asked without lowering the blade that could cut through this gathering like a silver tornado.

My wings...

Although Rhys didn't glance her way, some of his attention transferred to her.

"I may be an example of death warmed over," the vampire began, "but I have retained a few of my former brain cells. Enough of them to withhold that information until a deal has been struck."

Rhys rocked back on his heels, but she was the only one who could have witnessed that since he stood ramrod straight again in the blink of an eye. The heat of his anger radiated off him. He didn't yet comprehend that, if not for a transfusion of the same blood these bloodsuckers desired as part of the deal they were proposing, Rhys might have been like them.

Blood Knights. Named after the proclivities of their fanged Makers.

And yet Rhys had never used his fangs, and he had never looked back.

It was likely he and his brethren had never seen the occupants of Castle Broceliande in person, and had been invited, summoned there, by the dark magic those Makers possessed. Rhys also had been a victim of that dark time, as had his brothers. Avery vowed right then and there that she would never be the one to tell him any of this.

"What am I looking for?" she asked. "How can a deal be made without a sound basis for a decision that falls one way or the other?"

Out of the gloom stepped a bloodsucker draped in black velvet. The vampire's hair was gray and fell to its thin shoulders. An ashen face with sunken features held dark eye sockets hiding light-colored eyes.

This being was a rare and formidable sight among his kind. Without exuding enough power to be the creature vampires called their Prime, it still suggested a confidence that did not bode well for the vampire allowing itself to be struck down in any circumstance without a real fight.

Beside her, Rhys stiffened. "We meet again, vampire," he said.

"As I promised," the vamp returned with a slight nod of its gray head, before again speaking to Avery.

"You search for what you lost long ago," the vampire said to her.

"And that is?" Avery quickly fired back.

"Evidence of your species. The things that define you as a creature of the light."

Avery's insides had begun to quake. Keeping those quakes from spreading and becoming visible was a chore that required careful control.

"And that would be?" she pressed.

The wily vampire raised its bony arms to shoulder height and then lowered them, making an unmistakable flapping gesture. One horrid flap of its velvet-clad appendages and the horror of what Avery was seeing sent her insides skittering.

Rhys spoke again. "How would you know anything about that, if it were true?"

"One look at the angel's face, Guardian, will show you the truth about how much I know regarding what she has lost."

Angel. Flapping velvet gestures. *"This vampire knows too much,"* Avery's mind warned. It was all adding up to something foul.

"No," Rhys said adamantly to the old vampire. "No deal."

Avery didn't look at Rhys. Couldn't look at him. She understood that by making such a deal, by offering a few drops of her blood to this parasite, a new breed of vampire would be born in this century. That breed might become as strong as Rhys. As strong as she was, until she found her wings. All hell would break loose in the world if that happened. Vampires would win in the war against humans in less than a year.

"It's too late," she said. "I have already found the information about what I need."

"But can you get in?" the vamp challenged. "Will you be admitted to the darkest place you've ever seen, or welcomed there?"

"You're implying you'd be welcome," Avery said.

"Oh, yes. I can guarantee that."

"And we always believe what a vampire says," Rhys chimed in. "Due to the fact that your kind never lies or shifts the truth around for personal benefit."

The vampire shook its pasty head. Facing Avery directly, it said, "He does not know. One might find that pathetically intriguing."

Avery fingered the handle of her knife. The creature in front of her indeed knew a hell of a lot more than it should have, and had just offered her proof of that. Its pithy remark alluded to Rhys's connections with the creation of this vamp's species, and the slip of a fang by one of Castle Broceliande's infamous Makers.

"No deal," Rhys dangerously reiterated.

The vampire again raised its arms, this time in a gesture of acceptance of that decision. "So be it, Guardian."

The beast had the audacity, as well as just enough left of its human features, to offer Avery an expression of sympathy and commiseration…as if they were pals.

"So be it," the vamp repeated as it backed away slowly.

Rhys strode forward, going after the vampire. Avery stuck out a hand to hold him back. With her fingers wrapped in his coat, she shook her head. "No. Let them go."

When he turned to her, she said, "I wasn't kidding about finding what I seek. We're almost there, and this meeting proves it."

"If that fanged beast knows where you're headed and what we can expect when we arrive, what makes you think others won't know and be waiting there? Damn it, Avery. This place you want to go might be crawling with them."

"I have to take that chance."

He knew that was the case, of course, and he would have done the same thing in her place. Avery felt his emotions shift toward acceptance.

"All right. Where are we going?" he asked.

Avery pointed to the ground. "Down there. We just have to find a way in."

* * *

"We could follow them," Rhys suggested, waving at the empty darkness the vampires had disappeared into and dreading what they might find in those tunnels. "What sort of black market carries on in such a location?"

Avery's expression was grim. He hadn't voiced any opinion she hadn't already considered.

"Markets dealing in supernatural treasures that attract other monsters would relish a creepy space to ply their trade," she said. "Weaker monsters might be for sale, as well as Lycan pelts from unturned purebred Weres. Vials of blood from old saints. Holy relics." She looked at him directly. "Angel wings."

"Christ," Rhys said. "We'll have to do a one-stop mop-up of the whole event. That way, we'll rid the world of a whole mess of pests at once."

They were facing a daunting situation. An unknown one. He watched the corners of Avery's mouth twitch. She was worried—not for herself, for him. He had to wonder, given how long Avery had kept to the sidelines of everyone else's life and the reasons she skirted the fringes of society the way he did, if she had ever asked anyone for help, and why other angels hadn't come to her aid before now.

"That's not the way it works," she said, with that uncanny ability she had of reading him. "One angel, one mission. There aren't many of us to go around."

"Not even when that mission was one of high priority?"

Her eyes brightened with his challenge. "Do you think the Grail is the only mission worthy of our attention, Rhys?"

True, he hadn't stopped to think about that. The Grail was the only relic that had concerned and consumed him since his rebirth.

"Whoever sent you assumes you'll finish this," he said. "However long that takes."

Her smile was a sad, joyless one that confirmed his hypothesis. This Grail challenge was her deal, and hers alone.

In her favor, possibly the concept of time wasn't the same in the heavenly realms as it was on Earth, and centuries here meant nothing to the other place in the long run. Only Avery, grounded, wingless and relatively undaunted about the task she had been given, had to live through the endless years on Earth while pursuing her goal.

"We are, indeed, strange bedfellows," Rhys muttered, moving beside Avery, heading for the path through the shadows the intelligent bloodsucker and his minions had taken—a path that wily vampire would have set with the understanding that the immortal duo would follow.

"This will be a trap," he said. "There's no way around it."

Avery nodded.

"I doubt if our fanged friend wanted a deal," he observed.

"It wanted a closer look at its enemies, and got that," Avery agreed, picking up speed as they both strode forward.

"We can't take them all down at once, Avery, if that place is crammed with bloodsuckers."

That remark earned him a wry sideways glance. They had to try, Avery's expression told him. They had to take the bait and follow the fanged parasites to that underground black market. Doing so was their only way in.

"At least we're immortal," Rhys said, half in jest. "That's in our favor."

"Yes. We are that," Avery whispered back with the sigh of an angel hiding something from him. That sigh was all the notice Rhys needed about Avery continuing to keep some secrets to herself. Secrets that might have shed more light on how they had arrived at this point in time, together, side by side, as well as what they could look forward to.

It was too late to ask the questions bogging him down.

The damn vamps had set a path that was so easy to track, it was as though they'd tossed a trail of bread crumbs.

The symbols carved into Rhys's back flared to life, scalding his skin, firing his nerves, readying him for the next fight as only symbols wrought by magic could. Those inky, scrolling marks had no special allegiance to Castle Broceliande. They had been carved by Far Eastern sorcerers with clever, clearer means.

Through the sigils, Rhys could call his brothers, and they would come. Avery's cause was worthy of the pledges he and his brothers had made. It involved all of them.

But just as Avery had confessed about the missions of her kind, the Knights also had their own agendas and were scattered round the globe. With the Grail safely hidden and the strongest of his brothers standing guard over it, everyone else was doing their best to turn back the tide of monsters in the shadows.

He and Avery were on their own here.

The scent of fangers grew noticeably stronger near a dim, narrow alley. Rhys slowed. Beside him, Avery, Heaven's warrior angel, was outrageously beautiful. Rhys couldn't imagine what her wings would be like and how she'd look in them. If the image he'd seen of those gigantic feathers turned out to be an indication of the real thing, she'd be truly magnificent.

"We will get them back," he said to her. "Every damn feather."

They walked together, knowing that in minutes the real fun would begin.

Chapter 20

Five vampires showing their teeth stood in the shadows of the entrance to an unused back door that would have turned off most of the people unlucky enough to find it.

There was no human presence here. This was vampire territory and lethal to any living thing with red fluid in its veins.

Boarded-up buildings and glassless windows gave the place its eerie, abandoned vibe. Graffiti sprawled across brick and pavement alike, as if the street had seen gang activity before these vampires moved in. Maybe the vampires they were facing had been one of those gangs, with a new drug of choice. Blood.

Human blood.

Avery halted several paces from them without her knife in her hand. Rhys followed suit, opening and closing his fingers around his blade's hilt.

These bloodsuckers didn't advance or speak. Minions, servants of their Prime, they were guards in an unnatural lineup that told Rhys they had found the entrance to that black market gathering without a hell of a lot of effort.

Behind where he and Avery stood, shadows closed in to darken the area, making the night seem blacker than it already was. Shades were doing this, creeping in to wait for vamp leftovers. The presence of Shades meant there were mortals at this underground gathering, taking their lives in their hands by being part of such an illegal escapade.

"Is there a magic password?" Avery asked drily. "Or will a silver knife in your chests be all the invitation we need to get inside?"

Rhys didn't actually expect a response. The pasty bastards looked like statues in advertisements for London's wax museum.

Avery was a determined seeker, though, and had a lot to gain by coming here. Fearlessly, she walked right up to the bloodsuckers and looked into their faces as if this were nothing more than troop inspection. Rhys stayed close to her, uneasy about what lay ahead if they made it inside.

When Avery flashed a smile, all of the vamps stepped back at once. They might not have known exactly what sort of being was facing them, but they wanted no part of whatever she turned out to be.

She was all fight now—fierce, competitive, daring and brilliant at getting what she wanted. When she waved a hand, the vamps parted as if mesmerized. Two of them shielded their eyes from the inner light she radiated so artfully.

"So much for needing an invitation," Rhys said. He felt the need to add, "You do understand what we'll find down there?"

"Stolen goods," she muttered. "Belonging to me."

The door was made of iron, and heavy. Its composition alone would have prevented the passage of some supernatural species, unless it had been closed behind this market's invited guests to seal them inside. Not many supernaturals could stand to touch or be near iron or steel.

Was that how things worked? Rhys wondered. Money came in and never left, expanding the coffers of whoever ran this shindig? With a reputation like that, who would dare to attend a gathering of this kind, where the odds of surviving might be dismal?

The answer that came to him was that Weres wouldn't find a place like this to their liking, and neither would the Fae, if London housed any. Who, then, could they expect to find here, besides vampires desiring to use Avery for some unknown purpose?

Rhys didn't care about his own safety. Only hers. Come to think of it, he'd never worried about surviving the wars he'd participated in or facing down the hellhounds often sent his way. If anyone had found the key to ending his life, getting around the whole *immortal* thing, and Avery were to cart the Grail away, he might actually welcome the peace he'd find by permanently closing his eyes.

Not here, however. Not in some dark den that reeked of vampires.

Darkness swallowed them when they entered the hallway behind the door. The tight space rang with an echo when the iron door slammed shut. Lanterns lit the passageway ahead, looking like strings of electric lights. Half of them had burned out.

Avery didn't seem to notice either the darkness or the smell. Rhys supposed the only scent in her lungs was the rich fragrance of an imminent victory. He wasn't so sure he felt the same.

"You'll go," he said, leading the way down the passage and toward a set of steep concrete stairs. "Those wings mean your freedom."

"They mean fulfillment," Avery explained. "Wings aren't simply feathers tacked onto an angel's back, Rhys. They are tied in to my system. Part of my system."

She stopped him with a hand on his back, on the burning sigils that chattered instructions to his nerves beneath his clothes.

"Do you think I used to look like this?" she asked as he turned around to face her. "Pale and white and colorless?"

"I like it," he confessed. "You're beautiful."

She was quiet for a long time before finally speaking again.

"This..." She ran a hand down her almost iridescent cheek. "This is the result of losing an integral part of myself. I didn't look like this when I came here."

"To Earth, you mean?" Rhys asked.

She nodded. "Each decade drains more color from me, slowly, insidiously, bit by bit, as if someone were siphoning it off."

"Angels aren't..."

"Angels have no form in our realm. When we take form, it's with the beauty and color of the places we're sent to."

Rhys tried to wrap his mind around what she was telling him, but couldn't. Who could imagine Avery without a body? Or any being of intelligence without an outline of some kind?

Her eyes had softened. Those big blue eyes.

"You would have liked me then," she said. "With my wings."

Rhys shook his head. "Hell, I like you now, just the way you are."

"I'm being drained, and there's not much left of what I was. My wings will replenish what's been lost. My power will triple."

"I've seen the gashes where those wings were, Avery. Are you sure they can be reattached when we find them?"

Sadness again, in her eyes, on her face. "One can only hope," she concluded. "But hope often shines brightest in the darkest places."

In the middle of an upcoming showdown with the worst sort of creatures on the planet, and while cursing his Makers for the atrocity they had committed on such a beautiful being, Rhys wanted to take Avery in his arms and offer comfort. He wished for the time to do that and more time to be her lover. He wished he possessed the kind of sight that would allow him to believe she'd come out of this damn tunnel unharmed and with her coveted prize.

Avery walked on, taking the lead with her knife in one hand. Honor demanded he follow her, help her. However, honor wasn't the main driving factor here. His heart and his soul couldn't be separated from Avery. What he felt for her seemed very much like love. Respect, awe...and yes, *love.*

Bolstered by that thought, as well as the tiny glittering lights Avery began to throw off as they traversed the steep staircase into what seemed to him like the bowels of the Earth, Rhys repeated an earlier voiced sentiment.

"We will get them back."

As if on cue, and as though his promise had set off a hidden alarm in the dark hole they moved through, the lights and lanterns above their heads sputtered out.

Avery swore as blackness descended. Other than the angel light she was still strong enough to emit, it was difficult to tell which way was up, and which direction was down.

She heard Rhys utter an oath behind her.

Taking the steps one at a time, she continued on, able to feel her way along the wall, listening to the scraping sounds her knife made on the rock. Rising anger made her scars tingle. The inked wings began to itch. She ignored all of that, aware, as she moved, of the high-pitched humming noise coming from everywhere at once. She knew what that sound was, and after all this time, she really had found those missing pieces of herself.

Rhys was quiet now. Did he also hear her wings keening for their rightful owner? That hum filled her head, echoing, calling, luring her downward. Her heart was in her throat.

The floor leveled out eventually. Her fingers came away from the wall gritty. This section of the tunnel was composed of chalk, and chalk was a conductor of supernatural energy. That was why whoever ran this black market had chosen such a place, and how that creature had been able to hide the wings from her. Anyone with a sensitivity to paranormal phenomena who stumbled down here would equate the sounds and feelings with the presence of ghosts. Severed angel wings wouldn't warrant a thought, because who would believe such things existed?

"I'm coming," she whispered. "Almost there."

The tunnel led to another just like it, with stone columns propping up the ceilings every few feet. Darkness had swallowed them, but her angel light lit enough of the floor to assure they didn't tumble into a hole. And immortals all possessed the ability to manage the dark.

More sounds reached her, drowning out the keening.

"Do you hear that?" Rhys asked.

"Yes."

"Are you ready for what awaits us up ahead?"

She said, "I've been ready for hundreds of years."

"All right. Let's crash this party, angel."

The sliding ping of Rhys's knife leaving its sheath was a comfort to her when she knew he didn't really need a weapon. Rhys de Troyes was, in essence, a weapon himself. Immortal Rhys would shed his human-like persona when confronted with real danger, true danger, and stun the world with the parameters of his immortal soul's transformative powers.

She had seen this transformation once before, and had loved him more because of it. That had been the real Rhys, not the tamped-down super-mortal image he usually projected. As her own light had waned, his had grown. From the background, and from where she'd hidden, she had witnessed the fact that Rhys de Troyes was an unparalleled being, exquisitely fine to behold and totally outrageous at the same time.

It was so with each of the Seven. But Rhys…

"They're coming," he warned.

His chest touched her back. The sinewy thighs she had seen in all their bare fineness that very day, pressed to hers.

Just one more kiss, Avery wished she could say to him. *For luck.*

She felt his hands on her hips. His warm breath stirred her hair.

"Showtime," he whispered gamely in her ear.

Chapter 21

The place came alive with shadows as the light in the lanterns flared. Shades poured into the tunnel like a black tide—more of those creatures than Rhys had ever seen.

He and Avery were surrounded again by ghostly forms that circled without coming within reach. Even now, with so many of them taking up residence in Rhys's personal space, the creatures knew better than to take on an immortal. They also seemed hesitant about treading too close to Avery's heavenly light.

"I'm guessing you are to be our guides," Rhys said, back-to-back with Avery now, both of them assuming fighting stances. "So go ahead. Lead the way through this hellish maze."

"Come, Knight," a voice lured from inside the swirling circle of Shades. "Follow."

Avery spoke to that Shade. "I know you. We've met before."

Thin black veils of filminess created a long shadow that

stretched along one wall. But the Shade didn't respond to Avery's taunt.

"Follow," it said again, and the ring of monsters opened up at one end, showing the entrance to a tunnel that branched off from the one they were in.

Avery didn't hesitate. These Shades were seemingly of no consequence to her. Her eyes were trained on the tunnel. Rhys strained to pick up the sounds she appeared to be hearing that led her farther and farther into the dark.

Behind them, Shades filled in the space from floor to ceiling. This second ghostly welcoming party did little for Rhys's confidence in what lay ahead.

Avery moved quickly, surefooted now, confident in her direction. Her boots were as silent as she was. Her silver blade flashed now and then under the flickering lights. He could stop her, Rhys reasoned. He had the power and the strength to remove her from all of this. *And then what?*

Will you fade away completely in time, angel?

What comes after all that paleness? Complete transparency?

In truth, he couldn't keep Avery from what she wanted most because of his fear over what might happen afterward. The very real fear growing inside him was his worry about losing her.

I want this for you, Avery. I do.

He chanted those words over and over as he walked, trying to rationalize what went so heavily against his need for her.

Under a great stone archway she stopped, then spun to grab hold of his lapels. Pulling herself closer to him, Avery looked up, moved both hands to his hair and led his mouth to hers.

In this place, where danger reigned supreme, she kissed him.

As if she had heard each of his thoughts and desired to reassure him of the importance of her quest and her trust in him, she kissed him with a feverish passion.

A last kiss?

A gesture of farewell, since they both knew the dangers of what they were doing, and that things might not turn out as planned?

For a few brief seconds, somehow removed from time, they were transported to a place of pure sensation. Lips touching. Mouths merging. She tugged him closer. Her tongue swept across his teeth, and her breath was pure fire.

Rhys's senses expanded to encompass an image he'd seen before.

Pale, beautiful Avery, bare from the waist up.

This time, in his mind, when she turned her head to look at him in the doorway, he heard a distant cry like the one that had haunted him at Broceliande. A sound he had not investigated at the time. The sight of Avery's inked wings had moved him. She had moved him.

Half in and half out of this dream, Rhys understood Avery was showing this image to him. She was letting him see what waited for her up ahead and how much she needed it. She was also confirming that she admired and loved him for being here at this time, and for sharing in those moments, however tenuous those moments were.

She was radiant in the gloom of the cavern. In the dark, her light was like the sun's corona. She was excited, jazzed. Avery truly expected this to be the culmination of her long search.

Her heat was extraordinary, her mouth fierce as it took from him and gave back double. Their bodies were close enough to be one body, pressing, straining to be closer still.

And just when Rhys thought they'd stay entwined forever, in the space between one thundering heartbeat and the next, Avery pulled away. Cold air rushed in to cool Rhys's fever. Darkness returned to envelop them both.

She looked at him with sadness before she turned from him and walked on as if nothing had happened…when, for Rhys, everything had. He had tasted starlight, been embroiled in sunlight. If this was to be the end of his time with Avery, he wasn't ready to go on alone.

"Avery," he said softly as the Shades urged him to move.

But she was beyond hearing now.

Avery had drawn strength from that kiss. She had allowed Rhys to see her whole and as she used to be, as she again needed to be. Winged and angelic. Not the calm-hearted little cherub of children's dreams and religious doctrines, but one of Heaven's defenders against the fallen hordes. A member of Archangel Michael's fighting forces responsible for keeping the dark side at bay and within its set boundaries.

Fighter. Soldier. Merciless defender.

As such, it was impossible for her to ignore the closeness of that dark side now. She was in their territory. Walking through it. The walls gave off foul odors of sulfur and brimstone, which had always been the devil's calling cards. Her reactions to that were primal, visceral, familiar.

No ordinary black-market dealer would have dared to enter such a place without a guarantee of safety. That dealer had to have something for sale that the Fallen Ones wanted badly, and currently there were only two things on this planet that filled the bill. The Holy Grail, a vessel that possessed some of the spirit of the man some called the Son of God, and the severed wings of a once-mighty angel who had gone by the name of Aurian Arcadia.

Au. The symbol for gold, for the heavens and what she had been before becoming a colorless freak.

"Slowly," Rhys whispered to her, but it was a word she no longer recognized. The hum she perceived had gotten louder, calling to her, pleading with her to hurry. Her pulse was skyrocketing. Her skin had gone cold.

She charged ahead, traversing the dimly lit darkness effortlessly, led by the inhuman cries of her severed wings.

Those wings had screamed when the occupants of the castle had cut them from her with a hot silver blade…the same blade she carried now in her outstretched hand.

Rhys's Makers had covered their ears to dull the sound. They had fallen to their knees as the cries of two halves of one being, torn apart, became deafening. Yet the powerful, greedy threesome had carried on anyway, cutting, slicing, hurting her in ways she'd never dreamed of before wrapping her in iron chains.

And one man, she later discovered, when he had not yet been indoctrinated into the world of immortality, had heard her cries. Rhys had heard her and been haunted ever since.

"I'm coming. I'm here," Avery said, choking on memories and losing the battle with the instincts warning her to take care.

"Avery."

Rhys called to her again. There was wariness in his tone and a sense of urgency she had to ignore. The tunnel opened up suddenly. The security of close walls gave way to a huge, open orifice filled with dozens of motionless creatures. Shades. Vampires. Demons. Humans. Plus a few monsters Avery couldn't classify or put names to.

Fire roared in a metal grate in the center of the cavern, with red-orange flames leaping several feet high into the dank, moist air. Heads turned when she and Rhys stopped beneath a heavily runed archway. Those runes, carved into the rock, were symbols of power meant to neutralize the tricks of each member of this odd gathering, and probably worked with some of them. Standing beneath the arch made her skin ache.

Other than those annoying little reactions, Avery didn't feel much of anything at all, except excitement.

Her gaze strayed from the crowd to the ledges of the cavern above their heads, where iron cages were suspended on thick iron chains. Iron was used here to ensure none of the buyers present could grab hold of what those cages contained and run. The abundance of that particular metal, scattered around the cavern, smelled like death.

Rhys, beside her, muttered something that got lost in the gloom of the terrible scene being played out. Mesmerized, Avery watched as a man stepped forward to greet them.

"Bloody hell…damn…" Rhys stuttered, inching forward for a better look, obviously recognizing that man before this gathering's host had taken ten steps.

His world was dissolving into one long lie that countered everything he had believed to be the truth.

Rhys stared with disbelief at the creature parting the crowd. Not a man. Not this one.

"No," he protested with a sideways glance to Avery, whose face had settled into an unreadable stillness.

"Welcome friends," said the creature coming forward.

This welcome compounded the lies made real by Rhys's familiarity with that voice. The moving entity in red velvet robes was his Maker; the eldest of the nameless three that belonged to Castle Broceliande, and who were all supposed to be dead.

That had been the deal. The seven Knights were to replace the Makers. Only a few immortals could exist at one time, those Makers had explained. Too many of them, too strong, and the world's balance would tip in the wrong direction. As it had done since then, anyway.

And here, at the heart of this hellish cavern, lay the possibility of a reason why. His Maker was a liar and a cheat.

Avery's expressionless face suggested she also recognized this luxuriously robed creature. She had been correct in her hints about things at that bloody castle being far different than his memories of them.

Had she known how different? Yes. Because his Makers had taken her wings. The creature walking their way had taken them.

"Mordred." Avery's voice was flat when she addressed their host.

The sound of that name raised chills on the back of Rhys's neck. Flashes of more memory returned, images of red robes spreading over a verdant landscape by moonlight and hushed voices that vibrated through thick stone walls.

Still, this couldn't be the Mordred of the old tales, Rhys's mind protested. Maybe it was another being, because Mordred was said to have been King Arthur's son. Tales told of Mordred turning on his father and dealing Arthur a final death blow in the last battle for possession of the crown. The Blood Knights, prior to their transformation, had sat at Arthur's table, where they offered their fealty and swords to their king.

"Aurian Arcadia," the robed creature said, his attention on Avery. "I was expecting you."

Hell…the creature had just offered up another name to fill in the blanks. Avery's. Her angelic moniker was Aurian, a name that rivaled her beauty and shouldn't have crossed this robed bastard's lips. Names had power. Merely muttering real ones could give the speaker an advantage.

"You have something that belongs to me," Avery said, her voice hazardously calm in light of what was going on and who they were facing.

The cavern was curiously quiet, its air supercharged

with the electricity of this meeting between old foes. Rhys could hear that electricity crackle.

"Yes, perhaps I do," the robed creature said.

One long glance showed Rhys that dozens of Shades had moved to block each entrance to the cavern. He counted four branching tunnels and carefully noted the location of each. Personal experience told him that Shades were not the problem here. The numerous species of creatures salivating for what was in those iron cages were the ones needing cautious observation. Or maybe there was only one real monster here—the butcher that would harm an angel to such an extent as this one had.

Strategy demanded that Rhys pay attention to details when he wanted to look at Avery. A swift exit, if necessary, would have to be in a safe direction, so he scanned the cavern, ignoring more personal needs.

Two dozen bidders were present at this market, all of them seeming to get along for the moment, at least until the action began. Opposing forces on the streets above these tunnels stood side by side without tearing each other apart. The only group with no representatives was the werewolves.

Passing seconds seemed like hours, and Avery hadn't spoken again. Seeing into the hanging cages was impossible from where he and Avery stood. Did one of them hold a pair of red-tipped wings, or would those wings have faded in the same way Avery's color had faded without them? She had been right. If they called to her, those wings had to be here somewhere.

There was one added problem, of course. Avery had been expected to show up, and someone had correctly predicted that. Possibly it was the same creature that had lured seven men to a castle with the promise of abiding by God's will.

The whole thing stunk with the sulfurous stench of a

trap, but he and Avery had figured this out before stepping into the dark.

"Now might be a good time to give them back," Avery said at last.

"Have you come to bargain or to spend?" his Maker asked.

"Neither."

Murmurs rustled through the crowd. This gathering thought too much time was being wasted. The comely, black-haired, velvet-clothed creature facing Avery was too perfect to be anything but *Other.* His smile was evil incarnate. Rhys had never seen an expression like that, so cruel and calculating. This creature wasn't like the one in his memory. The Makers must have played their parts well back then.

"And look who accompanies you," his Maker said, fixing Rhys with a stern gaze. "Hello, Perceval. It's been a while."

His instinct was to slide his blade into the madman's chest and get this over with. Too much distance separated them, however, which likely was a purposeful attention to detail on his Maker's part. Two immortals with blades would make a hell of a dent in this unnatural gathering. The question here was how much power this robed entity had and which species he had sprung from.

"Vampire," Avery said, answering Rhys's silent question. "Another rumor that had truth at its core."

Vampire...

What was it Avery had told him, early on?

Legends say the Blood Knights were created by three magicians who were also the earliest form of what we know of today as vampires. If that's true, it would explain a lot about you.

Rhys rocked on his feet and ran his tongue over fangs

that had dropped, he supposed, because of the extremes of the danger confronting him and the reality of what those fangs meant. Somewhere in his tweaked DNA sat the reason for his unused teeth.

If what Avery said was true, the tarnished blood of the undead swam in his veins, but the outcome of that had to have been altered somehow by drinking from the golden chalice that had captured the blood of a man on a cross. He and his brothers had been resurrected to a life of immortality and had followed golden rules when everything else was a lie.

Avery took a step, listening. Rhys couldn't hear anything beyond the anxious fluttering of the crowd. His world had been turned upside down but he had to concentrate on what was going on now, with her. His angel. When Avery took a second step, the red-robed creature across from them lifted a pale, languid hand. As if summoned, several more vampires emerged from the shadows. Young vampires, fully fed. Beautiful creatures. Aggressive. Deadly.

"You know what I want in exchange for that which you seek," his Maker said to Avery. But Rhys knew the Maker's attention had been divided, and that half of it lay on Avery's unexpected companion. A Blood Knight had discovered the falseness of his origins and by accompanying Avery had found his Maker still very much alive.

"Nothing he says is the truth," Rhys sent to Avery, sensing her tuning in to his thoughts.

"No one understands that better than I do," she sent back.

"That thing you want so very badly," Avery explained to the creature in front of her in a clear, strong voice, "is something you will never get hold of again."

"What a shame," his Maker remarked with another casual hand gesture. "Without your permission, I will now have to use force."

"Like hell you will," Rhys warned, prepared to do everything in his power to thwart that threat.

Chapter 22

The humming sound produced by her wings had become a body-piercing vibration that threatened Avery's level of concentration when losing focus was risky.

Where are you?

Show me.

Her gaze never left the creature Rhys had called his Maker. She knew this black-hearted, ancient bloodsucker well, and remembered everything he had done to her. She remembered each taunt he'd made while she lay in chains in the dungeon carved beneath those tall white castle walls, and all his threats.

The three ancients at Broceliande hadn't killed mortals regularly in order to fuel their strange, extended existence. Instead, they fed on those of different origins. Capturing Fae folk was their specialty. An angel had been their crowning victory. How had they accomplished that? By luring her to the castle's garden, where a golden chalice sat submerged in a golden fountain. And then ensnaring her with a net made of fine-linked chain mail.

They had dragged her to the castle, across moonlight-dappled grounds. Securing her in chains had taken the effort of all three supernaturally strong creatures with the help of a conjured fog of gray, numbing smoke. Mordred's mother had been the sorceress Morgana, and she had taught her son well.

"Vampires are nothing," Avery said to the captor facing her now, in the present, without bothering to check out the minions the freak had set in place to test her reactions. His little army of vampires didn't matter to her. Mordred didn't matter. She had come here for one thing only, and the result was in sight.

More rustling sounds ran through the cavern. Other creatures gathered here were expecting an auction, and weren't keen on patience. Even ancient Makers with one-track minds had to be cognizant of the danger in leaving this crowd on their own and without entertainment for too long.

"One drop of blood is all I ask of you," Mordred said to her. "Two, at most."

"Do you imagine I actually believe you'd be satisfied with that, or that you'd give me anything in trade?" Avery said.

"Or that you'd allow her to leave this place," Rhys added, his attention also riveted to the black-haired monster. "It would seem that you are unable to keep your word in any circumstance. Wouldn't you agree, *Maker*?"

Rhys's hand brushed Avery's. The handsome Blood Knight stood very close, and the simple, brief touch of his flesh to hers made her skin burn. In spite of the situation facing them, her insides throbbed with an overarching need for him that refused to fade.

Emotions ran high. She wasn't alone here, surrounded by darkness. Like her, Rhys had broken this Maker's chains. Like her, his incredible body was also a vessel for the light. That infusion of her blood into the Seven had been this Makers' biggest mistake. Mordred's sorriest regret, she would have guessed.

"Wings!" Avery called out.

Her voice echoed in the giant cave, the sound eerily magnified by the conducting properties of the chalk in the walls.

In reaction, Rhys made a slight movement of his shoulders before settling back to stillness. This was his fight, as well. He'd been fooled by three master tricksters but had been able to avoid the kind of control they had planned for him. Instead of saving the Grail for Mordred and his beastly companions to barter with, as had been their plan, the Blood Knights created at that bloody castle had taken it away, hidden the chalice and continually defied all efforts made by anyone who tried to find it.

In the end, Avery thought, as Rhys's heat bolstered her courage, Rhys would have to relinquish that coveted item. In doing so, he and his brothers would be free of the bindings of their vows and promises. When they were no longer Guardians whose paths had been set, their futures would be theirs—more than they had been for some time.

"Wings!" she called again, and was rewarded. A rush of wind reached her that turned her head. Up high, near the invisible ceiling of the cavern and behind the orange licks of fire in the grate, came the unmistakable sound of her wings trying desperately to flap again in an enclosed space.

Before anyone could blink, Avery bounded across the floor, past the robed monster that had not only dealt Britain's most famous king a death blow, but had been responsible for setting this centuries-spanning game between them in motion.

Pushing off the central grate with both booted feet, she jumped up and caught hold of the chains. Climbing the forged links hand over hand, she reached the edge of the cage.

Momentum made the cage swing. Avery held on, ignoring the angry rumblings of the crowd. Some of those monsters might have come here tonight for the same thing. Parts of an angel. Or, hell, possibly Mordred had sold tickets, and they had only come for the show. Either way, she was not going to be anyone's bitch.

She swung with the cage, feeling the rise and fall of the gust of wind her wings were creating without being able to spread to their full ten-foot width. Hoisting herself up, tucking into a ball, Avery shoved both of her boots between the cage's heavy metal bars, absorbing the agony that left her hands branded.

Chaos had broken out on the cavern floor. Mordred's monstrous gang was on the move, pushing into the crowd of angry onlookers. Some of the other monsters began to fight the intrusion with fangs and claws, realizing this night wasn't going well and Mordred had lost control.

But the runes etched in the walls had stolen some of their power.

Rhys's Maker's vamp squad was doing some damage, by the sound of things. In the distance, and seemingly in a different world from the one she was in, Avery heard Rhys's knife strike a monster's body with a *schwang* and a *thud*.

Her heart continued to pound.

"Seize them!" Mordred shouted, his tone reflecting hints of anger tainted with surprise. He might have expected her, but obviously didn't count on the kind of strength she still possessed or the prowess of the company she kept.

Should have known better, Avery thought, high enough now to see a pair of wings that were white as snow and looking peaked. The red tips were gone, faded along with the rest of each wing's magnificent color. They fluttered when she spoke to them, recognizing Avery, welcoming her as if they were her pets.

"Like the rest of me, you have been drained and diminished, but we're together now," she crooned, searching for a way around the lock that sealed the cage.

Although she was strong, the lock was six inches in diameter and made of tarnished silver. There was no way to tear it apart with her bare hands. The cage bars were too close together for her wings to slide through. She had hit a snag and shouted a curse.

With action all around him, Rhys dodged two sets of fangs and parried with a successful double thrust that took out two of the young vampires. In the thick of the fighting that had broken out on the cavern floor, his Maker raged.

Enlightenment brought Rhys pain. More of the story of Castle Broceliande was needed, and yet those answers weren't going to be found here tonight.

Revenge would have been sweet, Rhys supposed. It would have been warranted, and dished out in honor of his brethren who had also been fooled. But that would have to wait. He had lost sight of Avery. In a show of strength he never would have imagined her fragile body contained, she had lunged away, her tracks covered by a mob of creatures for whom fighting was a drug.

She had jumped and disappeared into the upper regions of the cavern. Clearly, Avery had found what she came here to find. The desire to be with her at that moment had been fierce and was now lost.

"Avery!" he shouted, fighting oncoming creatures with both hands and listening for her reply with senses that had been tuned to her thought frequency.

There was no reply.

He fought harder, spinning in place, slashing at the oncoming tide of creatures with his knife and his sharp wooden stake, two weapons most of these monsters could not stand against, weapons wielded by a Knight who had, like a few of these creatures, been a man before answering the call of a higher power. Or so he had believed.

Another vampire exploded in a blast of foul-smelling gray ash, which left him a few seconds of breathing room. When he turned back to the scene taking place at the heart of the cavern, his Maker was no longer in sight.

“Have you run?” Rhys whispered, searching for a glimpse of red robes among the rest of the blood that was flying in every direction. Monsters were tearing monsters apart. All the humans were dead.

Very few of the two dozen guests were left standing, and Mordred wasn’t among them. Three of his vamp guards were biting everything in sight. As talented as Avery and Rhys might have been, the demons present at this shindig had the upper hand. A demon’s touch was a sampling of the fires they hailed from.

Time was of the essence. He had to find Avery and get her out of here. Demons and vampires would be ravenous for a pale angel from the opposite camp, and they would soon tromp the vamps.

He glanced up.

The cages these monsters used to seal off their goods would have presented a problem for anyone. Avery’s wings were in one of them. Did he want to know what kind of things were in the rest?

His blood sang in his veins with unparalleled sadness for whatever those cages hid. His heart ached. Still, if he couldn’t reach Avery, there were demons to face. He’d have to keep them off her back. Demons exemplified the worst of the world's nightmares.

"Time to change things up."

Rhys shook his head and rolled his shoulders, allowing his sigils to blister his back. The burn caused a secondary reaction that spread in his body like wildfire.

Muscles twitched and shuddered as they elongated and stretched to form new shapes. Sinewy ligaments snapped to allow the quick expansion of bone. Catching the burn, his hands began to shake. Fingers tightened on the weapons they held until the hilt of the silver blade also picked up the heat.

His hair grew with incredible speed and now reached his shoulders, falling over him in curtains of brown and gold. He tore off his jacket and opened his borrowed shirt to give his arms room to move.

Rhys's human semblance was peeling back layer by layer to make room for the thing hidden inside, the thing nestled at his core that the creatures he'd called his Makers had manufactured and then set free. A fiery being so impossibly strong that the cavern couldn't contain his anger for what these monsters had done to his angel. He was the Guardian now, protecting his own.

When he walked forward, the remnants of fighting ceased. As he lifted his head, the remaining two vampires backed into the shadows. Rhys trained his attention on the demons, both of which refused to clear his path to the grate.

When he became aware of Avery's struggle overhead, he signaled for the demons to approach him, wearing a smile on his weathered, acutely chiseled face. They came at him, one after the other, hissing curses with their webbed hands raised.

But demons had no place here. Although they were below the surface of London's streets at the moment, and in a darkness similar to the place they'd sprung from, hell's citizens were weaker in any kind of light, and were blinded by his.

They didn't reach him. A long silver blade caught them from behind and impaled them both like meat stuck on a skewer.

"You didn't presume to think I'd leave you here to fight alone?" his Maker asked, effortlessly tossing both devilish creatures, each as large as he was, into the fire in the grate. "Have I taught you nothing…Rhys, is it, these days?" the black-haired vampire added, wiping the demon blood coating his sword on the front of his flowing robes.

"In fact, perhaps you taught me too well, vampire," Rhys returned, moving forward in a blur of speed.

Chapter 23

Avery kicked at the lock on the cage until she had to give up. Below her swinging perch, Rhys was speaking, and she didn't need three guesses to figure out who he was speaking to.

She was afraid for him. The castle's creatures were terribly strong, and although she had seen to it that none of them could return to their home, she hadn't succeeded in finding her captors once they had abandoned their posts. Realizing she was about to escape from their torturous chains, all three had disappeared as completely as if they had never existed in the first place.

She looked down.

Ten feet separated the Knight and his Maker. They both held flashing silver blades. She had to hurry up and get her wings. There was no way she'd leave the wings here. No way she'd be separated from them again.

And Rhys…her glorious Knight, sans the shining armor of a former age, had changed. He was Rhys, and yet not

Rhys, taller, leaner, incredibly sculpted and lethal. An aura of light hugged his outline. His sharp silver blade shone with a supernatural sheen. She had only seen this kind of transformation once before, and had been as awed as she was right then. Rhys de Troyes, always handsome, always dangerous, looked every bit like an angel. Her soul pined for him, fluttering the way her wings did.

Those wings were pulsing in time with her escalating heart rate. Avery whispered assurances to them as she thought hard about what to do. Rhys could take care of himself. He had grudges to work out. Her wings were helpless and trapped.

Must hurry...

As the silver blades glinted on the cavern floor, an idea came to her. Avery drew out her knife. The iron cages had been conceived of the same darkness she had escaped from so long ago, and were Mordred's handiwork, no doubt. The knife in her hand had once been his property.

Her scars and wounds picked up the pulse as she inserted the tip of her blade into the lock and raised her face to the carved rock ceiling. "Let this work!" she shouted, putting all of her energy into the plea. "Open this damn cage!"

Using both hands, she twisted the blade clockwise. The mechanism turned as the blade snapped in two. The lock's sealed magic had been unraveled by whatever kind of spell the iron contraption recognized in Mordred's old blade.

The gate swung open. Bars gaped. Uncertain of what do next, or how to reattach the wings after so much time had gone by, Avery stuck out a hand to touch the snowy-white feathers as the clang of two swords meeting reached her from the below.

Rhys parried, holding off a thrust that would have made him a brochette. But fighting was absurd, really, when both he and his Maker knew no sword in the world could terminate a Blood Knight's charmed life. There was only one way to do that.

Rhys's off switch was unknown to him, that knowledge placed in the possession of some other creature that could have resided anywhere on the planet. What were the chances that special soul was in the room with them here? Maybe it would have been present if Mordred had expected Rhys instead of Avery. Lack of foresight had proved to be another of the Maker's mistakes.

The same kind of eternally unending life span couldn't be said in regard to a vampire's existence, in spite of how old and talented the one fighting Rhys was. Vampires could be killed. He had killed plenty of them.

The creature Rhys had called his Maker wasn't fighting with all his considerable might, aware of those discrepancies. So what was the point of all the playacting? Was this meeting of swords merely a ritual to make them both feel better about the way things had turned out?

Letting this black-haired beast escape wasn't in the cards, but if Mordred were to be killed, too many answers would die with him. After surviving...thriving, actually... for centuries—maybe even a few centuries prior to the creation of the Blood Knights—Mordred's story had to be a good one. How had those three become three of the first vampires? What came before that event? Which one of them had started the whole vampire thing rolling?

Rhys pondered that maddening puzzle, as well as the way to accomplish a takedown without dusting this strong vampire. Problem was, he couldn't concentrate fully when Avery was suspended from a cage above him in a long-awaited reunion with her wings. He shared her hopes. His heart rate continued to interact with hers, matching hers beat for beat the way it had ever since their bodies had joined together so blissfully.

Her shout had come to him above the slicing arc of Mordred's sword. "Let this work! Open this damn cage!" Avery had pleaded just moments ago.

She had found her wings in this damp, murky cave, and only one thing kept him from her.

Rhys again crossed blades with the creature that didn't deserve the mercy Rhys had wanted to show him.

His Maker stepped back suddenly, lowered his sword and gave Rhys a small, quick nod. When he looked up, Mordred wore a smug smile. "I can't destroy that which I've created, Knight, and that fact has been my deepest nightmare and the bane of my overextended existence. I made you too well, it seems."

He turned his back, waited a beat and added, "Neither will you kill me, I suppose, since I hold the key to your past, and I have now given your friend the very thing she has dearly sought. Wouldn't you agree I should get some kind of credit for that?"

Rhys's heart boomed in his chest. His arms flexed and tightened with the need to run this wise, wily creature through. Nevertheless, he couldn't do that when the freak's back was turned. There was a possibility he wouldn't have dealt that death blow anyway, not without knowing why he and his brothers hadn't turned out the same way these Makers had.

Conflicted, he watched Mordred disappear into a tunnel. Then Rhys looked up at Avery, who was smiling down at him with the loveliest smile he had ever seen. It was an expression of victory, like a ray of sunlight in a dark place. It was like a sign from the heavens Avery had fallen from that they were on the right track in whatever would happen now.

The cavern was empty. The market's multitude of hovering Shades hadn't joined in the fight. They had quickly deserted their posts after the first sword had been drawn. This unexpected disappearance was another puzzle in a long line of them. Rhys had roots to dig up and past transgressions to investigate. Avery's mission had been accomplished, but he had an eerie premonition that everything wasn't so perfect and that more rough times lay ahead.

"Need help?" he called to Avery, expecting her to wave off the offer.

"Yes. They're sick, weak, white," she said. "We have to get them out."

"We carry them along the street and hope people don't stare?"

His remark hadn't been serious, but Avery took it that way.

"I've seen stranger things. It's likely you have, too," she said.

"You're right about that," Rhys noted, searching for the mechanism hoisting the cages.

But something nagged at him again, interfering with his image of Avery uniting with her wings. His sigils hadn't lost their fire. His hold on his blade tightened.

"Trouble," he said, scanning the cavern for the location of the darkness the marks on his back were warning him about.

Avery stilled. The chains quieted. Rhys heard a whisper and looked questioningly at Avery, whose gaze slid to the cage next to where she still clung.

What was in those two other cages? What other hellish atrocities had this black market, hosted by his Maker, dug up?

"Avery," he said, and that was all she needed to understand what he was asking her to do.

With one more glance at her wings, she planted her feet

on the bottom bars of the cage and rocked until the cage began to swing sideways—enough so that she could see into the cage next to hers.

When the momentum stopped, she looked down at Rhys with an expression of horror that stripped away some of the joy of her long-awaited reunion with her wings. From the look alone, Rhys was sickened with dread.

Avery quelled the sudden chill of seeing what was in that cage with a warning to Rhys, who was looking for a way to join her. She shook her head, hoping that would make him take heed of the expression on her face.

A gaunt creature with long stringy hair the color of Mordred's velvet robes lay curled up on the cage floor, clad in tattered strips of cloth. Pale, bare legs contrasted with the cold iron of the bars. Burn marks lashed this creature's skin in huge welts that were proof of Otherness. Like other beings of supernatural origins, this creature couldn't stand the touch of any kind of metal.

The half-starved creature was sick and very out of place in the darkness of the cavern. An almost nonexistent glimmer of light emanated from it that Avery recognized.

"Fae," she whispered. "Don't worry. You will soon be free."

The upturned face was all bone and stretched skin. Ice-pale eyes peered at Avery from beneath faded red lashes. Avery saw recognition in those eyes. This creature, whose species dwelled in the Earth's green spaces, knew what an angel was.

Mordred had outdone himself with this elite selection of treasures. Angel wings. Fae. And from the sound of the rising growl on the other side of her, a wolf. Not just any wolf, but a large one, rare and black as the night.

Rhys was already lowering the cages one at a time. First

to reach the ground, Avery urged him to hurry. But the rattle of the cages and the clank of chains brought shudders that rocked her. Those shudders also ran through the Fae creature. The wolf howled.

Intuition needled her insistently, along with an extraordinary sense of kinship with these Others that wasn't to be explained.

"Get them out," she said to Rhys. "Get them out first."

Rhys freed the wolf. But Avery wondered what that wolf was going to do in the city and how it would find its way to a place better suited to it.

When she looked up, Rhys had the Fae creature in his arms. She couldn't tell if that creature was male or female, but that was often the way with elementals.

"Go," she said. "Hurry. I'll be all right."

Rhys didn't move. She hadn't actually expected him to follow any directive that didn't involve her safety. The Guardian was guarding her. How she loved him for that.

She had always loved him.

"Will your wolf detective help them? Can he help?" she asked.

"He will."

"I'll follow. Please, Rhys. Help them."

He understood this, with or without her suggestion. When he turned from her, Avery's heart sank. She now counted on seeing him, being near to him. Each step he took toward the tunnels hurt her in ways she'd never dreamed she would feel again.

She withheld a shout that would have given form to that hurt. Then she reached out a hand and issued another directive to her almost lifeless wings. One feather at a time, they began to spread—as much as they could within the confines of the cage. With a big intake of breath, Avery climbed back inside the cage and slipped to her knees. She tore off her jacket. Bare from the waist up, she rolled onto her back, on top of the outstretched feathers, and prayed for a miracle.

"Come to me now," she said softly but adamantly, and felt the first piercing sting of wing bones burrowing into her shoulder blades, seeking to reconnect with her spine.

Chapter 24

More monsters had not appeared. And there were too damn many tunnels.

Rhys strode swiftly through the rock maze of alleyways, following the distant scent of fresher air. The bundle he held didn't speak or move. Whatever this creature was, it was as light as one of Avery's feathers. Fae, Avery had said. In all his time on Earth, he had never seen one of them.

Red hair spilled over his arms. Bloodred. It was odd how that made him think of Griffin, one of his Blood Knight brethren, whose hair was a similar hue.

Now that he thought of it, the black wolf following him, whose growl reverberated in the space, had fur the color of another Knight's hair. Mason, who, with his black armor and shield, had once been known as the Obsidian Knight.

Shaking off those thoughts, Rhys reached a doorway to the street and found it standing open. Another strange detail. He expected vampires to be waiting. At the very least, the disappearing Shades. But the street was clear of monsters, unless some of the mortals passing the shadows where he stood met the standards for that category.

He had to get to Avery, but she had put the safety of others ahead of herself and had tasked him with seeing that through. He had to remember how strong she was, and that she had managed without him for centuries. She probably didn't need his help now, but that didn't matter. Avery was both the game and the endgame, for as long as she stayed.

Which might not be long now.

Tightening his hold on the Fae creature in his arms, he whispered, "Soon," and took off like a streak of lightning, leaving the shadows, needing to find a safe place where this little Fae creature could heal and thrive.

After that, Rhys promised himself, he and Avery had some unfinished business to tend to that didn't include making love like two creatures possessed.

Well, he quickly amended…maybe they could get the mad, passionate love thing out of the way first and get to that other business afterward. He was all for that, because how else were two immortals going to say goodbye? With a handshake. A big hug?

Goodbye...

The word made his heart tank.

The sensation of her wings reattaching was similar to being impaled by spikes. In a good way. Because it was nothing compared to the horror of having them sliced off.

As she lay on the floor of the cage, waiting for the process to be completed and hoping it actually could, the sound of the rush of blood in her ears and the tearing noises of her wings working their way into her skin left her tight-lipped and breathless.

She gripped the horrid iron bars for support. The pain of that touch added to her determination to see that this deadly game had a satisfactory culmination. Rhys had let his Maker go, and that was unacceptable. Imagining the damage that sucker had done since using his knife on her left her feeling twice as ill.

Still, the fact that Rhys had cared more about what happened to her than his own moment of revenge meant a lot. It spoke volumes about the fact that Rhys was starting to sense they had more than a brief connection and that something much more substantial and important lay behind their insatiable attraction to each other.

Insatiable. Yes...

They hadn't spoken more than a few hundred words to each other since they'd met, yet somehow their blood bond made it seem like they had been lovers for years. Maybe they could have had more time together if she hadn't held a grudge against everything that had come out of Broceliande. She regretted now that all those years had been wasted.

Pain and all, she wanted Rhys with her. Wings or no wings, she desired Rhys more than she ever had. But was that enough to change things? Change the ending of this story?

"You must take me to the Grail," she said aloud.

She would have to take the Grail back to the Creator of the Heavens, where it would remain safe forever.

The hurt didn't stop when the wings stilled. Tentatively, Avery sat up and rolled her neck. The wings fluttered weakly, unable to tap the blood flow they needed without time to adjust.

"Time to go."

She used the bars to get to her feet, having forgotten how heavy the wings were after being without them for so long. She picked up her jacket, though it was of no use at the moment and couldn't accommodate her new shape.

"Half naked it is, then," she muttered.

Rhys had reached the street. She sensed it. His thoughts were for her. The heat of his rapt attention was a welcome temperature change from the icy cold of the hellish cavern they had invaded tonight. Rhys would be waiting. She had to reach him.

"On my way to you," she whispered, afraid to speak her mind in that way when leaving him eventually would be hard. She wasn't sure she could leave him when her mission, in spite of how long it had taken, depended on her leaving the world that had become Rhys's playground. He was tethered here, without his own means of escape, forever.

She wobbled as she exited the cage and staggered forward, balancing the weight on her back. The whole black market carried with it a particularly foul stench, and yet parts of the scene didn't make sense. Where were the monsters? Why had they so easily been bested? Why had Rhys let the red-robed ringmaster go?

"We'll have to clean that up," she said to the wings. "Tighten those loose ends. It's what we do. What we have always done, even if it's too late to stem the tide of Broceliande's madness."

Rhys had been part of that madness. He and his Blood Knight brethren had proved that some mistakes can turn out well.

"Avery."

Rhys was calling. He was showing his respect by using the most current name she had chosen for herself, when having her real name would allow him extra power over her…a power he didn't need and never would, because she was fully onboard and bending to his will, to his call, by picking up speed.

* * *

There was havoc on the streets, Rhys discovered as he turned the corner that led to the penthouse. Sirens blared in the distance. People were stopping to look for the cause, alerted to the added pressure in the night that Rhys felt in his bones.

He had to be careful about being seen. The Fae creature in his grasp didn't look anything like a human being. He/she was moving, lifting an androgynous head, encouraged by the streetlights and the damp air after the close, airless cavern.

There was no way, with a clear conscience, he could set this delicate creature down in London. The city itself would eat this Fae alive, if the Shades and vamps didn't get there first.

The black wolf's presence pinged his nerves. Like another shadow, it tagged along behind him, a creature also out of its element. Avery's struggle to run was another constant pressure that sparked his nerve endings, as if her struggle were his.

Hell, he had become a magnet for the displaced. Nevertheless, he wouldn't have had it any other way.

Police cars were arriving on the block, coming fast, their shrill sirens and flashing lights polluting the night and instilling in Rhys a sense of impending chaos. Trouble lay ahead. Had the vampires regrouped near the building's front door?

Having had his fill of trouble, the only way he could see to avoid it was going up to the rooftops he had lately become so familiar with. From there, he could wait for the trouble to disappear. Avery would find him there. She would know where to look, and she would be in need of an escape route now that she had transformed. With those wings, she'd be a standout in any kind of company. *No more hiding. No more need for tattoo parlors.*

"We have become a little circle of freaks," he said to the frail bundle in his arms that clung to his neck.

As he began to climb, Rhys sincerely hoped monsters had nothing to do with whatever those cops were chasing, and that London's mortal population would never know the truth about the predators among them that had a foothold right beneath their feet.

But as he climbed, he heard a familiar voice say, "Never let it be said that a Shade can't help to turn the tide."

It was the Shade from the rooftop. Contrary to everything he'd believed, that Shade, along with its kind, might have caused the commotion on the street so he could get safely away.

Could that be true?

Damn it. The night, Rhys wanted to shout, had become one spectacular contradiction.

The squeal of sirens made Avery's muscles seize. Burdened as she was, she reached the rooftop before Rhys did and watched him climb to meet her.

"Not vamps this time," she said by way of greeting when he faced her, wanting to say so much more without daring to, trying not to be jealous of the way he held the bundle in his arms.

"No," he agreed. "Not vamps. Not this time."

The heat that radiated from him drew her closer. What a picture she presented, half dressed and with her wings folded up.

"You've lost your coat," he noted lightly, when the situation called for seriousness. They weren't in the clear. They were hovering on the brink of chaos at the moment, with the city loud and crime laden beneath the rooftop.

"I like the new look," he added softly. "It's spicy."

Afraid to address the grin that played on his lips in spite of everything they had been through, Avery turned her head. Rhys was used to fighting. He had only moments ago found out his Maker was a fiend, yet his outlook remained optimistic.

He was a delicious sight, with his shiny hair in tangles and his arms full of black-market Fae booty that those demons had salivated over.

From their rooftop perch, and underscoring the sirens, she heard the low, guttural growl of the black wolf that couldn't have followed Rhys's upward climb. That wolf was the only member missing from this little group of tonight's survivors, and against its wolfish nature, seemed to want to join in.

"Do they work?" Rhys asked her.

Avery shook her head, understanding the question. "Not yet. The wings need more time."

"Can you help to fight our way out of London, if it comes to that?"

"I can, yes. Do you have a way to help the creature you're holding?"

"All of us have to get out of the city. We can do that, now that you've found your wings and there's nothing to hold you here."

"And go where?" Avery asked, alerted to where Rhys was heading with this.

"Back to where it all began. I believe there might be some scores to settle."

"There's nothing left of that place," she said, giving him another piece of the puzzle he wouldn't yet be able to make into a cohesive whole.

Rhys was eyeing her intently. She knew he'd be going over hints of the truth that had emerged tonight in that dark cavern. As she watched, enlightenment began to reshape his handsome features, all of which once again resembled the Rhys she had first seen on the street.

"Nothing's left of Broceliande?" he finally asked. "You had something to do with its demise?"

"That castle could not stand. Not after..."

"That's where you must start the story," he said when she didn't finish her statement. "That's what I need to understand. You do get that? I have to know what happened there and how it involves you. I can't rest until I know."

"I once told you that you would be sorry about the truth."

"I believe I deserve to be sorry if that's what it takes to fill in the missing details of my past and yours. Won't you trust me with those details now that we know each other better?"

He didn't wait for her answer before he spoke again.

"We go. The Fae and the wolf go with us. There, they can be set free. Outside of the city, their folk can find them or they can find their way home. You are complete. That's what you said. You needed to be complete. Now I need the same thing."

Avery understood that kind of need. Rhys could make that journey with or without her, but he wouldn't find the truth he sought if she didn't let him see it. Besides, she'd be damned if she'd let him out of her sight.

Atonement was demanded of her for her part in what had taken place in the castle. The glint in Rhys's eyes demanded she fill him in. He was right. He deserved that. Other than Mordred, she was the only creature on Earth that could satisfy that need.

The wan creature in Rhys's arms stirred. A pair of huge eyes turned to Avery. The thin mouth opened and words came out. "You will be rewarded for taking me there," a soft-toned female voice announced. "This, I promise."

It was a lyrical voice with the consistency of trickling water. Easy on the ears. Joyous to the heart. Avery had heard voices like this before. More specifically, she had heard this one.

"You know the place of which we speak, Fae?" she asked.

"The white castle with a black heart."

"And how do you know that place?"

A breathy, hesitant reply came. "Were we not there together in that dark place, angel, pinned like bugs to a board?"

Rhys moved. He was trying to follow what was going on and not liking any of it.

"Yes," Avery said to the Fae creature. "That is where the dark masters took something precious from me."

"And from me," the Fae creature returned.

The next word tainted Avery's mouth with a sour taste before she spit it out. She would have given a lot to have avoided speaking it.

"Blood," she said. And the scars on her back ached with the remembrance of what that word meant.

The beautiful creature nodded her head once, and then, energy spent, nestled against Rhys's chest. Rhys's heart was beating as hard and as fast as Avery's was, still connected to hers as he looked back and forth from her to the dainty creature in his arms.

"So we go," Avery agreed. "It's time."

She strode to the rim of the roof purposefully and looked back. "I suppose we will have to fight our way out of here if those sirens mean anything. Shades and vampires probably made a mess of things on their way out of the cave, and people are scrambling to get out of the way."

"Not the Shades," he said. "And modern times call for desperate measures."

Avery knew he was remembering that his Maker had wanted her blood in that dark cavern. With the mention of blood now, he'd be looking for a connection.

Like her, however, he must have sensed that the danger on the streets was only faintly tinged with the supernatural. Crimes the mortals committed were not a Blood Knight's province, and therefore could be skirted without guilt. He would have been all over an aggressive vamp attack, so he was waiting, motionless. Perhaps he was sharing her next thought…about Mordred being out there somewhere, free to go where he pleased. And that Mordred wanted their souls.

In the face of more danger yet to come, somehow, and though it didn't seem possible, Avery loved Rhys even more for his show of patience as he walked toward her cradling the fair Fae creature in his arms.

His eyes were on her. Only her. And her heart sang with hope.

The black wolf was waiting for them when they reached the street. Sleek, strong and heavily muscled in spite of its recent captivity, that wolf joined their hunting party without getting too close.

"I know what you are," Rhys said to the wolf that wasn't merely an animal. Nor was it just a werewolf. It was an incredibly rare Lycan, black-pelted and regal. Able to shapeshift without a full moon and probably needing to retain its animal appearance due to the wolf's power to heal any wound Rhys hadn't yet seen.

There was no telling what this wolf looked like in its more human form, or if it could have survived Mordred's prison any other way than this. The feral growls that continuously rolled from its throat could easily be in reaction to the pain it had suffered at the hands of whoever had put it inside that cage.

Anger flared inside Rhys. His entire existence had been based on so many deceptions. Avery had been hurt behind those castle walls, and so, it seemed, had the Fae creature he carried that was still too weak to set down. Why hadn't the Fae been able to escape, if Avery had? The idea that such a delicate soul had been trapped for centuries behind iron bars made his stomach turn over.

Police sirens had stopped screaming by the time his boots touched asphalt. This meant the cops had made contact with their targets, and the Shades, if what he had heard was true, had instigated that distraction.

He and the others couldn't afford to be seen if they didn't need to jump in and fight. Avery was shirtless and had a pair of folded wings stuck to her back. A nonhuman being was tucked into his arms. The black wolf, larger than any those cops would have seen in their lifetimes, the Weres among them included, was tagging along. They could have made headlines or been the embodiment of a comic-book series.

Avery had drawn her knife. Half of a knife. Its blade had been broken, but it still gleamed menacingly under the streetlight.

"Let's hope you don't have to use that," he said.

Her eyes were alight with blue sparks. "The blade will heal itself in time, just like we do."

Rhys frowned, refusing to take the time to ask how that could happen. If Avery said it would heal, it would likely be so.

"More Shades," she hissed, stepping forward with a full display of the warrior she was, hands raised, face set.

"I'm fairly sure they aren't the problem, at least this time," he muttered, searching the shadows where Shades were gliding along the facade of the buildings en route to another location, ignoring the threat at their backs.

Avery's gaze met his. They turned in unison and, with the black wolf at their heels, took off to look for a safe way out of the city.

Chapter 25

"What the..." DI Crane said when he returned to the penthouse.

"We need a lift," Rhys explained. "Obviously we can't be seen."

"Obviously," Crane agreed, taking in the strange gathering. His gaze stopped on the wolf by the windows. "Aren't you a little lost, my friend?"

"Long story," Rhys said, understanding that Weres were territorial and never breached the borders of another pack without consequences. "Suffice it to say that none of these folks would be here if they didn't have to be. None of this was their choice."

The black wolf was quiet now as it eyed Crane.

"You can't shift back?" Crane asked, tuning in to the wolf with the internal radar all Weres possessed. "I see," he said moments later. "I'm sorry."

To Rhys he added, "How can I help?"

"Safe transport out of London. Tonight."

Crane's glance slid to the Fae female on the couch. He took in a big breath and let it out slowly before transferring his glaze to Avery, who had covered herself up by wrapping strips of cloth around her torso from pieces of Crane's shirts. He shook his head first, then said, "Hell, Rhys. Give me an hour and I'll take you out of here, myself."

Rhys saw Avery relax. She didn't speak.

"I'm thinking we'll need a van. A large one," Crane said thoughtfully. "Where are we going?"

"France."

"In that case, we'll need a plane. Can I know why we're going to France?"

The room was quiet, everyone's attention on the detective.

"All right," Crane said, breaking the silence. "I'll need two hours and a short flight plan." He headed to the door mumbling ridiculous phrases punctuated with curses about supernatural creatures eventually being the death of him, even though he was one of them.

"That went better than I thought it would," Rhys said.

Avery remained silent.

The black wolf growled menacingly.

But Rhys had to appreciate how many things had worked in their favor tonight, and how many things in this world weren't much like they had always seemed.

They were let out of the van Crane had commandeered several miles from the small French airport cops often used for going back and forth from England to France when other forms of transportation weren't possible. After assurances that they would be okay, Crane had left them on their own.

It was very late, or very early. Rhys could no longer tell how much darkness was left until the arrival of a new day.

The presence of the others accompanying him messed with his inner clock.

In order to keep out of sight, they had to hurry, and moved silently through the dark. Castle Broceliande had been set deep in the secluded forest of the Bras de Fer on French shores. Back when he'd first seen it, there had been no reason for the castle to have been guarded. The creatures that had strolled its lavish gardens would have been reason enough for others to have avoided such a place. It was often accepted, back then, that royalty often kept to themselves.

He wondered what he'd find now, and how he really felt about going back there. Broceliande was a black spot on his memory. He had trepidations about it even now.

As they walked, he remembered other things he had put from his mind about those times. The images were vivid enough to touch.

Like his brothers, he had accepted the invitation to the castle on the assurances of its reputation for bestowing favor upon knights in service to the crown. The invitation to attend those who dwelled at the castle had been written on costly parchment, delivered into his hand by a handsome young squire.

He had been intrigued.

He had found the white stone edifice beautiful. It was surrounded by perfumed gardens. Tiered fountains sang watery songs of welcome. Rhys recalled thinking how strange it was that he seemed to be the only guest, and that no other people milled about, enjoying the rare beauty of the place. Odder yet was how no one waited in the great hall to greet him.

As he walked, Rhys winced at his own naïveté. He wasn't sure why the memories were so painful. After all, he had agreed to the pact that had been offered to him there, even if not completely willingly, at first. In truth, he had believed in the necessity of the offer the castle's occupants had finally made him.

The strange countenances of those who dwelled at Castle Broceliande were, he had thought, part of some sort of charade. All courts loved games. They had come for him at dusk. Three beautiful people, perfect to the last detail. Jewels glittered at their wrists and throats, highlighting pale, perfect flesh. Three people who, it seemed, slept the daylight hours away, only to rise at sundown…a fact that hadn't seemed to matter since his questioning intelligence had not seen through their disguises.

Physically, he had fit right in, with his tall, sinewy physique sculpted to hard muscle on the fighting fields. But Castle Broceliande's occupants, who may indeed have been royal by birth and were as handsome as fallen stars, had been no longer human, he had found out tonight in that cavern. And it had been no game they played.

Rhys tilted his head back to look up at the moon. Even so far from that distant place in his memory, the chill persisted each time the image of the castle's inhabitants came to him.

How had he not known what they were? Not guessed?

Those white faces. The scarlet lips he now knew had covered unnaturally sharp teeth. The thick red liquid swirling in their golden goblets…

In that windowless castle, he had been handed a challenge, a quest, and he had paid for its acceptance with his life. In return for their favor, he was given the opportunity to behold the holiest of all relics. Whoever viewed this relic, legend foretold, would be blessed. Whoever drank from the chalice would be resurrected, as the Grail's original bearer had been. Born again.

He had sipped red liquid from that chalice, as had his hosts. The difference was that he had been made immortal, but with his soul intact. And those he had called his

Makers had become creatures that later would come to be known as vampires.

When Rhys looked up, he and Avery were alone. The Fae creature, so recently in his arms, had disappeared. The black wolf was gone.

"We're close," Avery said. "Not everyone is as strong as you or I, or as happy to be here."

"Hell, Avery, I'm not too happy about it."

She nodded. "Yet you asked for the truth, and this is where you'll find it."

The scenery was green, forested and dense. There were no roads leading to this place, nor well-used pathways cutting swaths through the foliage. Rhys studied the forest by the light of a moon tilted low in the sky. Morning wasn't far off.

"You must hate this," he said to Avery. "Returning here."

"I have made some peace with it. More peace will follow."

"When?"

"When you see the truth and love me still."

His heart was racing again. Blood pounded in his ears. Avery had used the word *love.*

Light shone from her—all those little dancing particles, so like stardust. But when her mission was completed, she would leave him. She would be welcomed by the bigger light, and he'd be alone again, in the dark.

"We both have demons to slay," Avery said.

Rhys nodded. "Your mission is nearly complete."

He again took in his surroundings, noting the wild tangle that probably hid a giant pair of gates.

"Let's finish your mission, Avery. Let us do that first, before setting foot in that place."

She came closer, looked up at him. "Where is the Grail, Rhys?"

He countered. “Why don’t you know?”

“You are my bond with the Seven. I only see the chalice through your eyes, and you have never been to the Grail’s final resting place.”

“What bond?” he asked. “How would you know I’ve never been there? Explain.”

“I can’t. Not yet. You…”

“Yes. You’ve said before I won’t like the truth. But that’s no excuse now. We’re here, Avery. We’re very near to those blasted gates and I am the only one of us who doesn’t know what that really means.”

She continued to stare up at him, glowing from within like the first time he’d seen her. Confusion creased her brow. He thought there was a delicate pink tint to her cheeks, something he hadn’t seen there before.

“All right,” she conceded warily. Her wings, still folded tightly to her back, fluttered as if ruffled by a breeze. “All right, Rhys.”

When she averted her face, Rhys felt the return of a foreboding chill that clashed with the burn of his sigils.

“I will give you more of the truth,” she said. “I was there.”

He could see how difficult this was for her.

“I know that,” he whispered.

“We were there together, you and I. At the same time. But I had been there longer. I wasn’t kept in a fine room with a servant to minister to my needs.”

“It’s your scream I hear in my memory,” he said when her voice quieted.

She nodded. “They lured me here with a golden promise. The three of them had found the Grail.”

“And you were sent to retrieve it.”

“But the castle’s occupants had used it. They had used the Grail to extend their lives.”

"The Makers."

"You called them that."

"How did they do that? How did they use the Grail for such a purpose?"

"By drinking each other's blood from that holy cup, drawn from their dripping veins, and assuming that blood was the key to their success."

Rhys blinked slowly, hating the image that presented him with. The red liquid he had seen in their goblets. The red fluid he had ingested. It was all coming back with a stark clarity.

"It worked," he said. "They became immortal."

"And in the process, lost their souls."

"What about you?" he pressed, closely observing Avery's reactions. He saw the shudder shake her and was sorry the truth he sought was so terrible.

"I was a source of new blood. With me, there was no need for more cannibalization. Light ran in my veins, when they had already sunk far into darkness."

The horror of that explanation forced Rhys to close his eyes. But he had already pieced some of this together.

"So they took your blood, drank your blood," he said in disgust.

"No. They couldn't take my blood for themselves. The blood of light could not help to heal the soulless ones. It made them sick when they tried. They barely survived. So they lured you here, as they had lured me and the other Knights in your brotherhood. All their promises were false and for nothing, except where the seven of you were concerned."

Rhys's sigils seemed to claw at his neck in preparation for what was to come, that awful announcement that contained the seed at the center of the truth he sought.

"They gave your blood to us?" he asked her.

She nodded. "The other Knights got an infusion of something else to go along with my blood and the blood of the Makers. The Makers were experimenting, you see."

"You said the other Knights. The other Knights got something else, as well."

"Yes. You," Avery said, hesitating before delivering the blow Rhys felt coming. "You, and only you, received only my blood, along with the blood of your Makers."

He couldn't take his eyes off her. Didn't dare speak.

"The blood of the angels is what you carry inside you to counteract the Makers' blood gift," she said. "Because of that, the souls of the Seven were retained when you all died as mortals and were resurrected as immortal. Because of the mistakes the Makers made by using an angel to further their agenda, they lost control of all seven of you."

She paused for a breath, mustering the courage to go on.

"Their only hope after that was to hide the Grail so no others could find it or use it against them. Only the Knights were strong enough to stand against them, but none of you knew the truth. You believed their lies and willingly obeyed the vows you had taken."

"We hid the Grail," Rhys said.

She nodded again. "You hid it well from the world, and also from them."

The picture that puzzle was presenting to him was a terrible one.

"We did their bidding," he said, sickened more by that idea.

She nodded. "And the blood they tampered with has kept the Grail from them all this time."

"They've been looking for it?"

"Oh, yes. For as long as I have."

"That's why one of them wanted more blood from you tonight, so that he could…"

"Start over. Find someone who could help them find the Grail, using me as the link to gain control over the world's most powerful holy relic. There's no telling what they might have done with it after that."

Rhys's mind was turning, spinning, to access more pieces of that puzzle.

"What about the Fae? She was there with you at the castle?"

"I think maybe her blood was used in one of you."

Again an image of Griffin, his blood brother, came to Rhys. Griff had red hair, like that Fae creature's. Griffin's eyes held a similar gleam.

"Damn," he muttered, without speaking the rest of the stream of curses that came to his mind. "Damn them all to hell."

When he opened his eyes, Avery was there, close. Her words were as sharp as the knife she carried. Her fragrance was as sweetly unsettling as ever.

She said, "You beat them at their own game, Rhys. Once I have the Grail, you will be free of all that."

She had said the same thing before, only now it made sense. Mordred was after the location of the Grail he had lost. If Avery took it away, beyond the reach of any being tethered to the Earth, Mordred would never get his hands on it again. Maybe, eventually, the old vampire would stop looking.

"He will come here," Avery said, assessing his thoughts. "Mordred will find us here at Broceliande, if he isn't here already."

"Then we must see that he doesn't find what he seeks."

Avery's hand was on his sleeve, resting lightly. "You can find it? You can find the Grail? Take me there, Rhys. Make me welcome. The Grail has to be given up willingly. I'm finished with taking what others don't want to give up."

Rhys thought of his six brothers, now going by the names of Lance, Mason, Ladd, Christopher, Alexander, Griffin…and what they'd say about an angel taking over as Grail Guardian. He supposed that when Avery showed up they'd be as surprised as he had been.

All seven Knights had to be in accord in order to relinquish the vessel, but they didn't have to be present. Only with a full mental accord could the Grail be released from its place of repose.

He was already stripping off his coat and his shirt. Barechested, angry, wary of everything he'd heard tonight, Rhys offered his back to Avery while the power of the Blood Knights again surged to the surface.

Avery let out a breath. "The sigils are moving."

"The symbols on my back will lead us there," he said.

"All this time, your marks were a map," Avery whispered, tracing the scrolls with the tip of her finger.

Rhys knew that when he exposed that secret, the other Knights would be alerted and on guard. Mason LanVal, brother, Knight, Grail keeper, Guardian and the strongest of the Blood Knights, was the Grail's current champion. Some called him the Guardian of the Night.

Distantly, with nothing more than a thought and an angel's brief touch, Rhys felt Mason's attention turn his way. His sigils responded with a new flare of heat. Avery stepped back.

"Close," he said. "All this time, it was closer than anyone would have guessed."

Taking Avery's hand in his and calling on the power the Makers had mistakenly given him that had served his vows well, Rhys called up the thunder in his soul. With his sigils pulsing, he and Avery headed out to find where in France the Grail was hidden…knowing that place wasn't far.

Chapter 26

The wings on Avery's back fluttered softly, the life in them making a slow comeback. They still felt weighty, and she was no longer used to the need to balance them, which made walking difficult.

What was left of the night was cool. There was no breeze. She and Rhys walked for what seemed like hours, but that couldn't have been the case since dawn hadn't yet arrived.

Close, Rhys had said. The Grail was close by. She didn't like the possible repercussions of that. If Mordred was here and got wind of where they were headed, the next battle would be the worst. Spilling immortal blood on the chalice would bring down the wrath of the heavens, and no one, be it angel, Blood Knight or ancient vampire, would want to witness that.

She followed Rhys closely, observing how his skin gleamed in the moonlight. The dark, intricate marks on his neck and upper back continued to move, as if, like her wings, his marks were alive. But that had to be an illusion, she reasoned, since those symbols had been deeply etched into his skin.

She shelved the impulse to run her hands over all that fine molded flesh and tamped down the urge to run her tongue along the curved edge of each muscle's perfection. She tried to focus on what they might find ahead, but kept coming back to the way Rhys's golden-brown hair, longer now in his latest incarnation, softly caressed the ridges of his shoulders.

Who couldn't have noticed how gracefully fluid this Knight was in motion?

He had faced his Maker in that blasted cavern, and Mordred had chosen to run rather than go up against the sheer brilliance of this Blood Knight. All seven of the Knights, together at the same time, could have ruled the world if they had chosen to. People might have thought them gods. Instead, the Seven hugged the shadows, remained separated from each other and did their best to keep out of sight in an endless, ceaseless circle of life.

Rhys...

Rhys would walk this Earth forever.

When he slowed, Avery slowed with him. His head tilted. He was listening to a sound she strained to hear. The forest had grown thicker, making it impossible to see anything beyond the unending labyrinth of trees. She heard nothing at all, and quickly realized why Rhys had hesitated. It was the total absence of sound he was tuning in to. The forest had gone quiet. No hint of bugs. No birds. No rustle of leaves.

When Rhys stopped walking, Avery's alert system kicked into high gear. Her fingers tightened on the hilt of the knife she held ready at her side.

"We wait." His voice was low, like sifting gravel.

She didn't have to ask what they were waiting for. Avery also felt the soundless vibration of something moving in the periphery. That vibe didn't tell her whether the moving presence was going to appear, or if it would be on their side if it did. Mordred making an appearance would have fired off a hundred inner alarms. This was different.

Two deep breaths later, Avery recognized why. As the new vibration connected with hers, she muttered, "Knight."

"Yes," Rhys agreed without taking his attention from the trees. "Blood brother."

Relief was short-lived. The brother Rhys was speaking of was the least familiar to her of all of them. This warrior possessed the kind of power that enabled him to pass in the darkness undetected by all but a chosen few. Animals, birds and insects either feared him or became quietly reverent when he drew near. This was the raven-haired brother Rhys had called Guardian of the Night. It seemed now that he was also the Keeper of the Grail.

Instinctively, Avery moved closer to Rhys without sheathing her knife. If, due to the nature of her quest, they weren't welcome here, she hoped to regain enough of her balance to make a convincing statement to the contrary.

"Avery," Rhys said with a nod of his handsome head. "It's all right. I promise."

With tight, cautious control over her nerves, Avery watched and waited for another of Broceliande's creatures to show himself.

When he did, the impact of his appearance drove the breath from her lungs.

Rhys didn't have time to hold out a hand in greeting. Mason LanVal, much changed since they last saw each other and more formidable than Rhys remembered, stood in front of them with a finger held to his lips.

They had faced so many battles together in the past, always fighting side by side. Seen here, wearing jeans and a faded blue shirt, the image Mason presented didn't begin to take the edge off the special being those clothes contained. No matter what else they both were, or how long they had been apart, Rhys was glad to see Mason.

Long, shaggy hair, the color of night, curtained a bronzed, angular face. Sinewy muscle threatened to tear apart the seams of his shirt. Light-colored eyes were trained on Rhys intently.

Avery whirled around to glance behind them. She also now perceived a further disturbance in the forest atmosphere.

Mason beckoned with a gesture that meant they were to follow him. No greetings were spoken. Not one word was said out loud.

"Come, brother," Mason silently sent. *"It would seem that we have more than one unexpected guest tonight."*

"The Maker," Rhys returned, glimpsing the trouble at hand.

"Maker?" Mason repeated the word as if it left a bad taste in his mouth. *"What a surprise. I just got rid of one of those bastards, and now we have another one? It would seem they lied to us, brother."*

"He wants what is hidden."

"Don't they all?"

Avery hadn't been introduced to Mason, and Rhys was sorry for that. Mason, however, didn't question Rhys's choice of a companion. None of the Seven would have purposefully brought danger to the Grail site, exposing the secrecy they had worked so hard and long to maintain.

"You got rid of another?" Rhys silently asked.

Mason nodded without explaining, saving that story for later.

Tonight, Mordred was going to push his luck, and Rhys was determined to end that vampire's reign, once and for all.

They walked on, Mason in front, Avery in the middle, Rhys bringing up the rear. He doubted if Mordred could sense them, since the lying beast wasn't yet close.

The forest thinned slightly when they came to a dirt road that was heavily rutted. Rhys raised an eyebrow when Mason turned.

"Wolves that way," Mason said aloud, waving a hand to the south. "The remains of an old chateau lie to the north."

"I take it we're going to the chateau," Rhys said. "You live there?"

Mason shook his head. "It's where I found the other one."

Rhys said, "The other Maker?"

"Vampire maker," Mason said. "Isn't that what they became?"

"So you know about that." It was the first time Avery had spoken.

Mason's gaze drifted to her. "I know far more than I'd like to, angel."

Avery didn't respond unfavorably to the intensity of Mason's attention. It was likely, Rhys thought, she wasn't often intimidated. But then, her blood ran in Mason's veins as well as in Rhys's. As with himself, part of Mason's strength was due to that blood.

Standing tall, with her bare arms tense and her hands at her sides, she said, "Does the item you've hidden draw them here without the bloodsuckers knowing the reason?"

"Perhaps," Mason replied.

"I have come to take it away," Avery said.

"I know that," Mason returned. "I've wondered how long it would take one of you to get here."

Rhys wasn't quite as taken aback by that disclosure as

he should have been. Through the marks carved into him that connected all the Knights, blood to blood, Mason must have discerned their approach and the reason for this visit. The Grail's Guardian had been waiting a long time.

"I have seen you," Mason said to Avery as he started walking along the old road.

Avery was silent. She was contemplating Mason's remark.

"Or thought I had seen you," Mason amended. "I see now it wasn't a dream."

"You will let me take it?" Avery asked. Her question was backed by a steely determination to counter any argument Mason might put up.

"Hell, I will gladly hand the damn thing over," Mason said, "if it means a few moments of peace."

"Don't you mean millennia?" Rhys suggested.

"Oui," Mason agreed. "Haven't we all wondered what a long, lengthy span of peace would be like, even while knowing we must move on to other things?"

The first distant sound reached them before they had gone far, echoing in the rapidly diminishing dark with a familiar, haunting chill.

"Wolves," Rhys said.

Mason turned toward the echo. "A warning that company has arrived."

Avery strode to the edge of the road. "Which will we find first? Mordred or the dawn of a new day?"

"Mordred," Mason said with a glance at Rhys, but Mason wasn't responding to Avery's question. He was simply repeating the name Avery had spoken and frowning over the implications of what that name meant.

Whatever was coming their way was going to have to be postponed, however, because the sky, seen through the branches, had lightened several shades.

Reading his concern, Mason said, "A fang bearer won't be able to handle the sun. Still, what's left of that old place in the north since it burned has plenty of holes for him to hide in."

"Burned?" Avery said.

"A bad mistake on the part of its former night-loving occupants helped me to clean the nest of bloodsuckers out," Mason briefly explained.

Rhys understood that another of the three Makers had been ruling that nest at the time. *Bastard* is what Mason had called that one…which meant that besides Mordred, there was still one Maker left of the three. The female. What were the odds that female had killed herself, according to the original plan, when neither of her companions had adhered to their vows to the Seven?

"So we go there after daybreak and find him," Avery said.

"I'm afraid that won't suit me, angel," Mason said. "I would prefer to look my enemy in the face. I'd like answers and to know where the last Maker is."

Mason again looked to Avery with a question. "Did Mordred do that to you?"

He was noting her scars and how many edged the strips of cloth she had wound around herself.

She turned to Rhys. "You didn't let the others know about me?"

"I've kept your secrets," Rhys replied. "You were adamant about that."

Their eyes met, held. What he saw flickering there made Rhys take a step toward her. They had come a long way in such a few short days, and tonight had been particularly eventful. Avery's shoulders were hunched, as if her wings weighed her down, and fine lines of weariness still surrounded her eyes. He wished he could ease her burden.

His head came up when another sound split the silence of the night. “Wolves again. Closer this time.”

“Come.” Mason backed to the center of the road. “I have a place for you to stay where she will be safe.”

Rhys didn’t bother to argue with that. Mason had formed his own opinion of Avery and what she could handle. The black-haired Guardian knew what her scars meant. The sheer number of them would have told him exactly what kind of fighter she was. Mason was merely being polite.

Rhys decided, as he observed Mason, that his blood brother couldn’t have received Fae blood along with his dose of Otherness. There was an intrinsic fierceness to Mason that was more like…wolf.

Like a rare black wolf.

Rhys craned his neck to see beyond the trees bordering the road, scenting the distant wolves and wondering again if those animals recognized something similar to themselves in Mason LanVal’s DNA.

All the speculation was forgotten, however, when the sudden awareness of a vampire presence washed over him like the icy tide of an oncoming plague.

The look of surprise on Rhys’s face quickly faded when Avery’s eyes again met his. If they had expected normal behavior from a nest of vampires controlled by a powerful ancient immortal Prime, they wouldn’t have been ready for what was fast approaching along with the early light of dawn. But everyone here understood what a Prime named Mordred was capable of.

Avery straightened as the buzz of her inner anxiety returned.

“He’s turned them into superfreaks,” Rhys muttered, taking a protective stance next to her.

“Fae,” she said. “He must have fed his vamps Fae blood.”

"Wolf blood would be toxic to the undead," Mason added.

Unless it was given prior to a mortal's final breath, Rhys thought, still watching Mason carefully.

"So, with a little Fae in them, what can we expect?" Rhys said.

"Daywalkers." Avery raised what was left of her broken blade. "Bloodsuckers able to tolerate some sunlight and negotiate their way through a forest."

"Mon dieu," Mason muttered with a perfect French accent. "The other one said he had watched his companions die."

"Liars. All of them," Avery remarked. "No one knows that better than I do. They lived. All of them lived."

Rhys had closed his eyes. "North. They are heading north."

"And so, it seems, are we," Mason said.

Their sprint through the trees was silent. They trod the earth lightly, even in boots. Avery had recovered some of her flagging energy. Her body felt feverish, as if the wings were providing heat.

Mason's knowledge of this area gave them an advantage. If they could beat Mordred's vampires to that chateau and keep them from finding shelter when the sun grew too hot for even their Fae blood to endure, the vamps would be trapped.

Depending on how many suckers Mordred had brought with him, three powerful immortals designed for fighting could cut out that little army's heart. And Mordred would face the wrath of his alchemical creations.

Running felt good and served to lift Avery's spirits. There were no buildings here to search or to hinder their progress, and the road they traversed looked like it was seldom used. Her wings seemed lighter and less of a burden.

By the time Mason slowed, she figured they had gone three or four miles. Again, Mason held up a hand, then he pointed to a spot beyond the brush where the skeleton of a large building sat. The area smelled of smoke. The burned-out chateau's facade was mostly intact, with blackened walls and gaping holes where its windows had been. Its roof was gone. The upper story had caved in.

Dawn light did nothing to rid Avery of the bad feelings attached to this place, but they had succeeded in beating the vampires here.

Without much time left, they strode to what was left of the chateau. With their backs to the front steps, the three of them waited for the arrival of Mordred's twenty-first-century gang of fangers.

Chapter 27

They arrived in a bunch. Twelve vampires, without their leader. Mordred's minions. Stranger looking than usual when viewed by the rising light of a new day.

Rhys's fingers were glued to the stake in his hand.

"Rather disappointing turnout." The seriousness of Mason's features belied the light tone of his remark.

"Maybe they're just the welcoming committee," Rhys suggested.

"No. That's all there are," Avery said, as if he didn't already get that. "They're meant to be nothing more than a pain in our backsides."

"They certainly meet that requirement," Rhys agreed.

"An aperitif," Mason said. "Before the main course is served."

The blood-tweaked vampires stopped where the trees ended and the swath of old grass began. Rhys heard one of them whine eagerly for the fight that lay ahead. He got the impression, however, that they weren't completely sure about leaving the shade of those trees, and Rhys wondered if Mordred's newbies had been recently created for just such a purpose as this one.

"Big time waster when the ringmaster is a no-show," Mason muttered.

"Which begs the question of where he is," Rhys said.

"He wouldn't have known where to send these vampires if he hadn't followed us here," Avery aptly pointed out. "He must have stored these new monsters at..."

"Broceliande," Rhys finished for her.

He frowned, pondering the tactics Mordred may have dreamed up in order to remain behind the scene when he was very likely the strongest vampire in the world. One of an elite few, anyway. Still, vampires couldn't really harm any of the three immortals here, so what was the point in sending them?

Distraction? To keep them from what?

He struggled to comprehend what Mordred had in mind. What was it that beast had said to him in the cavern?

I can't destroy that which I've created, Knight, and that fact has been my deepest nightmare and the bane of my overextended existence. I made you too well, it seems.

All of a sudden, those words began to makes sense.

"He can't kill us," Rhys said.

"Of course not. We're immortal," Mason returned.

Rhys shook his head. "No. That's not all of it. Mordred can't kill us for some other reason."

"He doesn't yet have the Grail," Avery said.

"So why isn't he here?" Mason queried.

There had to be a reason Mordred wasn't joining his minions. If he couldn't kill any of the Knights outright, how did he plan on taking the Grail from them?

Coming up with that answer had to be postponed. The moment had come for the vampires to attack.

They came in a staggered line, baring their fangs and wielding dark blades. The blades were yet another unexpected anomaly in a long line of them. Still, no blade, cursed or otherwise, could seriously harm either of the beings beside Rhys, especially now that none of these gaunt bastards had Avery's wings in a cage.

The first of them ran for Avery. The poor bastards had another thing coming if they imagined she'd stand for being singled out. She moved forward to greet those fangs and adroitly fended off the attack with a slick sideways glide, followed by a practiced arc of her partially broken blade. Rhys heard the jagged blade strike bone…and they were one vampire down.

He and Mason strode forward together, forming a pattern they had long ago perfected in the holy wars that came to be known as the Crusades. Circle to the right, then come in from behind. One twist of the torso, another lunge, and three more vampires were dust.

Exploding vampires heralded the rising sun, but taking them down wasn't quite as easy as usual. These bloodsuckers' bodies had been tweaked by a master puppeteer. More effort was required to dust them, along with careful timing and a bit of sweat.

Rhys fought his way to Avery, surprised to find her wearing a tepid smile. She, too, had been created for fighting and was very near to completing her earthly goal. Avery, reunited with her wings, was a dangerous avenger. She might have been the best fighter present, and had nothing to lose.

Two more vampires were gone.

Six to go.

The sun was rising faster than Rhys remembered. Even after feeding on the Fae, these fanged opponents were visibly growing weaker. Their reactions had slowed. Haunted faces showed strain. Two more went down beneath Rhys's blade and another by stake.

That left four.

Two.

Mason's silver blade hummed wicked death songs in the early morning air.

"Mine," Avery whispered to him, facing the remaining vampires. She had done this before when claiming the right to a kill. Her need for vengeance appeared in the lines of determination on her beautiful face.

Rhys hesitated. Mason waited. Backing off, as Avery had requested, and staring at the exquisiteness of her skills.

Avery's wings were moving, quaking with a struggle to expand. As she sliced with her blade and whirled in a spectacularly fluid death dance, those wings began to open. But it was merely the stretching of a few feathers.

Beside Rhys, Mason made a surprised, appreciative sound. Some of the color he had seen in his dream-like image of Avery had returned. Blue feathers were still pale, perhaps only healed, yet their whiteness had gone, and they looked stronger.

Seeing the flutter of her wings, the last vampire standing growled in protest. Then it, too, was reduced to smoky gray ash.

Avery turned, still holding her blade…which was no longer a jagged shard, but whole again, just like she was.

She had been right, Rhys thought, about everything.

Avery scanned the area looking for other opponents without finding any. There was no scent of the master, the vampire maker, and that, too, was strange. Mordred would know why she and Rhys had come all this way and that the Grail was near. That madman had sent in his troops to deter the immortals from figuring out his next play.

Behind her, Rhys was anxious. The ground was covered with ash. Sunlight was spreading. From his vantage point near the steps of the old chateau, Mason LanVal was watching her.

"We can't wait much longer," she said to Mason. "The danger of keeping the chalice here grows with each minute we hesitate."

"The Maker hasn't yet shown his hand," Mason returned.

She lowered her blade and turned to Rhys. "How can he end you? What's the key to taking down an immortal? You and the brother who stands as a barrier between Mordred and what he wants?"

She inched forward to stress the importance of gaining this information. "Now is the time to share that detail, Rhys. It might be crucial."

He glanced to Mason, then nodded.

"Each Blood Knight has a counterpart soul responsible for turning us off, ending our existence once and for all. None of us know who that is, or where in the world our counterpart resides. We weren't expected to find those other souls, and aren't designed to meet."

After again glancing at Mason, Rhys continued. "Our Makers planted fail-safe switches in seven other souls who are ultimately responsible for dealing each Knight a final death blow if called into action."

She said, "How would they do that?"

"We don't know. After all this time, I doubt if those creatures housing the souls would know, either."

"What if…" She started over. "What if Mordred has found them and that's his plan for getting the Grail?"

"Those souls could be anywhere in the world, Avery. He wouldn't have allowed them to get too near to us."

"But you travel around," Avery argued.

"If we were close to those other souls, I think we would have recognized them somehow, in some small way. Besides, he was surprised to see me in that cavern."

"Then maybe," she said thoughtfully, "the rise in monster activity in cities like London has been carefully choreographed to lure you and the other Knights to places where those hidden souls aren't located. Maybe Mordred didn't want you to glean any information about what he was up to, hoping to keep you out of his way."

"He'd have to face me when he came for the Grail," Mason said.

Avery nodded. "He lured me here with the wings. He exposed them to me in order to relieve me of more of my blood. Blood for what? Creating more Blood Knights? Enough of them to overpower the world and set Mordred up as its ruler? All he'd need to make more of you would be two things—angel blood and the Grail. He could start over, hoping the direction of his new Knights wouldn't get out of hand."

The idea seemed right. Everyone here realized those things were viable possibilities. Avery could see them mulling that over.

Mason said, "I think it's feasible Mordred has company and isn't in this alone, whether or not he has found those counterpart souls, and whether or not it's as you've suggested about a force of new Blood Knights. He never did like being on his own."

She watched Rhys's expression change again.

"The third Maker," Rhys said. "Mordred's female companion might be here as well."

"Still, you can best them," Avery pointed out. "No matter how ancient they are, they're vampires. That's their weakness. Their souls were dark before they drank from the chalice and once they were soulless, they became even darker. Your souls are light. You're stronger and able to work in the daylight."

"And the light side always wins?" Mason asked.

"You all have the breath of the heavens in your lungs, and my side doesn't give up or give in."

"The Grail and angel blood?" Mason queried. "Mordred would need that...why?"

"Long story," Rhys said, noting Mason's sudden restlessness. "And true."

"Then we go and get the thing you all want," Mason suggested, without demanding an explanation for that second small hint that things weren't as he might have always imagined.

"I have to try to take it," Avery said.

"Are you ready, brother?" Mason addressed Rhys.

Rhys nodded.

How many years had he walked the Earth without knowing the truth? Rhys wondered as he reentered the forest. Hundreds? Thousands? Now that he had discovered the truth, would that mean the end of his extended existence—or the start of a new chapter?

Avery marched ahead with Mason, each long stride causing her wings to rustle softly. Now and then she turned her head, as if the wings were whispering to her.

The tips of the feathers had already darkened to a dull red hue. His angel's hair picked up a slight golden sheen, seen when they passed in and out of the sunlight.

When Mason stopped, Rhys's first thought was that this couldn't be right, because that blasted chateau was still right behind them. They were standing on a mound of dirt surrounded by stones. Trees leaned in from overhead, blocking out most of the day's early sunlight. It was a small clearing, unworthy of what he now supposed might be buried beneath it, and because of that had been the perfect hiding place for one of the world's greatest treasures.

Avery looked at the ground and then knelt down. Her pallor was ashen, more so than usual. He knew her well enough now to note that, and also that her expression seemed strained. Could she feel the golden thing buried here? Her quest was nearly complete.

From her position on her knees, she looked up at him with the sad eyes of someone torn by indecision. At the moment, Rhys couldn't have said anything if he'd tried. Give or take the next fight—and surely there would be one—she'd have the Grail. And she'd be gone.

He wasn't sorry he had helped her get to this point. He only wished it had taken longer.

"Do we dig?" he finally asked.

"If this is truly the way it has to be," Mason replied.

"Will you truly be glad?" Avery asked Mason without looking up. "Glad to be free of this burden?"

"Some," Mason said. "It's brought me luck, Faith and a pack of new friends, things that are rare in our world."

"Faith?" Rhys repeated.

Mason smiled wearily. "The name of the love of my life."

So, Mason had found love, as had a couple more of their brothers. The lucky ones. Rhys didn't want to look at Avery in case she could read him and understand why his heart was racing. Nevertheless, he couldn't keep his eyes off her.

Love wasn't in the cards for him. In his long lifetime, he had never found anyone like this angel. In her, he had found his soul mate. He would never have given his heart so willingly and completely to anyone else. It was hers for the asking.

As she continued to stare at the ground beneath her knees, Rhys almost expected Avery to address those personal thoughts. Instead, she said, "Darkness is upon us."

Chapter 28

Darkness is upon us.

Words to chill the soul.

Rhys and Mason spun around with their weapons in hand. Avery didn't move. The clearing had begun to vibrate—little ripples running underfoot, overhead leaves rustling. In this holy place that Mason had carved for the Grail, there was going to be a war of intentions. No one realized that better than Rhys and his two companions, whose lives had been consumed by the fallout from this golden Grail Quest.

Clouds were rolling in—huge black clouds coming toward them in an unnatural wind to eat up the sunlight.

The first monster arrived by itself. It wasn't a vampire, or didn't look like one to Rhys, in spite of its sharp, snapping fangs.

"More of that bastard's experiments," he muttered, waiting, gauging where to strike a quick death blow to this extraordinarily tall beast's body when it attacked.

The thing appeared to have been pieced together from

parts of several monsters. Hideous face. Broad chest. Its Frankenstein-like image wavered on the outskirts of the clearing, as if it were half Shade, when that wasn't possible.

A roar from above them announced the visit of a second monster as it dropped from a tree. Anger flashed across Avery's face. She said, "They think they can just waltz in here and take it from us."

"Guess they don't know us very well," Rhys remarked, ready for whatever these creeps were going to do next to try to make Avery's prediction a reality.

The third odd beast that showed up had a face like a demon—red skin, slits for eyes. The rest of it was a more familiar shape. Mordred had successfully crossed a human and one of hell's citizens, and however daunting that idea might have been to some, it was a further mistake, and an example of the Maker's susceptibility for tinkering with the wrong kinds of monsters. Demon, sure. But humans were always vulnerable to intimidation and a show of greater strength, and this latest visitor's body was mostly human.

The newcomers didn't attack. One by one, more freaks appeared until they surrounded the clearing. Wide-bodied creatures. Ugly as sin.

"Great odds," Mason said.

"Seven of them," Avery observed, as if that should mean something. "He's toying with us."

Seven...

Rhys went inward to find more details.

Seven monsters for seven Blood Knights. The number seven was a magic number in fantasy, religion and metaphysical belief systems. There were seven deadly sins and seven heavenly virtues. Seven days in a week. In Christianity's book of Revelation, there were seven churches, seven angels, seven seals, seven trumpets and seven stars.

Scholars suggested the number seven depicts completeness and perfection. And on the seventh day, God rested…

But these monsters weren't Blood Knights and were nowhere close to perfection. So it was a mockery of the seven Knights that Mordred was offering here. More of his ridiculous game, since the Maker knew that one Blood Knight, on his own, could easily mop up the motley gang facing them and think of it as a walk in the park.

Rather than joining them, as Rhys and Mason stood alertly on the mound, Avery stayed where she was, staring down. She pressed her fingertips into the dirt, and the earth quaked. Soil sifted through her fingers when she raised both hands, and the sky darkened further.

The ground rocked. The monsters watching Avery shifted uneasily without pouncing.

"What are you waiting for, reinforcements?" Rhys said to them.

"They're waiting for him. Their Maker." Avery's voice was hushed.

Rhys could sense that this was true. His nerves began to buzz along neural pathways as if galloping toward a fire. A smell he knew all too well drifted past the trees. He almost choked with recognition.

"Here we go," he said, anxiously awaiting the arrival of the mad, sadistic vampire and the unearthly, undead queen that would surely be with him. The end game was now in motion, with all the pieces on the board.

Avery had to concentrate on what she was doing, which was a chore with monsters raining down around her. Still, unless Mordred and his companion had grown much stronger since they last met, showing up here was of little consequence to her. Desire for vengeance still sat heavily on her soul, and she'd get to that. First, she had a holy relic to collect and remove from Mordred's reach. She needed all of the Blood Knights in accord in order to have it, and two of the seven were going to be busy for a while.

The monster's monsters hadn't moved. She wasn't sure they could speak. Like silent sentries, they also awaited the coming of their masters. When viewed through the lens of the physical beauty Rhys and his blood brother possessed, those creatures looked like poorly made life-sized voodoo dolls.

Rhys had lowered his weapon. He was on guard, on edge, his senses attuned to what was coming. She could stand beside him, touch him, whisper assurances to him that things would be all right. He would like that and appreciate her closeness. She would have loved the feel of her hand on his arm, her fingers on his back. But she might also be a distraction for him when his full attention was necessary.

Everyone wanted more answers than they already had, except for her. The Grail was within reach, and she felt its vibration. The chalice was calling to her, light to light. It had helped to mold Rhys into the creature he was. The glorious Knight with a heart of gold. And here it had rested for a very long time.

There was no reason to consider how much darkness that powerful relic had also caused. The hurt, pain and suffering its continued existence on this plane promised if it was found again by the likes of Mordred. So she pushed her hands deeper into the soil and closed her eyes. "You know what I'm here to do, and why. Blood Knights…can you hear me, through this Grail?"

The earth shook again. In the periphery, she saw everyone take a step to ride out the aftershock. Her senses wrapped around the golden chalice Mason and his brothers had sealed inside a metal box. That box wasn't buried deep. She could reach it by shoving aside a few handfuls of dirt and bracken. But she had to wait for the rest of the Knights to answer her call.

Mordred was there, suddenly, his presence crowding them all. Avery looked up to see the other fanged viper of Castle Broceliande had, indeed, come with him—a perfect pairing of majestic wickedness with terrific acting skills.

Their beauty was deceiving. Their hearts were blackened by greed and all the blood they had ingested. But they had never shown either their fangs or their true natures to the Knights they had recruited. Most onlookers would have thought them fair, if they didn't look too closely.

Decked out in velvet finery, they approached the clearing as if they owned it. Although there was no more Broceliande, chances were good they had found another lair to replace it. The world's vampire population was proof of their continued existence. The monsters they had brought along were examples of how far astray their genetic tinkering had gone.

No shame showed on their white faces. The midnight-haired female that had helped to slice Avery's flesh to pieces in the deep dungeons of Broceliande spoke first.

"Blood or no blood, we should have killed you when we had the chance, angel."

Rhys took a small sideways step toward Avery. A protective move. Her hands weren't free, so she couldn't have drawn her knife. Both hands were buried to the wrists in the earth as if she would, in fact, dig the chalice out of that mound. Her folded wings were motionless.

In his mind, he heard her silent message. *"Release your claim."*

"Perhaps you have forgotten about the light," Rhys suggested to Mordred and his mistress. "And how hard that light is to maneuver. Because of your deceptions, there is always evil to face."

Their attention veered to him through red-rimmed eyes that could tolerate the darkness of a cloud-covered sun. Rhys wondered briefly if they had gotten rid of that sun moments ago, or if Avery had done it to pave the way for this face-off. Although his angel hadn't moved, he could have sworn he felt her hand brush his. While she hadn't blatantly looked his way, more of her thoughts came to him. *"I have it,"* was her next message. *"I will take it home."*

She had found the Grail. She had her hands on it. It was the end of an era. The end of hundreds of eras.

"What is it you expect?" Rhys asked the manipulators of this monstrous gathering. "That we could allow your nasty machinations to continue now that we know what you truly are?"

Mordred smiled. "Do you include yourself in that sentiment, Rhys de Troyes, as well as your silent brother, when we made both of you?"

"Yes," Rhys replied. "We now understand what we are."

"Then you will be happy to hear that we've come to end all that pain and drama. Right here, now."

"And how do you plan to do that?" Mason asked.

With a dismissive gesture, Mordred waved a long-fingered hand that might have been used to cut away Avery's wings. Rhys could see in his mind the chains and the knives they had used. Or maybe he was tapping into Avery's mental images of the past.

Mordred said, "Give us the Grail, and all will be well."

"You know that isn't going to happen, Mordred."

Hearing his true name spoken caused Mordred's eyes to narrow. He lowered his voice and spoke to his ancient paramour. "You're right, my dear. We should have killed the angel."

"You did try, as I recall," Avery said.

She held a carved silver-and-bronze box that Rhys estimated to be twelve by twelve inches in size. As she brushed away the dirt, the damn thing began to shine as if it hadn't been buried for hundreds upon hundreds of years.

Mordred let out an appreciative gasp. The female beside him lunged, using a wave of her hands to unravel the silence and unleash her lust for what rested inside that box.

The trees surrounding the clearing shook free of their roots and began to fall. At the same time, the ring of Mordred's monsters sprang to life.

The demon hybrid was the first to reach Rhys. Like the vampires they had fought earlier, this creature that never should have existed also carried a black blade. It moved with unexpected swiftness, going after Rhys with a relentless series of slashes and forceful thrusts. Rhys dodged each attack and parried with his knife, calling up skills from many old battles as he rallied to the challenge.

The clearing was engulfed in a sea of motion. Mason was grappling with two more of Mordred's creatures. The rest were heading toward Avery, alongside the chatelaine of Castle Broceliande. The fanged vixen reached to take the silver box from Avery but drew back, howling. The box had protections, wards that scored the vampire's white flesh. She hissed when her skin began to sizzle.

Avery, Rhys reasoned, had known about those wards.

More sounds joined in with the dark mistress's shout of pain, coming from all around them. Rhys feared Mordred had, indeed, brought replacements, but the female vampire's howl had set off a recognizable string of others.

Howls. Close by.

Wolves.

* * *

With the silver box tucked under one arm, Avery fended off attackers. She deftly fought her way to Rhys's side, striking down one mindless beast with a well-placed stab from behind and ramming another with her shoulder. Rhys finished that one off with a smooth spin and a blade to its throat.

Her pulse raced. Her heart ached. These monsters felt pain the way any of the beings present did. She, Rhys and Mason were killing them, but Mordred pulled the strings. Mordred and his companions had set all of this in motion, the fights, the aches and the need for revenge. Yet Mordred was standing back, happy to let his minions do the work.

Something else rode the wind, however. Wolves were coming, moving fast and on all fours. Sensing how their minds worked, she realized these were Weres, furred up without the kiss of a full moon. Lycans that could shift at will. Lycans were werewolf royalty, and she had met one of them by freeing it from a cage.

She felt their approach, watched as those wolves sprang from the forest with their teeth and claws bared. Ten of them. Larger than regular wolves, fiercer, with the unmistakable gleam of intelligence in their eyes. She had seen others like them in the city. Detective Crane's pack. Leading these feral beasts was the black wolf they had rescued, here to repay a debt.

The wolves leaped into the fight, biting, clawing, tearing apart what was left of Mordred's monsters as they fought side by side with Rhys and Mason, somehow getting the fact that the Blood Knights were the good guys.

The closer they got to Avery, the more her own wildness blossomed. Slowly, with fighting all around her and Mordred's mistress about to return for another shot at the box, she faced Mordred.

"How do you plan on getting that chalice back to where you'd take it, Aurian Arcadia?" he asked. "Your wings don't work. The pathetic things are nothing more than show for a fallen angel whose side deserted her long ago and still pays no heed."

She heard him clearly amid the sounds of fighting. The female version of Mordred was getting too close.

"You don't suppose what's in this box will heal me?" Avery said.

"It's a pity you won't have time to find out," Mordred warned.

"Isn't it more of a pity that you showed up here and brought your paramour with you? That you have played into my hands at last, and I get two for the price of one?"

A flicker of doubt crossed Mordred's pasty features and lingered. "You did not call us out," he said.

"Didn't I? We're all here, monster. The beloved Knights who unknowingly betrayed your trust now see what you are and what you've done. Do you suppose they will allow you to get away with more of the same? In the game of Mordred versus the Holy Grail, which side do you think they will continue to back?"

Rhys was listening. His share of monsters was gone. Mason stood beside him, LanVal's stern gaze pinned on the raven-haired vampire queen who had paused, suddenly uncertain about victory.

The sound of the wolves ending the unnatural life of the last creature to oppose them was a gruesome reminder of Mordred's need to dominate. Together, Avery and the two Blood Knights faced Mordred, each of them with a weapon in their hands.

Chapter 29

"Perceval." Mordred's voice was low and well-practiced in the art of using true names to reel in his prey.

"It's too late for that," Rhys said. "Your cover has been blown and look where the fallout has landed us."

Mordred wasn't ready to concede any of his power. That much was obvious in spite of the fact that he had nowhere to go at the moment. The tables had turned. The Maker was trapped.

When Mordred's gaze slid to Avery, Rhys inched closer to her. She wasn't sending messages, and he couldn't read her. The strips of cloth she had wrapped around her torso were stained with dark blood that wasn't hers. It couldn't have been hers, because her blood was as colorless as her skin. Her newly reattached wings, though more colorful than when he had first seen them, seemed a long way from being useful. Maybe it was as Mordred had suggested, and they never would be useful again.

What then, my love?

They'd find a new place for the Grail and continue guarding it? It would be his turn to watch over the relic this time, and he'd get to have Avery for a while longer?

Avery stood next to him in all her pale glory—tall and beautiful, holding tightly to the box that protected the item she had suffered through all of this to find.

"She can't take the Grail," Mordred's mistress warned, backing up to stand by her lover.

"Her wings will heal," Rhys said. "When they do, you won't be around to stop her."

Avery's appreciation came to him in the form of a wave of familiar warmth...and as quickly as that, Rhys remembered where he had seen her before. Her warmth had given her away.

On the sidelines. Always on the sidelines and out of reach, he had glimpsed her hovering. Here and there, year after year, with a few breaks in that span of time, this angel had been around...a pale ghost who disappeared when he got close to noticing her. That is what he hadn't remembered until now, and why her scent was familiar.

Power. Scent. The search for her wings. Hell, had Avery set this whole thing up in order to get what she wanted, as she had just intimated, or was she playing this by ear, like he was?

He didn't dare look at her with the Makers so close. They had the ability to move like lightning. He had seen this before. Could they take the box from Avery with so many Grail guards watching over it and watching over the angel who held it? Maybe not. Because in order to break the wards sealing the Grail inside, Avery had needed permission from all of his brothers. Without that permission, Mordred could no longer touch the item he sought.

Trapped as he was, Mordred smiled again. "What my queen means is that the angel cannot take the Grail, even if her wings were to heal—which, by the way, is unlikely. She would have to get past us first, and if you think those creatures you faced here were the only ones standing between her and Broceliande, you are not as smart as you have led us to believe."

"There is no Broceliande," Rhys said.

Beside him, Mason's muscles twitched.

"You saw to that," Mordred said to Avery. "But a house is not a home if the people living in it have already moved on."

"The only *people* there were half demon," Avery countered. "And now there is nothing for them there at all."

Mordred nodded. "Yet I believe in order to set things right, you have to go back. Isn't that the way these things go, angel? That is where you landed and where the Grail lured you to us. In order to return to the heavens, you'd not only need wings, but also to stand in the same spot where your feet first touched down."

He smiled as he continued speaking, assured of their full attention. "When you arrived and had set both feet on the Earth, wasn't that point of reference stapled to the castle's grounds?"

Rhys wanted badly to look at Avery. He wanted her to explain what the madman was talking about.

Mordred went on as if he read Rhys's puzzled state.

"And once the wings were removed, you no longer had a connection to your friends. They couldn't help you because you were no longer an angel. You were no longer enough like them for the heavens to track you among so many others requiring their attention."

So, Rhys thought as sickness rolled in his stomach, that was it, that was why she had been alone. If Mordred's take on things was true, Rhys had his answer as to why other angels hadn't appeared. Finding the Grail had been Avery's assignment. Only hers. Each angel has a mission, she had told him.

Perhaps time wasn't the same in the heavens as it was on Earth, Rhys reasoned. Maybe only seconds had gone by up there since Avery had left the clouds. Possibly there was no such thing as time, at all.

Is it true? he wanted to ask her. She hadn't countered Mordred's remarks.

"So," Mordred said smugly, "unless you can fight your way back to Broceliande, where this whole thing began, through an army of creatures at my beck and call, your Grail is not safe."

Avery moved at last by nodding her head. When she looked up again, she was smiling. That smile told Rhys she had more surprises up her sleeve and that she wasn't through yet. He watched Mordred's grin dissolve.

"There are two things wrong with your thinking," she said. "The first is your belief that all of my power is tied to the wings. The second is that you have forgotten about something else that stands in the way of your victory."

"And that would be?" Mordred's mistress asked, confident in her lover's explanation of the way this was to go.

Avery's smile did not falter when she said, "Daylight."

On cue, the clouds rolled back to reveal a bright yellow sun. Thunder cracked as those clouds hustled away. And the sound of monsters dying in the distance rang in Rhys's ears like the chimes of a golden bell.

It wasn't quite so simple, Avery knew. Mordred, a being conceived of darkness, also had the ability to bring back the clouds. He tried to do so now, shocked at having overplayed this hand. It was too late to save his little army of vampire freaks, however. Daylight was their enemy, and therefore Avery's weapon of choice. That, and an angry wolf pack of

Mason's friends. There could have been more monsters hiding in the shadows of the trees, but she didn't sense them.

Mordred and his mistress had backed up, seeking shelter. Their velvet clothes protected them only slightly from the burn their faces and hands had received from the flash of yellow fire. Avery didn't let up on her command for the clouds to keep away, and with her wings in place, her new power shone as brightly as the silver box in her hands.

Mason and the wolves that had proved themselves good allies surrounded the pair. The black wolf growled a greeting. Without the darkness, the vampires, no matter how strong they were, or how cunning, were as good as chained in place.

"It's all connected, you see," Avery said calmly. "I am the Grail, and the Grail is me."

Rhys turned to her, surprise lighting his face. Avery knew what he was seeing. Her color was returning. Her skin felt flushed, and hotter than ever. Strands of her hair, blowing in the wind, were changing from white to gold.

On her back, her wings began to unfold. This time, there was no flutter. With a sound similar to shaking out a blanket, they extended—a full span of blue, gray and crimson that picked up the wind and lifted her inches from the ground.

Rhys didn't speak. Maybe he couldn't, but then, neither could she. This moment marked the beginning of the end for them, and they both realized it. Maybe, for the first time, he was seeing the angel. The whole one.

Funny, she now thought, as she had before, how close love and pain truly were when weighed on the scale of emotions, and how much pain one sometimes had to endure in order to find the right kind of love. The look on Rhys's handsome, angular face reflected a similar belief. The sadness in his eyes said everything he couldn't.

When she could speak again, Avery dragged her attention from Rhys. "They're dangerous," she said to Mason. "Those monsters are too dangerous to have hanging around."

Mason nodded. "Do you want them?"

She took time to ponder the question.

She had wanted vengeance in the past. Lived for it. She had dreamed of tearing them apart limb by limb as they had torn at her. She had dreamed of stringing their fangs on a necklace and offering it to anyone else thinking of daring to pit their strengths against those of the light. Because, in answer to the question Rhys had once posed, she had truthfully replied that the light didn't always win, but it came out on top more often than not.

Rhys was waiting for her to answer Mason's query. But the truth was that by meeting Rhys, and by loving him, she had given her demons back. She had sent them where they belonged, and the desire for revenge had gone with them.

"No," she said solemnly. "Would you like the honor, Mason?"

Mason nodded. "It's a decision for all of us to make. All of our brotherhood, together."

"You'll call them?"

"Oui."

"And until then?"

"Let caring for them be my mission," Mason replied. "Now that I have no other, it will give me something to do."

Rhys's shoulder offered support that Avery took. In his touch, a whole bunch of sensations returned with astounding speed. Remembrances of the beauty of his mouth on her mouth, the hardness of his chest and how she had briefly nestled against it. Memories of the way his muscles danced when they had made love on the debris-covered floor of an abandoned building, their bodies meshing perfectly, fitting together as though they had been made for each other.

"I'll accompany you there," Rhys said. His voice was unsteady. "I must make my own peace with Broceliande."

"I want to be with you for whatever time we have left," he silently added.

Their eyes met. Light streaked through Avery, as it did each time he looked at her like that. She almost wished her wings would carry her away now, so that the pain of parting from Rhys wouldn't be postponed. Yet she didn't really want that. Each moment with him would, from now on, be a gift.

Stop, she wanted to say to her glorious Blood Knight. *Stop looking at me. If it weren't for the Grail, maybe...*

If I didn't need to take it where it will be safe...

She blinked slowly, barely able to catch hold of one decent breath. Hell. Vengeance was wasted on Mordred and his mistress, because love, it suddenly seemed to her, was the strangest beast of all.

Chapter 30

Rhys surveyed the landscape.

Pieces of the castle's white walls remained, but not many. Here and there a polished stone punctuated the brown, overgrown space of what had once been a garden to rival any garden on Earth. There, bloodred roses as tall as a man had bloomed by starlight, and the sound of water had hidden the cries of an angel trapped beneath the ground.

Aurian Arcadia.

She had been quiet on the return to this place, and he hadn't wanted to disturb her thoughts. Her appearance had radically changed. Her hair was fair, and hung to her waist like threads of 24-karat gold. Her face, once so pale, bloomed with color. The mouth he had found so full and lush was a rosy pink.

Those lips had been on his lips, as well as so many other delightful places on his body. He could remember and relive each nibble of her tiny white teeth along his rib cage, and feel each flick of her tongue. Her breath had been fiery and, oh, so sweet.

The body he craved was still ultra lean, and yet a few of her starker angles had been replaced by curves. All she was missing from the picture book of angels was a halo. Yet, if there were such things, he very much doubted warrior Avery would have accepted one.

She was stunning. Different, but also the same. Instinctively, Rhys bowed his head, honoring this transformation while unready to face it. Avery would go now. She'd fly home using those incredible wings. He didn't see how he'd be able to go on without her, alone for all the countless years still ahead of him, though he had, he supposed, signed up for that.

It was easy to sense that Avery was smiling without seeing her lips upturn because he had always been connected to her. Avery's blood ran in his veins, she had said, but that was only part of their bond.

He looked at her now, noting how radiant her smile was and the way it beamed. Today, sunlight clung to the ruins, replacing former shadows. Avery didn't seem to mind being here, where evil had disrupted her course. With her by his side, neither did he.

Avery's wings were folded up again, tight to her back. They helped to feed her in some way, as if some special kind of sustenance ran through them. Her blood connected to the veins that attached each individual feather to the structure that supported them. They had healed in time to see the grand finale of her story. Finding the Grail had helped with that. She was again a unified whole. A heavenly creation.

He wanted her so badly, his body had begun to quake.

"You'll take the Grail away now," he said.

"It's why I came to this world."

Back when he had first set eyes on her, glittering light particles had accompanied her in the darkest places. Those particles were present now and reflected the sunlight.

"The Grail is precious," she said.

How many other angels had experienced the trauma and pain of being split in two, Rhys wondered, and continued to adhere to a quest? Could any other kind of being have endured the way Aurian Arcadia had?

Am I expected to wave goodbye, Avery?

Watch you ascend?

Go back to the life I'm relegated to continuing?

So all right, he'd do that and make it work. What else was there? He wasn't going to be the second immortal responsible for grounding her.

"You were right when you suggested that in being free of old vows, we'd also be free," he said. "However, I can't see how things will change for me or my brothers. We have been chasing the concept of *right* all this time, and won't give up on that."

"I know," Avery said softly. "Here is where you're needed."

Rhys strained to hold himself back when that seemed futile. He desperately wished to see those wings spreading and to feel the brush of downy feathers on his face.

"I can't go with you," he said.

His eyes found hers…still pale blue and dark-rimmed, like the earlier edgy, anxious, kick-ass angel version of Avery. He was happy to see those black marks. Still, he had to wonder what the rest of the heavenly hordes would think of that one leftover modern touch when she showed up.

Angels don't have forms, she had said. Unable to picture that, Rhys tried unsuccessfully to return her smile. "Can you travel like that?" he teased.

"Like what?"

Her red-tipped wings appeared to be nothing more than fanciful shadows in the afternoon light. The rest of Avery was now as naked as he'd wished her to be, having shed her cloth bindings. Rhys grinned, finally, unable to help himself. Avery had been a showstopper before. She was light-years beyond that classification now.

She would draw attention wherever she went if she stayed here with him. No one would be able to resist a second look and a third. She was just too incredibly beautiful.

"A question," he said, sobering, jealous of things that never were going to happen, missing her before she had left.

She nodded for him to go on.

"How did you get away from this terrible place? You never told me that part."

He glanced around at the remains of the castle that bordered the garden. Only part of one tower stood, choked by a tangle of vines.

"You did this, Avery? Took it down stone by stone?"

She was standing close to him. Her golden breasts brushed his chest each time she took in a breath. He didn't want to close his eyes, but had to. The pleasure of being near his angel made his soul ache.

"Maybe you can also explain why angels need to breathe," he added, needing to speak, seeking to quell the absolute necessity of reaching for her, kissing her, burying himself inside her.

"All living things breathe," she said.

The words she formed were puffs of warm air. In this cold, wicked space, Avery was the only warm thing.

"Then you are alive," he said.

"Like you, I am alive here, now."

"Hell, Avery…"

She placed a finger against his lips to silence him. That, too, was a familiar gesture. Rhys's pulse continued to race as her finger first slid between his lips, then tracked downward over his chin to the triangle of bare skin exposed between the sides of his shirt.

"Did someone help you to escape?" he asked with a sigh.

She shook her head, sending light particles dancing, and slipped her hand into that opening in the cloth. She laid her palm on his bare chest, above his thunderous heart. "I'm in there," she said. "Part of me fuels that beat."

"And I..." Rhys said in a deep, throaty voice as he angled his hand over her waist and hips, over her abs and beneath, where he softly stroked the V between her thighs. "I always want to be inside of you."

Avery threw back her head, accepting his stroke as if she had been waiting for it. Rhys held her to him with an arm around her waist.

It crossed his mind that this wasn't the time or place to prove to Avery how much he loved her. She had been tortured here, and had bled. She'd been wrapped in cold iron chains, alone, when he had believed his Makers to be good.

But Avery didn't protest this personal touch. By sealing their emotions and bodies together near what remained of Broceliande's foundations, they were overwriting what had gone before and truly laying the past to rest.

"I..." she began, as her eyes shut. "I tricked them, in turn. That's how I got away, and how I knew they could be beaten."

Rhys lifted her up, brought her closer, so that her face was level with his. He spoke haltingly. "It only matters that you did escape from this terrible place."

Her eyes remained closed. Her body was pliant beneath his touch.

"We will consecrate this ground, rendering it golden, erasing what has gone before, my angel. My winged lover.

The spell will be broken and, like us, whatever haunts this place will be free. We need never look back."

Avery's arms encircled his shoulders. Her scalding hot mouth found his. "Make it so, Blood Knight," she whispered, searching his face.

"All right," he said, holding her in his arms a moment longer before easing her to the ground where he'd have her one last time. One final time. Before she left him.

She had never seen Rhys sleep. Had never pictured him at rest. He looked almost peaceful when no one needed rescuing.

Perched on the chipped base of a pedestal that had once supported a marble statue of a maiden with a lyre, Avery carefully observed Rhys, noting each intake of breath and the way his broad, naked chest rose and fell.

She breathed with him.

He hadn't stirred for some time. Possibly this was the first night he had felt at ease in a long while, since no one would dare to trespass on this castle's tainted land now that Mordred and the other Makers were gone from here.

Soon enough, he'd waken. A new sunrise sat on the horizon. The sky was already a mixture of yellow and pink. It was likely Rhys hadn't enjoyed waking in daylight for years. He had told her something like that. Bad things came out at night, and facing down bad things was his business. It was his calling.

Avery ran a hand over her stomach, stroking every inch of skin he had touched. Last night, their lovemaking had been rough. She had demanded that of him, needing to experience everything he had to offer. She craved a rematch now. The desire to have all of Rhys, over and over, was primal, and only teased by having sampled his talents.

Rhys de Troyes looked like a sleeping prince in a fairy

tale, when the true nature of his existence was far from fantasy. He complemented the place as no other could. His presence on these grounds marked the end of one tale and the beginning of another. After centuries of trials and battles, Rhys was free of the Grail Quest.

Her heart, which should have been buoyant, hurt. Her soul, which should have helped her to ascend, struggled to remain rooted in the body of the creature Rhys loved so much and so well.

Straightening, standing tall, and as naked as Rhys was, Avery spread her wings. Allowing them the freedom to expand and to again taste the sunrise after their long hiatus from those things, she reveled in the sensation. She had dearly missed the sun. The rising warmth was like a dose of medicine for a wounded soul.

Dawn sang to her. Wind caressed her face. The clouds were calling. The Grail waited to be taken to its next resting place. And all she could think about was Rhys. Her Blood Knight lover was the most delicious thing in a world that looked better today, but was actually so incredibly sad.

When Rhys stirred in his sleep, Avery arched her back. When he made a soft sound, the one she loved, her hand slipped between her thighs.

One great flap of her wings, and she was in the air. One more and she was straddling her sleepy Knight, whose eyes slowly started to open.

"More," she whispered.

Almost magically, the part of his body she wanted rose to the occasion, hard, erect and willing. She slid over him, allowed him to fill her completely, absorbing the quakes and the pleasure that swelled within her. Only with Rhys had she experienced true bliss. Not even the glory of the clouds could rival this.

Tears collected in her eyes. She gave him one more

stroke, and with the Grail in her hand, free of its silver box, Avery began to drift away from all sensation. The rumble of a rising climax faded into the distance…and she felt herself go.

The sky rushed in, tugging her upward and away from her lover. She uttered a cry of protest, but it was too late.

Her wings carried her, soaring, lifting her up with the currents, until the castle was just a dot below—and then nothing at all. And in that final flight home, her heart shattered into a million tiny pieces.

Light surrounded her. Whispers of welcome came. She was fading again, fading more, losing the flesh, becoming pure spirit.

The angels were singing. The Grail was safe now, and where it belonged, but Aurian Arcadia wasn't happy or where she wanted to be. She knew that now. She had known this since meeting Rhys.

Her hands were empty. The Grail was gone. It had been taken away and her mission was complete. She floated as the last threads of her earthly existence separated into ribbons of light. Soon she would lose touch with the last few hundred years, when she didn't want to forget *him.* She didn't want to lose her beautiful Blood Knight.

Her tears surrounded her and felt like rain. The last wisps of her earthly consciousness were wavering. *No. Not yet. I'm not ready.*

"Avery."

Rhys's call reached her, resonating in her soul. She sensed the pain in his voice. Her hurt had become his. She had taken away his beliefs and left him with nothing but the leftover stone shards of a castle.

If he had used her real name, he could have commanded her to return. He hadn't done so. Rhys assumed this was what she wanted—to be free of earthly bonds, pain and dark memories. Rhys was accepting this separation because of what she was, and who she was. He was allowing her to be part of the greater good at his own expense. Rhys was sacrificing his happiness for hers, knowing he'd pay for letting her go.

While she…

Heaven help her, she loved him, and she was about to become one with the light until she was needed again.

Those thoughts were disturbing.

"Avery. I…I will always love you. And I will never forget."

He had issued his final farewell. Avery recognized it as the last.

No! she protested. *"Rhys!"*

Wind whistled at her ears. The angels stopped singing, perhaps in recognition of a heart in tatters. Another voice came, speaking to her spirit to spirit, and it was a beautiful thing, a peaceful conversation. But it wasn't enough. Not now.

She was determined to go back to her lover.

"Please," she pleaded. *"Please."*

A sudden jolt to whatever was left of her system began to draw pieces of her back together again. Hands, arms, legs all took form. Hips and waist were there, buoyant beneath a great pair of crimson-tipped wings that strongly and surely surfed the breeze.

She was being rewarded, after all. Someone had listened, she thought…

…as she fell.

Rhys uncovered his face, startled by the soft slap of flesh meeting with his flesh and the sound of his name being spoken.

"Rhys."

He looked hard at the apparition straddling him, certain he was dreaming.

Great wings, colorful and expansive, were outstretched. Centered between those wings was a naked female form he knew intimately. But that couldn't be right. Could it? Avery had gone away.

"Am I dreaming?"

"Yes," Avery whispered, leaning over him where he lay resting, tightening her legs around his sides.

Long golden hair tickled his ribs. Pert breasts brushed his chest as her angelic face came close. Familiar blue eyes looked into his. Lush rosy-pink lips parted. "I am nobody's sweetheart," she said.

"I know about the thorns," Rhys managed to say.

"I am a holy warrior."

"And terribly handy to have around," he said.

"They might call me back. There might be another quest."

"We'll tackle the next one together."

A beat passed before Avery said with a warm breath, "So, in the time left to us, may I make a suggestion, Blood Knight?"

Rhys's heart pounded. His pulse boomed. He wasn't dreaming. This was real. She was real. He felt her weight, saw the glorious wings, the golden skin and the challenging sparkle in her expression.

Avery had come back to him.

Her smile was like Heaven itself. Her hips were another story. They began to move, taunting him, teasing, urging him to take up where they had left off. Without understanding how or why, he had been granted his wish. Just one. And he vowed never to ask for another.

"Suggestion? Yes. What?" He hardly got that out. She

knew exactly how to arouse him, how to please him. The rhythm of her body riding his was pure ecstasy.

"Why don't you stop thinking and make the most of this reunion?" his angel coaxed with a sexy, very unangelic grin.

"That," Rhys whispered to her, his body more than willing to meet her challenge, his hands reaching up to draw her mouth to his, "is exactly what I plan on doing. Right now."

He added, barely, "You used up another trick to come back?"

Her lips trembled slightly when she breathed a final few words into his mouth.

"The angel and the Blood Knight, forever," she said, with the adamancy of a promise.

"Forever and a day," Rhys heartily agreed.

* * * * *